Books by Hilma Wolitzer

ENDING (1974)

IN THE FLESH (1977)

HEARTS (1980)

IN THE PALOMAR ARMS (1983)

FOR YOUNG READERS

INTRODUCING
SHIRLEY BRAVERMAN (1975)

OUT OF LOVE (1976)

TOBY LIVED HERE (1978)

In the Palomar Arms

IN THE

Palomar Arms

Hilma Wolitzer

Farrar / Straus / Giroux

NEW YORK

11/1983
gen'l

The author wishes to express her gratitude
to the Corporation of Yaddo

For Muriel and Marc,

in loving friendship

Their marriage is a good one. In our eyes
What makes a marriage <u>good</u>? Well, that the tether
Fray but not break, and that they stay together.
One should be watching while the other dies.

HOWARD NEMEROV / *The Common Wisdom*

In the Palomar Arms

1

"What smells like that?"

It is two o'clock on a Wednesday afternoon in July, and Daphne Moss and Kenny Bannister are resting in a grand, wet, postcoital tangle on her foldout bed. She extricates herself carefully and rises up on one elbow, staring into the constant orange flicker of the fake fireplace. "What smells like that?" she asks again.

"Like what, puss?" he says drowsily. Daph has been acting a little strange lately. She's always sniffing at everything: the furniture cushions, her own hands, even him. He wonders if she's developed an allergy to something, or a nervous tic. Ah, well. He runs his nipping mouth along her spine. Her skin is salty; his lips are pleasantly sore. When she doesn't respond to his questions or his kisses, he repeats, "Like *what?*" And then, more alert, "Is something burning?" That's all he'd need. He starts to sit up.

"No, no," Daphne says, pushing him back down. "Nothing like that. It must be my imagination." His immediate alarm should offend her, but it really doesn't. She understands that if they were to be rescued from a burning building in one another's naked arms, Kenny's divorce plans might be hindered. The prime and delicate matter of child custody would certainly be jeopardized.

Tax consultants are not known to make bedside house calls.

Kenny has a boy of four and a two-year-old girl Daphne has seen only in wallet-sized snapshots. They appear to be beautiful children, possibly exceptional children. In one picture, they're standing in marbled light holding hands, and look like Hansel and Gretel just before the betrayal.

Daphne strokes Kenny's chest in diminishing circles until he falls asleep. A short nap before the seventy-mile drive back to his office is important. A shower to erase the gorgeous and unmistakable stink of sex is even more important. She lies quietly next to him, drifting into a lazy flow of random thought, starting with a replay of their just-completed lovemaking—those kisses no less desperate than the first ones six months ago; the glorious boom of Kenny going off inside her, and the smaller jolts of her own orgasms—one, two, three! Four? She wonders when they'll have an overnight. How odd it will seem in utter darkness. They haven't even been to a movie together yet.

Something in the air conditioner flaps rhythmically, and Daphne muses about the course in television script-writing she's taking during this summer semester, pretending an impossible triumph when her work is read aloud the following week. Everyone, including Mr. Steinmetz, bursts into spontaneous applause. A voice from the back of the room yells "Bravo!"

Impossible, all right. She is definitely getting better at dialogue, though, giving her main characters, who are lovers, clearer speeches, never longer than the three prescribed typewritten lines. Sometimes this makes them sound strangely taciturn and distant, like a taxi driver and his dispatcher talking on a two-way radio. So she lets them gesture and smile a lot more.

The fat Tolstoy paperback she's reading for World Lit I is open on the night table, and its pages are densely black with descriptive prose. For a moment she sees her own existence, sparsely recorded in a cramped, limited hand. In Russian novels, miles of wheat fields are sown and threshed with the changing seasons. People make leisurely journeys during which their lives are carefully contemplated, and they even fling themselves in front of trains. There is none of the ticking monotony of real-life daytime drama.

Daphne glances at the digital clock. Time pulses from the afternoon like blood from a serious wound. She should get a clock that doesn't mark the passing of every single second in disgusting Day-Glo green. Soon she will have to get up and go to work. She sighs deeply. The atmosphere at the Palomar Arms is so depressing. The pay is rotten, too, and she knows that she's over-qualified; none of the other kitchen aides are college students. It was the only job she could find with a four-to-midnight shift, other than the one at the phone company, and she had not done well enough on the tests she'd taken there. The interviewer told Daphne that she was deficient in the area of complex numerical retention, making her an unlikely candidate for the opening in Directory Information. That, after a two-hour battery of personality, aptitude, and interest tests. Many of the questions had been boring, or seemed pointless or loaded. Would you rather be a florist or an exterminator? A court stenographer or a glassblower? Do you often feel that people are against you? Do you have blinding headaches? Never? Some of the time? Most of the time?

Daphne thinks now that blinding headaches are probably a prerequisite for a job with the telephone company. Look at all the wrong numbers she always reaches, and the phone calls she receives in the middle of the night for people named Tony, Rochelle, and Dr. Mandelbaum. She recalls bitterly all the coins she's lost in pay telephones, and the wobbly recorded voices that urge her to throw good money after bad and have a nice day.

"What would you say my strong points are?" Daphne had asked the interviewer.

There was a long miserable pause during which the other woman tapped a pencil against her own forehead. Then she smiled with aching effort, and said, "Well, you seem to show considerable interest in nature and in people."

But who didn't? Perhaps only Mrs. Shumway, the head cook at the Palomar Arms, who had hired Daphne in an instant, asking only if she'd ever had hepatitis or TB. Mrs. Shumway had absolutely no interest in Daphne's headaches or aspirations, her love life or her move to Ventura. She kept flogging a slab of meat while they spoke, and without looking up advised Daphne to get a uniform from Supply, and not to forget a hairnet.

The job is just temporary, until Kenny gets his divorce and Daphne is finished with her course work at

Ventura College. Both goals should be reached by the end of the year, before her twenty-fifth birthday.

In the meantime, there are all those old sick people. And that row of deadly, humming microwave ovens. The posted signs give warning only to those wearing a pacemaker. But Daphne's learned to hurl the trays in and step quickly aside, before she's zapped into sterility, or worse.

She tries to think of the inmates collectively as "them," an unfortunate club of aliens she will never be asked to join, and she moves in their midst with the swift, scissoring energy of youth, breathing out more often than she breathes in. She also sprays herself liberally with perfume to overcome the odors of urine and food, which are surprisingly interchangeable. The people, however, are not. Names, faces, voices declare their individuality, and inscribe themselves on the stone of her memory.

The Palomar Arms Senior Home is registered with the Buildings Department as a "convalescent and re-habilitation facility." But hardly any of its residents ever convalesce or get rehabilitated. Their major common complaint is extreme and irrevocable old age, and most of them are kept hostage until they die, or are moved at the last moment for that purpose to a conventional hospital.

One woman has been there for thirteen years, since the younger Dr. Rauscher took over. She is almost a hundred now, and although her skin is shirred into millions of tiny folds, and her vision and hearing are impaired, she's considered stable, and a likely candidate for a special centennial celebration. Daphne has heard that it will include fireworks on the lawn, and telegrams of congratulation from the Governor of California and the President of the United States.

She stares at her own smooth bare arm and slowly brings it to her nose. Then she smells her fingers, peeking slyly between them at the sleeping Kenny. Despite the perfume she wears, and the lingering scent of their bodies' work, the odors of the Palomar Arms are here, too, in the bedclothes, and in the long strands of Daphne's brown hair. She believes they have even invaded the shelves of her refrigerator. Every week she throws out something else—a head of lettuce or an egg —that seems perfectly good, but has a funny smell.

Daphne looks up at the ceiling she had recently painted a midnight blue. She'd pasted luminescent paper stars here and there to reproduce the heavens and a semblance of night for their daylight loving. The whole thing has the phony charm of an amateur stage set. Perhaps she should have followed the patterns of actual constellations instead of this random distribution. But when she's here alone, in the real night, the stars burn and wink and she swirls into sleep under their cosmic watchfulness.

Now she gazes directly at Kenny, and is impressed by how beautiful he seems, although she knows that he is only moderately handsome. He is, she imagines, the way men used to be before the sexual revolution—tender, grateful, and crazily aroused most of the time. Everything appears to turn Kenny on: the painted sky; the artificial fireplace, with its motor-driven fan and cellophane flames; the cheap white cotton panties she buys, three pairs to the package, at K-Mart; and especially her hair, which, when she takes him into her mouth, he winds and winds into a tight skein around his hand until her scalp prickles, and he lets it loose all at once, snaking and spilling over both of them. He slips into her like a thief entering a doorway, and she is rutted, exactly as she wishes to be. At the same time, he holds her face in his cupped hands as carefully as a thirsty man would gather water.

Kenny's marriage and fatherhood disturb Daphne, of course. She needs frequent reassurance that she is not responsible for the destruction of his family, that it was an inevitability before she and Kenny ever met. Still, she has shockingly nasty daydreams in which his wife and children are all killed instantly in a tragic accident. She is horrified by the cruel range of her imagination: their car diving off the edge of a mountain; the house exploding into dust just as Kenny clears the door on his way to work; an insane sniper in a shopping mall . . .

When the time is right, he will merely leave them. There'll be lawyers, recriminations, and the tearing wrench of parting, but no unwarranted violence.

It would be so much better if they had never been at all. Yet Daphne reasons that Kenny's domestic experience has helped to make him a lover of greater dimension than the single men she's used to. Often she's treated like a wife who is still in high favor, or like a treasured child. After the tumult of their first lovemaking, they kept smiling at one another, immodestly proud and happy. Kenny gently fingered her ribs and then the dancing pulse of her throat. He said, "Are you okay? No broken bones? No internal injuries? Oh, *Jesus!*" And they both laughed out loud until they turned serious again with desire.

He always covers her with the blanket when he must remove his own heat from the bed, and it floats and settles over her like a wide blue wing. The other, unmarried, men she's known were more like affectionate but competitive siblings. How marvelous it is to be cherished instead.

In turn, Daphne is sometimes inspired in her inventions of pleasure: wrapped candies under the pillows for after; love poems torn into pieces to be reassembled with wonderfully silly or lyrical results. Once, after the bed was folded, and he was dressed and about to leave, she did a naked cartwheel across the room, landing upright close to where he stood, trapped and dizzied by the spectacle.

Kenny's breathing is faint and mysterious, and each flaxen hair on his body is separate and remarkable. His lolling penis is a dear amnesiac she will not be selfish enough to restore with a kiss. Let it, let all of him sleep.

Red hair on a man can be a dubious asset, Daphne knows. There's the accompanying pale skin others might not like but which she chooses to think of as luminous. And the shower of freckles everywhere that look edible to her, but could be unattractive to some people. She vows never, never to tell him that taller men used to be her secret preference.

Daphne sighs again, even more deeply than before.

The best years of her infinite and promising life are about to begin, and almost everything is perfect. Then why is she seized by a clutch of fear and loneliness? She throws her arms around Kenny, waking him up.

2

As always, Kenny enjoys the drive back to Studio City after being with Daphne. He experiences an afterglow that would be visible to anyone, even a traffic cop, who would excuse him for speeding with a brotherly grin and a mild reprimand. Kenny starts to sing "Everybody loves somebody sometime" against a competing stereo tape of the Supremes. His Toyota is only trembling along at seventy-five, and there's a silver Mercedes bearing down on his tail. Through the rearview mirror he can see the other driver, who is also singing, or maybe talking to himself. Kenny laughs out loud and bangs the steering wheel in time to the Supremes, who have won out by the sheer force of their vitality. "Baby love, oh, baby love!" he shouts in unison with them. He can afford this brief indulgence in abandoned happiness. By the time he gets to his office, a metamorphosis will have taken place; he will be totally unmarked by love and hardly stirred by memory. The speedometer will soon quiver around seventy, drop to sixty-five, registering also the dissipation of magic. If he's pulled over later, he'll definitely get a ticket, and probably be frisked for grass or coke, besides.

Kenny has never confided to Daphne that his image of her and of their fevered meetings always begins to fade as he approaches Camarillo, and is almost gone be-

fore he reaches the Malibu turnoff. This is not a slight
to Daph or to their relationship. It is only a trick he's
learned to protect himself from the grief of conflict. He
is really mad about her, and often likes to think of how
she first appeared to him that evening in the Intro
Philosophy class at U.C.L.A. She'd stood to recite from
Aristotle about lovers finding their chief delight in gaz-
ing upon the beloved, and therefore preferring sight to
all the other senses. Kenny had been wandering inside
his head most of the past hour, hearing bits of what was
being said, about happiness, friendship, goodness, and
evil. His own sight was blurry—all of his senses were
dulled. The question had been raised earlier: How far
may a man love himself above others? The broad moral
dilemma was immediately reduced to a personal one, and
Kenny pondered his own selfishness. Hadn't he taken
this course as much for the night out from his marriage
as to come to some deep understanding of human existence?

And then Daphne, that low-voiced woman whose hair
fell almost to her waist, spoke about sight and lovers, and
Kenny's vision sharpened in a kind of ocular miracle.
She was tall and generously built, and her skin seemed
as finely textured as his children's. A slight, appealing
nervousness could be perceived in the hand that wandered blindly over a notebook while she spoke. She went
on to defend the narcissism of self-love that must precede
the love of others. It was as if Justice herself had ripped
off her blindfold and spoken in his behalf, and Kenny's
other senses woke, one after the other, like dreaming
schoolchildren tapped on their heads with a pointer.

On another night he saw her at the main library, sitting in isolated splendor on a high stool, stamping books. He remembers the unexpected and unreasonable pleasure of her smile when she looked up at him, and the low, whispering voice that directed him to the periodicals room. Unable to concentrate on the microfilm of the *Wall Street Journals* he had sought, Kenny took his time anyway, aimlessly browsing through obscure literary magazines—things called *Shove, Rutabaga Review,* and *Hermaphrodite*—expecting, *knowing,* that she would be there when he got back to the other room, her heels hooked over the rungs of the stool, giving her calf muscles that dancer's tension. He dared a bar with her near campus that night, still innocent of significant act or commitment, and then the riskier confinement of his car, and finally her apartment. His bravado faltered only when he recognized the strength and willfulness of his attraction. When he was with her, he was plagued by a demented yearning to be with her again.

And it wasn't just the sex, although that was sublime. It was also her rapturous attention, which gave him a second chance to be new, to be capable once more of fortunate surprises.

Daphne didn't ask him for several days. She wasn't stupid, he knew, just not eager to hear bad news. But eventually she said, "You're married, Kenny, aren't you?" They were sitting in the purring Toyota, parked near her West Hollywood apartment building. His silence was more telling than a rush of confession, but her dark eyes were steady and demanding. "Sort of," he said hoarsely, and groaned, reaching for her. When they embraced, it was like the signing of an agreement in which the fine print has been read and then ignored.

He adores Daphne and is sincere in his suit of her. But on the periphery of his heart there is premature nostalgia for the life he has not yet given up. Especially for his children.

The title "Daddy" pleases Kenny more than his given name ever has, more than any term of endearment ever could. It is what his son Steven shouts from a window when the Toyota rounds the driveway to their house, as if he's announcing the Second Coming. And it was his daughter Molly's first word, even before "Mama." Now she makes a little song of it each morning while she eats her Froot Loops and lays one small bare foot in his lap, under the table. He holds her foot, out of a tender urge, and to guard his balls against a possible sudden kick as her song rises in pitch and passion. "Oh, Daddy, my Daddy-boy Daddy!"

The real beauty of being a father is that it's a created job. The biological part can be hit-and-run. Nowadays you can even hit into a test tube; conception doesn't require two warm bodies anymore. Women have always been the heroes of childbirth, anyway. They bloom with it, they almost die from it. And they claim, without qualification, to endure the greatest possible physical pain.

Once, when Steven was a baby, Kenny broke his leg in two places, skiing. A few weeks later, he and Joy had three other couples in for dinner. One of the men said, admiringly, that Kenny's leg must have hurt like a sucker, and Joy smirked. The other women nodded at her, knowingly, without a word passing among them. Kenny was amazed and outraged. He said that the pain had been excruciating, and one of the women actually laughed out loud. She folded her arms and said, "It wasn't anything like labor, buster, you can bet on that."

Kenny said he wouldn't know, but that the bone had literally *pierced* the skin. It was whitish yellow, like a huge, emerging tooth. A seasoned ski pro had fainted when he looked at it.

"Ha!" the woman said. "Ha, ha," the other woman added, even Joy, who had wept in the ambulance and said, "Darling darling darling," until they'd put him under for surgery.

The mildest of the men said, "We get more heart attacks, more lung cancer, more sports injuries. I mean, that's statistics."

"My water broke with Steven hours before I began to dilate," Joy said. "It was a *dry birth*." She ripped off a ragged piece of bread and chewed it.

"Have you ever been shot?" Kenny asked no one in particular. "Guys in Vietnam got it in the guts, in the head." It was a weak, even a specious argument, since nobody at the table, including Kenny, had been in Vietnam. Joy hefted the heavy meat platter with one hand and left the room.

There was a long, troubled silence during which the wine was finished and crusts of bread were shredded into little hills of crumbs. Then one of the men said, "Hemorrhoids!"

Joy was carrying in the dessert, her lips a narrow pleated line. *"Please,"* she said.

"I know it's not a pleasant subject," the man admitted. "It's not dinner-table chitchat, like water breaking and dilation, so do forgive me. But the anus happens to be the area of the body that is more sensitive to pain than any other part of man."

"Oh ho, of *man*," his wife said, spooning her parfait. "*Man* couldn't take a half hour of hard labor. Not five stinking minutes."

Her husband stood up, his napkin falling to the floor. His face was dark with blood. "Why don't you shut your trap," he suggested.

"Hey, everybody," Kenny said, recalling that he was the host of this shipwrecked party. But he felt helpless, with that malingerer—his leg in an ankle-to-thigh cast—propped on a pillowed chair.

The evening ended badly; it was a long time ago. Two of the couples have since divorced, and Kenny's leg has healed completely. He has to use strong light to find the thin surgical scar. But the children are conspicuously here, are flourishing like trees.

And birth is the greatest drama he can imagine, one he had to watch from the sidelines, moaning and cheering like a football fan whose team is in danger of losing the playoffs.

Joy's labors were long and arduous, and her courage extraordinary. Her streaked blond hair that he'd always loved was dark with perspiration. The terrible, wanton ease of screwing, Kenny thought the first time he watched her writhe and pant and thrust. Whose asshole idea was it to let fathers in, anyway? A few months before, they had quarreled bitterly over an expensive lamp Joy had bought. If anything happened to her now, Kenny promised himself, he'd cut off his prick with a broken light bulb.

But it didn't. And he hasn't. Thank God.

When Steven was finally born, and held up for scrutiny in all his glazed perfection, Kenny had lost sight of his own long-past participation in this event. He was astounded and moved to see that the baby looked just like him.

Even before he met Daphne, though, things were not good in Kenny's marriage. This was the truth, not just a story he'd invented to console Daphne that day she'd wept in his arms and said, "I'm not a homewrecker, am I, Kenny? I'm not, am I?"

He and Joy argued about the most trivial matters. He often couldn't remember the details an hour later, but the anger remained, and a shameful appetite for revenge. Joy became more extravagant, pushing him into petty stinginess. She bought a white fox jacket, and he traveled five miles to save three cents a gallon on gas.

They were lousy together in bed, and each accused the other of simply getting off without concern for sentiment. Then she stopped having orgasms, hardly moved at all. He felt as if he were trying to resuscitate a drowned stranger. Had she faked it before? All those previous outcries and shudders struck him now as too convulsive, as theatrical and contrived. He started to come almost before he'd begun, or he lost his erection completely. "Well, I'm not a necrophiliac!" he'd yell, on his way to the bathroom, the refrigerator, the sofa. She wouldn't say anything. He had the conviction, though, that she was smiling secretly in the darkness.

Often they spoke to one another only through the children. "Give Daddy the mail, honey. There's an important bill in there."

"Tell Mommy I'll be home late."

Even when they were all in the same room, Steven delivered their messages with the cheerful willingness of a dog.

Kenny and Joy had been strongly in love once; he's certain of that. Years ago, when they were separated for the first time by a business trip, he had sent a telegram that simply said: I AM JOYLESS.

Yet it's difficult now to trace their history and find the very beginning of that love's dissolution. They went to a marriage counselor, but Joy became frustrated by the man's refusal to take sides, especially hers when she felt vehemently righteous. And Kenny resented the counselor's insistence that they argue only in his presence, as if they were children who could not be trusted alone with matches, with their dangerous combustible rage. Mutual dissatisfaction drew them together for a while, and they quit the counselor, but it was a false, temporary peace. With the loss of a common enemy, their own hostilities soon resumed.

A little over a week ago, on Saturday, Joy went into Beverly Hills to shop, and Kenny was supposed to be babysitting. He fell asleep in his chair, drinking a beer and watching a rerun of a Rams game. He woke in a panic and found the children playing safely and quietly near his feet. Kenny's chest was strewn with doll blankets and dish towels. Kids were always doing and saying things that could kill you later when you remembered them, especially if you didn't live at home anymore. He thought of Joy at that moment, in the dressing room of some exclusive boutique, avenging his failure to make her happy by attacking his slight tendency toward thrift.

When she learned about Daphne, wouldn't she strike back by trying to deprive him of the central passion of his life—Steven and Molly?

Three months after he met Daphne, Kenny privately consulted a lawyer. Bill Larkin, plucked from a prominent ad in the Yellow Pages—*Divorce/Civil/Real Estate/Criminal/Advice to Do-It-Yourselfers*—because the man he regularly used, whose office is right down the hall from Kenny's, is also Joy's cousin. Her whole family is crawling with lawyers.

Larkin told him to ease himself very slowly out of the marriage. "It's like defusing a bomb, you know?" he said. He had a handy metaphor or aphorism for everything. "Don't admit to anything," he advised. "She'll nail you to the cross if she finds out about what's-her-name. A woman scorned and all that jazz. Sometimes it's only the dough you've spent on your honey that gets them. They add it all up: motels, dinners, gifts, you know? It makes them crazy, especially if they've been stretching the meat loaf with soy beans, squeezing the yellow into the oleo."

Kenny bypassed the inconceivable notion of Joy on a household budget. And what motels? What dinners? He'd been so fearful of detection that he hadn't taken Daphne anywhere, at least not until he'd convinced her to move out of L.A. for a while. Even in Ventura, where no one else he knows lives or works, he chooses a dark, obscure restaurant for the occasional lunch they share. The menus can barely be read by the weak, flickering light of the memorial candle on each table. But he is so sick with love and apprehension he can hardly eat anyway, or make proper conversation. It doesn't matter; the fork in her hand starts to tremble less than halfway through the meal. They race back to Daphne's apartment and throw open the sofa bed, working faster than that kid in the Castro commercial.

Bill Larkin gave him a scenario to play out at home. He said, "When the time is ripe, put it to your wife like this: 'You're not happy, right? Well, I'm not happy, either. Life is short and misery's long. Why should we torture ourselves? Why shouldn't we be happy? Only not together.' Then make love to her a couple of times," Larkin advised. "Send her a dozen roses. Just remember that goodbye is a lot like hello." He leaned back and lit a big cigar, while Kenny searched the diplomas on the wall behind the desk.

As soon as things open up between Joy and himself, as soon as he feels they can speak sanely to one another, he'll get a proper attorney, a powerful and respected shark like Joy's cousin; somebody who will make sure he doesn't lose his kids. Until then, he must be careful not to say Daphne's name in his sleep, or even worse, when he's awake.

The silver Mercedes passes on the right, its horn screaming. The singing driver gives Kenny the finger.

Jesus, he must have passed Camarillo. When Aristotle said that happiness is good, he probably didn't mean this kind of happiness, taken on the sly. If only bigamy was an accepted practice. It could save so much aggravation, time, money. He doesn't have anything kinky in mind, either, like both women at the same time or anything like that . . .

He has a dual reverie of Daphne in the shower at her Ventura apartment, washing her seaweed hair, her full breasts sleek and running with water; and of Joy sitting fully clothed on a chair in their Sherman Oaks living room. He holds them together in his head for one thrilling moment. Then Daphne shuts off the water and wraps all of herself discreetly in a large towel. She disappears into a mist of steam. Joy continues to sit there, staring straight ahead, waiting for him to come home.

3

She's late again, only fifteen minutes this time, but Mrs. Shumway gives her a killing look. Daphne's partners, who chat together in Spanish, are already setting out the sectioned Styrofoam trays to be filled. Other aides are at their places across the kitchen.

After Kenny's visits, all of Daphne's reflexes seem slowed, as if the efforts of love are numbing. On these days, knowing that she might be late, she puts on her white uniform at home, something she prefers not to do because it arouses staring and comments from strangers. People want to know if she's a hairdresser, or a nurse. A woman in a supermarket once asked Daphne to remove a sliver of glass from her finger. Today, as she walked to her car, a drunk sitting on a bus-stop bench assumed she was a bride, and said that she should not wear white if she wasn't pure.

Daphne puts her hairnet on, and looks into the steaming pots and pans on the nearest stove. Some kind of fish tonight, and macaroni, and a cauldron of murky soup in which bits of vegetables rise to the surface like flotsam in a boiling sea.

The Rolodex file of dietary restrictions is on the counter, where Feliciana Juarez places a cellophane packet of plastic utensils on each tray.

Daphne calls out, "Aaron, Mrs. T.! 215A! No sugar! No salt! No fat!"

Feliciana's sister, Evita, staples a name and a room slip to one of the trays and intones, "Aaron, Señora T., doscientos trienta y cinco A. No azúcar. No sal. No grasa . . . Ay, qué vida!" Feliciana ladles it all out.

When Daphne gets to McBride, Mrs. N., who is only low sodium, there's a break in the assembly rhythm and a flurry of Spanish between the two other women. McBride is the ninety-nine-year-old. The whole place is in a state of excitement about the party planned for her hundredth birthday on September 6. There has not been such a celebration at the Palomar Arms for years, which isn't surprising, considering the circumstances. Loneliness and boredom might have carried off a few contenders, or the food alone could have done it. Mrs. Shumway roasts or boils everything until it turns black or white and lies defeated in the shallow grave of a serving tray.

And Daphne knows that mistakes are made, that dinners, and occasionally medicines, are delivered to the wrong patients. Last month, a severe diabetic, delighted by the sweet and unexpected change in his diet, polished off the ice cream and fruit salad meant for somebody else. He had to be revived with an emergency dose of insulin when he was found, slumped and stunned over his bed table, two hours later.

Mrs. McBride is well, though, and has attained the status of a local celebrity. Other patients and their visitors look in at the doorway of 227 and exclaim, "That's her!" as if they've sighted Elizabeth Taylor or

Jackie Onassis. Once in a while her photograph is taken with a flash camera, probably blinding the old woman for minutes afterward. Her good health is toasted by staff members with pint bottles in the linen room and the pantry, where bets are placed as to whether or not she'll make it. The latest odds are in her favor, and should increase as the days are counted down.

When the trays are all filled, they're placed onto rolling meal carts, and then taken up to the second and third floors for rewarming and distribution. As the aides wait in the basement for the two elevators, which are notoriously slow, they take turns hitting the call button, even though it's already lit. Sometimes they tell horror stories to help pass the time. It's a sort of open competition in which Daphne has never participated, except as an audience. She would like to join in, but has not yet come up with a worthy anecdote, or the necessary nerve.

Now she thinks of a story idea one of the men in her scriptwriting class presented the week before, about an aborted fetus that returns to threaten a wealthy beach community. It has enough incredibility for this occasion, and is suitably gruesome. But something, maybe the setting, makes Daphne feel it's inappropriate, so she doesn't volunteer to speak.

Instead, she listens as an older woman describes the ghost of a man who was buried without his dentures, and who haunts the Palomar Arms on the midnight-to-eight shift, searching for them in the night-table drawers.

It's a flat and familiar tale that's greeted with a mixture of catcalls and disparaging murmurs. The narrator shrugs and punches the call button.

Soon another woman begins. She worked at a nursing home in Chicago once where the cook poisoned every old lady who looked the least bit like her own mother. She injected their canned peaches with arsenic, and must have killed fifty or sixty of them before anyone caught on.

"Why did she do it?" Daphne asks.

"Her mother would never let her ride on the carpet sweeper when she was a little girl," the woman explains.

"Aaah, go on," the first storyteller says, but Evita whispers, "Dios mío," and Daphne looks back toward the kitchen, where Mrs. Shumway is starting tomorrow's soup from a pile of bones.

There's a thoughtful pause.

"Dr. Rauscher hypnotizes people into leaving him all their money," someone announces.

"Oh, who don't know *that*," Feliciana says, her disdain instantly silencing the other.

Then a black aide named Lucille James says that she doesn't know if she should even tell her story, because it's so disgusting it could give somebody permanent nerves.

It's a wonderful opening, and her best friend, Ruthann, promptly says, "Tell it, girl. I've heard everything; you won't get me."

"Okay," Lucille says. "But don't get mad if you're sick or something later." This story really happened, she states, to a friend of her cousin's, in Detroit. The person it happened to, a middle-aged lady, had this big dog—some brand name, an Irish or German dog. *Mean.* "But he loved this lady who owned him," Lucille says, "so she gets nervous when she comes home from work one day and he doesn't come to the door or anything."

"He's dead!" Ruthann proclaims.

"Naw. But the lady hears something strange, like a choking sound." Lucille pauses, surveys her rapt audience, and goes on. "She comes inside and that dog is lying on the floor, choking his head off. So she calls to him and says, 'What's the matter?' like you do, and then when she sees he can't even bark, and all his legs are twitching like a roach in Raid, she sticks her hand right down his throat. But she can't find anything. Whatever's in there, it's too deep."

"If it's a rat," Ruthann says, "just keep it to yourself. I can't stand when it's about rats."

"So she picks him up and runs out into the street and goes to the animal hospital. All this time that dog's choking and twitching."

"I don't even like when it's about dogs," Feliciana says.

Lucille continues. "The doctor has to open up the dog's throat to get out what's choking him, and that lady's standing right there watching the operation, so she sees him take out this finger and put it on the table."

"A finger?" Daphne asks. "A *human* finger?"

"Lord, Lord," Ruthann intones.

"You know any other kind of finger?" Lucille asks Daphne.

"Did the dog die?" Feliciana says.

"So the doctor says, 'We better call the police,' and they do."

"I'm not eating my dinner," Evita announces.

"Honey, you're gonna lose *weight*," Lucille assures her, before resuming the narrative. "The lady goes back to her apartment with the police and they notice these bloodstains she didn't notice before, because she was all upset about the dog. And they follow those bloodstains right to the closet in the lady's bedroom."

"Have mercy!" Ruthann cries.

But Lucille doesn't. "The police open up the closet door and this burglar's body falls out, every single drop of blood drained right out of it . . ."

"Oh. Oh," someone says faintly.

"And . . . one . . . finger . . . missing!" Lucille finishes in a hoarse, triumphant whisper as both elevators descend and open at once.

Daphne has only five more trays to deliver before she can go up to the staff lounge for her supper break. The first belongs to Miss Nettleson, the Dream Lady, who greets everyone with a recital of something she's recently dreamed, or invented. Most of the employees, and the other patients, ignore her, or listen with the nondirective attention of classical analysts. Sometimes, one of the floor aides brings in her dream book and offers direct interpretations. Dreams about gold portend disappointment; blood means money, or shame; a wedding in which the dreamer is dressed as a bride foretells heavy sickness and death.

In her youth, Miss Nettleson had been a movie actress. She has a scrapbook of her career on the shelf of her narrow closet, and once she showed Daphne stills of herself in romantic poses with John Gilbert and Nils

Asther. She was round-faced, dimpled, and appealing then, and although she worked steadily for years, she never became a star.

Daphne, who remembers a few of the Freudian dream symbols from last semester's course in general psychology, keeps them to herself and remains neutral. She suspects that Miss Nettleson has not quite given up the wonderland of the movies, in which made-up stories protect you from real life the way dreams are supposed to protect your sleep. "Fish tonight!" Daphne announces, and Miss Nettleson says, as if they had already been in deep conversation that day, "And then I'm in a place like a meadow. There are sheep all around, but they have faces like people . . ."

Daphne sets the tray down, and plumps the pillows behind Miss Nettleson's back. "And macaroni," she says before tiptoeing out.

The next two trays go to room 225, which is shared by a pair of widowed sisters. Their place is mobbed with personal belongings, like a room in a college dorm. Family photos hang on every wall next to crayoned landscapes with the word *Nana* scrawled at the top of most of them, and the name *Terri* or *Michelle* at the bottom. There are throw pillows with elaborate needlepoint covers, and a small forest of plants on the windowsill, crowding one another for space and light. Each night table holds a Kleenex dispenser and an eyeglass case covered in needlepoint like the cushions, and there are two ceramic mugs that say *Bank of America* on the side. A four-footed cane and a metal walker keep each other company against one wall.

The first time Daphne saw Mrs. Feldman and Mrs. Bernstein, she thought they were twins. They were sitting close together on matching chairs, wearing similar flowered housecoats and holding hands. Gradually, over the weeks, Daphne began to notice the differences between them.

Mrs. Feldman is older, by several years. Her hair is much thinner than her sister's, and the small hump of age just below the back of the neck is more pronounced. The widow's hump. Mrs. Bernstein has had a stroke, and the side of her face Daphne didn't see immediately is pulled down. It battles against the other side when it works to smile.

Both women are smiling as Daphne comes in with their trays. They're watching television, a game show that sounds excessively loud and frantic. As in all the rooms, the set is bolted to a ceiling bracket and aimed downward at the viewers like a riot gun in a prison tower.

"Look who's here, Pearl," Mrs. Feldman says. "Hello, dear. Oh, supper! That looks nice."

"Is it Betty?" Mrs. Bernstein asks, the sentence drawled and slow.

"Now, don't be dopey," her sister chides. "It's that nice girl, bringing our supper. Thank you, dear. Aren't you pretty today? Pearl, we'll have to introduce her to Richard."

"Is it still raining?" Mrs. Bernstein asks. Daphne has to lean forward to understand her. "He said it was raining." Mrs. Bernstein points her useful hand at the television screen, where the emcee is counting money into a contestant's outstretched palm. The whole audience counts along with him in a steady chant: "*One* hundred, *two* hundred, *three* hundred . . ."

"Now, Pearl, you know they tape that show. You know Jack Barry's not live. Look out the window. Is it raining?"

". . . *eight* hundred, *nine* hundred, a *thousand* dollars!"

"It rained a little bit yesterday," Daphne offers, but Mrs. Bernstein is examining her tray. "Oh, not *fish*," she says, and sounds close to tears. But that could just be the way she speaks.

Her sister opens both packets of utensils, using her teeth, and proceeds to cut up Mrs. Bernstein's dinner.

"Do you need any help?" Daphne asks.

"No, thank you, dear. We're just fine," Mrs. Feldman says.

"Well, I guess I'll be going then," Daphne says. "I have one more room to do. Enjoy your dinner."

"We will," Mrs. Feldman assures her. "We always do, don't we, Pearl? Have a nice evening now. Take care. And thanks a million."

"You, too," Daphne says, not quite sure what she's answering.

Before she lifts the last meals from her cart, she tries to imagine the two sisters as children, sharing a room then, too, with a different kind of clutter: dolls, skates, schoolbooks. But it's impossible to do. They are fixed forever in her head the way she's just seen them. Only her own, more recent, childhood is within reach of imagination and memory, and even that's uncertain. When

Daphne visits her family in Seattle, she and her mother argue about little points of family history. No, of course Daphne never had a pink tulle dress with a satin slip—does she think her mother has no taste at all?—and they moved before her grandfather died, not after, doesn't she remember?

Daphne takes a small perfume dispenser from her uniform pocket and sprays both of her wrists generously, and then the back of her neck.

She brings the final trays to 227, where the current star of the Palomar Arms is sitting in quiet darkness. The blind is drawn against the vanishing light, and the television set is blank and silent. It's clear that someone in here wets herself.

Daphne's eyes adjust and she finds Mrs. McBride, who is uncommonly tall and thin, sitting upright in her chair, asleep. Maybe it's the influence of all the centennial talk, but she looks monumental to Daphne, like the seated statue of Lincoln in Washington, D.C. Especially when Daphne throws the light switch, illuminating her. Such stillness! Daphne's breath catches. What if she's dead, with less than two months to go?

Mrs. McBride opens her eyes that are smoky with sleep and cataracts, and Daphne is held for a moment by their solemn gaze. Then she puts the two trays down, and adjusts Mrs. McBride's table over those draped angular knees. "Supper!" Daphne sings out, and hears muffled weeping from the other bed, where a large blanketed form is lying. That patient's daughter, who's usually there to feed her mother, must be out using the hall telephone, or the visitors' bathroom.

"Where's . . ." Daphne begins, and then she sees the ribbon bow. It's pink satin, and might have come from a candy box or an overdressed plant. Someone has tied it into the sparse white hair at the top of Mrs. McBride's head. It destroys her awesome dignity, making her look like one of those absurd little poodles that yap and dance around on two frilled legs. A playful nurse must have done it, or a phantom fan, while the old woman was sleeping. Daphne forgets her unfinished question. She reaches up and snatches the ribbon from Mrs. McBride's hair. It slides right off, and Daphne shoves it into her pocket, alongside the perfume dispenser. "There!" she says, and hurries out of the room.

Jerry Palumbo, one of the physical therapists, and Monica Mann, from Laundry, are sharing a joint in the staff lounge when Daphne gets there. They're already stoned, and smile like cats as Daphne takes her yogurt and fruit from the refrigerator. Two maintenance men are asleep in chairs, and Mkabi Wilson, a second-floor RN, is at a table, shuffling through a stack of index cards. During the day she attends a bartending school. It's a six-week course, and when she graduates she'll have a certificate that will enable her to work at private parties, where she could earn as much per hour as she does for nursing. Then she'll try to get a different shift here.

Mkabi and her husband Darryl are fiercely ambitious. He works two jobs now, and their small son Bobby spends much of his time at a day-care center, or with one of his grandmothers. It's for Bobby's sake that his parents are working this hard. They both grew up in the Watts ghetto and want to provide insurance against poverty for him. Money is being set aside for Bobby's education, with the ultimate goal of medical, dental, or law school. They want to buy a house soon in a more affluent neighborhood, so that the boy will have a natural sense of himself in a privileged environment. Mkabi is named for a Zulu princess and she looks royal, with her elegant neck and that dense crown of spiraling curls the tiny cap can't suppress. She waves at Daphne and continues to work through her cards, which contain recipes for various mixed drinks.

Daphne sniffs at her yogurt and begins to eat.

"Hey, baby," Jerry says. He holds the minuscule joint out to Daphne, who shakes her head, indicating the yogurt.

"Moss gets high on Dannon," Monica says. She refers to everyone by surname.

"Looking good, Daphne," Jerry says. He's compact, hairy, and limber, and reminds her of those illustrations in her anthropology text of that form of life midway between ape and man. Physical Therapy, or PT, as it's called at the Palomar Arms, shuts down before the patients' dinner hour, but, to Daphne's surprise, Jerry rarely leaves directly after work. He hangs around, coming on to one of the women or another in a blatant, almost ludicrous way. Can anyone take him seriously? He's wearing white pants and sneakers, and a white T-shirt with a picture of Joan Crawford on it, and the caption: *I Never Laid a Fucking Hand on Those Kids.*

After Daphne finishes her supper, she volunteers to

help Mkabi study. They face one another and Daphne takes the cards. "Pink Squirrel," she says.

Mkabi shuts her eyes and begins reciting: "Stemmed cocktail glass, mixing cup, ice. Two ounces cream, half ounce white crème de cacao, half ounce crème de almond. Blend and strain."

"Right!" Daphne says. "How about a Gin Presbyterian?"

After Mkabi goes back on duty, Monica and Jerry start to dance without music. Monica is a big blonde in a tent dress. "La-la-la," she sings, and Jerry bends her backward in an exaggerated dip, making her shriek. One of the maintenance men wakes up, stares blearily, and then goes back to sleep. Monica and Jerry collapse against one another on the orange couch.

"Mkabi manages to do so much," Daphne says. "She's absolutely amazing."

"Wilson?" Monica says. "She's a real dreamer."

"No, she's not," Daphne argues. "She and Darryl work harder than anyone I know, and they save every penny they can. Bobby's going to have a better chance because of them. How can you say she's a dreamer?"

"Do you know what's gonna happen to that kid?" Monica asks. "After Mommy and Daddy break their backs stashing it away for him? Do you know what little Bobby's gonna do?"

"What?" Jerry asks, kissing her on the neck.

She pushes him away. "Little Bobby's gonna drop out, drop acid, snort coke, and shoot smack. He's gonna rob banks, pimp women, and break his lovin' mama's heart."

Daphne is furious. "What a dumb, racist thing to say,

Monica! Bobby is a wonderful child. He's already a superior student in preschool, and he's going to have a terrific life."

Monica smiles, her lids heavy. She holds up her hands as if to ward off a mighty force. "Okay, okay," she says. "You win. I take it all back. He's a great kid, a real little genius. He's gonna grab all the honors, and Harvard and Yale are gonna fight over him. You win." She falls silent, yet Daphne is uneasy, as if something invisible but evil has entered the room.

"Then you know what's gonna happen?" Monica begins again. Her voice is husky with intent. "After they get him the best house in the best neighborhood? The best car? Little Bobby's best house is gonna burn down with him in it. Faulty wiring, he doesn't even smoke. Or a fucked-up white cop shoots him dead, by mistake. No, no! Wait! Some drunk is gonna jump the divider when Dr. Bobby's speeding in his 450SL to save another sucker's life. Crash. Bang. That's what's gonna happen."

Daphne feels ill, almost faint. Her whole body is swarming with anger and anxiety. "That's sick, Monica," she says. "Really *sick*. How can you say such terrible things?"

"Because that's how it works," Monica says. "Do you really think anything's fair? Do you think Ken's gonna leave Barbie in their dream house and marry you? What a whiny little feeb you are, Moss. Go out there. Go down the halls. Look in the rooms. *That's* what happens."

"She's stoned," Jerry explains, but his own face is pale, and he has edged away from Monica to the other side of the couch. He attempts to change the subject.

"They're closing in on Rauscher, you know, for Medicare fraud."

Daphne moves in an injured trance as she retrieves the dinner trays. Most of the patients are sleeping or watching television. She looks down toward the floor, avoiding their faces. The night-lights reveal discarded slippers, newspapers, and enterprising roaches darting off with fallen crumbs of food.

She regrets having confided in Monica and Mkabi the week before when the three of them were alone together in the lounge for a while. It was as if the secret of herself and Kenny could no longer be contained. Did love always call up a braggart's need to spread the news? Or was it insecurity that made her blab everything, for the confirmation of envy and support? Someone else to say yes, yes, it's wonderful, it's rare, it's true. Perhaps her only error was in the choice of confidantes, although that evening Monica had been mildly neutral, almost approving. Mkabi, on the other hand, had delivered a sermonette on the virtuousness of virtue. One didn't mess around with married men; it invariably led to tragedy. "Huh," Monica had commented. "Being *married* to a married man is what leads to that." She had hinted on previous occasions of at least two failed marriages of her own. After what she'd said tonight, though . . . well, she's crazy, that's all. This whole place is a madhouse.

Daphne's rubber soles suck at the floor, and her meal cart rattles and squeals. Oh, why couldn't she have gotten that job with the telephone company? The woman in Personnel had seemed to like her in the initial interview. Daphne's story about moving from L.A. to Ventura to be closer to her fiancé sounded reasonable and appealing. She'd explained that she would have an associate's degree in communications by the end of the year, mumbling the word "associate's" and carefully emphasizing "communications." The only real lie was a small one. She had actually moved here to be *away* from Kenny, or safely out of the radarscope of his wife's suspicion. Daphne hated the word "fiancé," though, and felt later that it was hardly appropriate under the circumstances. It occurred to her that other words relating to marriage were equally unsatisfactory. "Bonds of matrimony" could be a euphemism for S and M; and she hoped that when her wedding to Kenny finally did take place, no newspaper announcement would say that her nuptials had been held.

Unexpectedly, Daphne encounters herself in the mirror in 225, where the sisters are asleep. In the dim light, her simple white uniform is not unbridelike. She wonders at her patience with Kenny, that she has accepted with such good will his lawyer's advice of extreme caution, that Kenny still lives at home with his wife and children, that nothing has been hinted to that wife of his affair with Daphne. And that Daphne is displaced here in Ventura, here at the Palomar Arms, in on a conspiracy against herself. U.C.L.A. was a much better school. And she had been able to find more interesting work, on and off campus, that fit into her schedule.

She thinks of Allen Burdette, a doctoral student in psychology she was seeing just before she met Kenny. He looked a lot like Al Pacino, only taller, and after a date he'd phone her and recite Keats: "What can I do to drive away / Remembrance from my eyes? for they have seen, / Ay, an hour ago, my brilliant Queen!"

Daphne and Allen were on the brink of sexual convergence, and then Kenny showed up in her life. When she was packing to go to Ventura, Allen rang her doorbell. It was past midnight, and he looked drunk or high on something. She prayed that he wouldn't start quoting sonnets or villanelles at her while she wound her dishes in bubble wrap. But instead he paced among the cartons for a few moments before saying, "I really heated you up for that guy, didn't I?"

Still, she is weighted with homesickness. She misses her close female friends in Los Angeles, and has hesitated to ask anyone to visit overnight, for fear it will be the very night that Kenny's wife decides to go out of town with the children. So far, though, she's never gone farther than Rodeo Drive.

In the kitchen, a portable television set is playing. Mrs. Shumway is long gone, and the aides are watching the news as they clean up. The volume is low, but sound ricochets off the white tiled walls, giving everything, even the commercials, a strange profundity. It is as if God Himself is commanding them to buy Rice-A-Roni. On the local news, a municipal judge, convicted of conspiracy and accepting bribes, is led away in handcuffs. Daphne cools her face in the smoking frost of the freezer. How does she know that Kenny no longer sleeps with his wife, or if he's really seen a lawyer? How does she know anything?

4

Nora McBride has lied about her age; she is only ninety-seven years old and won't be entitled to the centennial celebration in her honor in August or September, whenever her birthday is. Still, she's the oldest resident of the home, unless someone is shaving off a few years. How easy it used to be to falsify or invent personal records. Births were often registered late, or not at all. Immigrants searched their bundles for proof of themselves, and then were handed new American names for their new lives.

These days, even wrong facts become the truth. They put them into those machines and then they can't get them out. That's why dead people get magazines in the mail, and notices of white sales forever.

Nora's lie about her age is not a recent one. It was made up for the purpose of her seduction of and marriage to John Nolan McBride more than eighty years ago. Eighty-three years, she thinks. He was a severely moral, albeit passionate, man, and would not have wanted to rob the cradle. Nora was the youngest of a dozen children, and her tired parents didn't thwart her fearful wish to marry at fourteen. They might have lost track of her age themselves—there were so many children. And the older girls were the ones they'd held on to.

Lying awake now in the middle of the night, Nora remembers, no, *feels*, the rough pull of her sister Catherine's hand on the way to school, to church. And the way Agnes brushed Nora's hair until it almost caught on fire, as if she wanted to yank it all out and be done with the chore forever. Well, most of it's gone now, and so is poor Agnes. Nora's fingers follow the bony definitions of her own skull and she thinks of Agnes, toes up in her coffin, and how she hated to get out of bed on those Boston winter mornings. Everything was luck— your placement in the family, your sex. The boys were sent off to school, the younger girls allowed to break away. Nora is the only surviving member of that large, urgent family. All that noise, once, and the food!

The meals here are bland and watery. When the new girl, the one who wears so much perfume, brings supper, the soup tastes like Evening in Paris. How can Nora be so ravenous, even want such food? How can she still want?

In one respect, at least, she remains the way she was as a girl and a young woman. She cannot believe, for more than a stricken moment at a time, in her own death. The stubborn forces of life, will, and denial all distract her, just as they did when she was a fourteen-year-old bride and a twenty-nine-year-old widow. Maybe it's because she never had any children, and has lost the logic of the generations.

But she must make herself know it soon, and be prepared; otherwise, she might be taken by surprise, something she's always hated. A frail, dreamy girl, she would beat her brother Henry with a wild infusion of strength whenever he jumped from behind a door and screamed "Boo!" at her. Pay attention, she orders herself as she falls into those abrupt and frequent daytime naps. She sleeps less at night, though, is often awake like this, and thinks, against all reason, that death will only come in filtered darkness, if ever. Fool. She has seen them trundle off enough bodies in the heart of the day, while meal carts rattled down the corridor in the other direction, and elsewhere in the world people boarded buses. There's no "Death" to come and get you, anyway, Nora knows, having tried on and cast off religion, mysticism, and any other possible form of consolation. It is you who go, ready or not. She should be ready, even eager, to fly from this body with all its traitorous parts, to be gone from this place with its dreary bingo games, the various therapies that only absorb time and don't fix anything. In PT she travels halfway across a long room, using a walker, and then she comes back. Perhaps it takes a whole day. In RT she's a constant winner of bingo, lotto, and keno. They tell her she wins, anyway; she can't make out the cards anymore. That blur of noise and numbers gets her fuzzy until someone shouts "Bingo!" into her ear, and raises her dozing arm to claim a prize. Every Christmas, Nora gives little gift packets of plastic rain hats, ballpoint pens, and sewing kits to the aides who awarded them to her in the first place. In OT she's making a multicolored potholder on a child's loom, but her wrist will never be bent again by an iron skillet.

Oh, butter, eggs! Jack McBride at the edge of a vast white bed, suspenders down, taking off one shoe. Certain images return with a physical rush and hot clarity, although she keeps losing and finding recent events, ideas, people. During all her years in this place, she's had so many roommates. Forty? Fifty? There were some early intense friendships, and a few wars, but most of the time it's like sharing a train compartment with a series of strangers on a distant, uncertain journey. Too many of them want the television, even when they're turned away from it, even when the picture rolls and rolls like the wheels of a train. Television is worse than life.

Now it's starting to be morning again; the sun isn't bored yet with its work. It rises in the east and throws light into the room, revealing the sleeping form of Nora's current roommate, an obese woman who's suffered a stroke. She hasn't been here long—a week or a month. Nora can't remember her name, and probably the woman can't either. She's aphasic, confused, heartbroken. As soon as she wakes, she starts to wail. Those who have lost everything but single phrases recite them now. Next door the Oh, God man begins his first lamentation of the day—"Oh, God! Oh, God! Oh, God!" There are other voices from other rooms—Nora hears only those at the highest decibels—the crowing calls of morning need and complaint: hunger, thirst, pain, toilet! Everybody wants something.

As the oldest, Nora is strangely like the youngest again. Her bare gums ache as if they're going to yield a third harvest of teeth. This bed has bars, the way her first one did, and she is cared for with the same grudging sense of duty. But the caretakers here are nursing aides, usually Chicanos or blacks who address every elderly female patient as Mama. They urge rattleboned behinds onto bedpans, crooning, "Come on now, Mama. Do it for me, Mama." And they press heaping spoonsful of food against lax or greedy mouths, sometimes when the old women are still propped on their pans or commodes. In and out, the first law of the body. "That's right, Mama. That's good."

Nora's last roommate, or the one before that, was a Jewish woman in her eighties. She was senile, but had transitory moments of a kind of lucidity. She would come to, astonished and not displeased to find herself the mother of such dark and exuberant children. She must have given birth to them in some twilight sleep of her old age, like Sarah. But how good they were to her. "Ziseh kinder!" she would exclaim, and blow kisses after them, using both hands. In less rational times, she would inquire suspiciously of her handler, "Du bist a Yid?"

Seen through the bars of Nora's bed, the people in the hall go by in flickering motion, like dancers in those little books you flipped through.

The new roommate, who is crying now, will probably cry until she loses the ability to do that, too. Her broken sounds are like the bleats of a newborn lamb, or the noises from that radio down the hall someone keeps dialing and dialing.

What am I doing here, Nora wonders, her meaning as unsure as ever.

If the weather is good, her birthday party will be on the lawn. "Ahhh, Mama," she tells her roommate. "Cheer up, will you? What's the use?"

5

The red light behind the bed glows like the end of a cigarette. Neither Kenny nor Joy smokes, although both of them did at one time. In those days, after lovemaking, the cigarette they shared burned like a firefly in the darkness, at her lips, at his. Now they don't smoke, they don't make love.

She had been such a passionate girl once, almost comically so, wanting more and more, shouting her demands and her satisfaction. "Oh, do it, *do it*, I said! That's good, that's wonderful. Don't stop, my darling, don't stop or I'll kill you!" Even several months ago, just before things began to go really bad, there was clear evidence of a hard, leftover lust—quieter perhaps, maybe less violent, but certainly there.

They lie far apart on the large bed, as far as they can without falling off. The distance between them is like a desert, or an unswimmable body of water, and Kenny wonders for the first time if Joy, too, has taken a lover. It's been weeks since they've touched one another, except by accident, sparking only embarrassment then, or the electric current of their tempers. Has she been doing it with someone else? He cannot imagine the reality of that, although the idea takes hold, with tentacles, in his head and chest. Another man, meeting Joy elsewhere in utter secrecy, as he meets Daphne. Discovering that lovely skin under the lovely skins of her extravagant clothing. What does Kenny feel? So many things at once that he can't define his reaction as a single feeling. Unreasonable fury, denial, a moment of cold detachment, culpability . . . relief? Maybe she's simply doing *without* it, uncharacteristic as that may be. People change. Their moods change, the intensity of their needs.

Tonight, Joy's parents are asleep just down the hall, in the guest room. They'd arrived that afternoon from New York for a two-week vacation. On other, earlier, visits, Gus and Frances's presence in the house seemed to stimulate Kenny and Joy into sexual action. A carryover from the parental taboos of their courting days, probably. The danger of committing the forbidden act in the unknowing/knowing nearness of Mother and Father. Then Joy had usually been the instigator—they were *her* mother and father—but Kenny's fervor was heightened, too. He just had the good sense to keep the noise level down.

Now the house is very quiet. The children are sleeping. Gus and Frances are out of it, too, tired from their flight, from the excitement of reunion. Kenny thinks again of how much he cares for them, and how they, like the children, have come into his life by the merest chance. And could be lost the same way.

Joy is motionless on her side of the bed, Kenny on his. The red light behind them locates the panic button for the burglar-alarm system. It was an option he had argued against, in vain. In fact, he had not wanted the whole system installed, at first. Jesus, she bought so much stuff it needed a bodyguard! *Joy's her name and acquisition's her game,* he'd say to himself, almost aloud. But he was already involved with Daphne then, and too beset by nervous guilt to provoke strong new quarrels about money. And maybe a burglar alarm *was* a good idea. The crime rate in Los Angeles was rising with phenomenal speed. There had been numerous break-ins in their general neighborhood, and finally one right next door. Pros, apparently, who went directly to the jewelry, the silverware, the money. Scary. Except that material goods were not what Kenny worried about—only the physical safety of his family. He was old-fashioned in that he'd always enjoyed fantasies about protecting Joy and the kids against attack from the world of crime and perversion. Pow! Bam! Take that, you creeps! He wouldn't admit this to anyone because it was so childish, an extension of those secret boyhood games in which he saved his parents and brother from outer-space creatures, from imaginary enemy bombs. Sometimes he let his brother be the only one killed.

Joy made an appointment, and one Saturday afternoon in February a man from On-Guard, Inc., came to demonstrate his wares. There were choices to be made: wired alarms, or wireless ones; keys, or computerized panels; direct police dialing, or a connection to a central switchboard whose operator dialed the police for you. And a variety of ludicrous options, like the panic button behind the bed. Joy was pre-sold before the guy's arrival, but he showed them everything anyway, using a psychological sales pitch that was careful not to challenge Kenny's ability to defend his own household, single-handed—*bare*-handed, if necessary. It was as if the salesman could see into those dumb fantasies, or even had them himself. He called Kenny "sir," although, balding and potbellied, he was at least fifteen years older. It made Kenny smile. The salesman smiled back, encouraged, and opened an oversized attaché case to reveal a heavy cardboard replica of the front of a ranch-style house. It reminded Kenny of Molly's dollhouse, in which, with her baby's vision of domesticity, she would bed down the doll family along with toy elephants, trains, loose crayons, and her brother's lead soldiers.

"This is your average unprotected home, sir," the salesman said. "Oh, you've got your cylinders, your double bolts, and your dead bolts; your chains, your police locks, and your window screws . . . even your watchdog. You feel *safe*. In fact, you don't even think about it too much. I mean, it's your house, right? *And* the bank's, heh-heh. So who's gonna violate it?"

You, asshole, Kenny wanted to say, but it had only been a rhetorical question. The salesman took a deep, wheezing breath and went on. "In L.A. County alone, in 1980, there were 170,289 illegal entries. Reported, that is. Because of the nature of some of the crimes, plenty of them don't get reported, if you know what I mean. The crook, *crooks* enter the house—middle of the night, broad daylight, you name it. They get in through a window, a door, the basement . . . No alarms go off, no warning to the man of the house, to the police, to nobody."

Kenny peered into the attaché case and saw, near the lower left corner of the house façade, a black metal box with two exposed wires dangling from it—one red, one blue.

"But," the salesman said, deftly twisting the red and

blue wires together, using only one hand, "with an On-Guard Protect-All System, the family is safe. *Let the intruders enter!*" He said that last with the corny overkill of a kid in a school play. With his free hand, he lifted the housefront to reveal a realistically drawn and painted interior of a living room. A woman was seated at the piano in the picture, her hands poised gracefully above the keys. A man stood just behind her, a proprietary arm around her shoulders. His mouth was open in the perfect O of joyous song. Two children, a boy and girl about the ages of Steven and Molly, were frolicking on the rug with a large German shepherd. A lively fire danced in the hearth behind them.

"Thirty seconds after entry," the salesman said, "the alarm is sounded." Right on cue, there was an earsplitting series of screams from the attaché case. It was one of those maniac whooping sirens, and Kenny winced, while Joy held her hands over her ears. Thank God the kids were playing down the street at a friend's house; it would have scared the hell out of them. The salesman let the siren continue for several seconds after his point was obviously made. "The police are there in no time!" he shouted over the din. "If the homeowner has private weapons, he's ready in a flash!"

It was such a relief when the wires were disconnected and the siren cut off in mid-wail. Kenny wondered briefly if homeowners with guns ever kept them in piano benches. He was grateful that the demonstration was over.

But it wasn't. "*Now,*" the salesman said, "here's the same house, without the System." Again, he lifted the cardboard façade, but this time he revealed a scene of mayhem and plunder. It was only another page, only another richly colored painting of the same living room. Again the rendition was terribly realistic, especially the blood. The woman was still seated at the piano, but at a strange, unnatural angle. Her sheet music was scattered all around her, and splattered red. Cupboards and drawers hung open, their contents tangled and spilled. The man was undoubtedly dead; no one could possibly be alive with such extensive wounds, with wide-open, staring eyes like his. The O of his mouth was shock, not song. The children were still alive. Their eyes were wide open, too, but with unmistakable terror. They were in the clutches of two masked men. There were four or five masked men in the room, one of them holding a smoking gun over the felled dog. Before the salesman let the housefront drop over this scene of carnage, Kenny noticed that even the fire in the hearth had gone out.

He argued with Joy about a few of the options—the panic button, for instance, and ignition cutoff devices for both of their cars—but gave in finally on the whole package. In truth, he could afford it. Kenny is in business for himself, and business has been good. He knew what he was really buying, anyway, understood the bargain he was making with fate. And maybe when he and Daphne were deliriously fucking some afternoon, the burglar alarm would actually save his family from disaster. He thought about getting a dog, too. The On-Guard demonstration had been imbecilic, as hard-sell as possible. But you only had to open a newspaper to know that you couldn't invent anything more terrible than reality.

He hates that glowing button, though, the last image on his eye before sleep. It triggers dreams in which the siren goes off in the middle of the night, and the police don't come, and the central switchboard doesn't call demanding the code word to signal a false alarm. How Joy had agonized over choosing the *right* code word, one they'd both easily remember, and one an intruder, like Rumpelstiltskin's maiden, could never guess. Her procrastination drove him crazy. "It's not your goddamn *mantra*, for God's sake!" he'd cried, and they finally settled on Gus, her father's name.

One night Kenny did set the alarm off himself, by opening a window without disengaging the system first, and when the operator at the central switchboard promptly called, he answered and said, "It's okay, only a little accident. This is Gus." He felt like such an impostor. Gus is one of the nicest men he knows. He and Frances had taken Kenny on immediately as the son they'd always wanted, and offered unconditional love that thoroughly pleased and amazed him. After all, Joy was their only child, their golden girl, and he had carried her three thousand miles away. His own parents, who live on Long Island, and who are divorced but still at war, had never accepted him without the insidious imposition of judgment. Frances calls him Kenneth, or "dear"—a rare mixture of respect and affection. Once, a long time ago, he'd mentioned that he missed the sand tarts from William Greenberg's bakery on Madison Avenue. Since then, she always brings a box of them in her hand luggage when she and Gus come to L.A.

Gus, who is a dentist, brings a small case of his tools,

and checks out everyone's mouth by the light of the gooseneck lamp in Kenny's study. "Ah, beautiful. Great," he murmurs, peering inside, gently sounding each tooth like a chime. Two years ago, he'd had an operation for lung cancer, had "beaten the big C," as he put it. Without self-pity or misplaced rage. "No sweat," Kenny told the operator after the second false alarm. "I opened the window again. Sorry—this is Gus, signing off." But he was only himself, far less than the hero whose name he took.

Sometimes he dreams that the siren is screaming and he is screaming with it, frozen, of course, unable to act. The painted intruders come to life in those stupid masks. There *is* a dog that won't or can't bark. Kenny is helpless, too, as impotent in his horror as he has been sexually with Joy. Or in his dream the phone rings and rings, and he can't answer it to say that he *isn't* Gus, we're all in trouble, in danger, come save us! He wakes, unconsoled for minutes by the silence, by the way he can move his quivering arms and legs if he needs to. And he feels ashamed. He is, after all, responsible for his own dreams, isn't he? How long it takes for his breathing to become normal once more, for his pulse to calm.

That afternoon, while he and Joy and the children waited for the plane, which was a half hour late, and then an hour late, he murmured something about the men's room and hurried around the corner of the lounge to a bank of telephones. Of course, he'd spoken to Daphne days before about Gus and Frances's upcoming visit, but he felt a sudden panic during the flight delay, a need to explain it all again to her and be reassured again by her patience and understanding. While Joy's parents were in town, he wouldn't be able to get to Ventura very often. Gus and Frances would want to take the whole family out to lunch whenever possible. Since Gus's surgery, they tried to find cause and occasion for celebration every day. They'd want to go to Knott's Berry Farm, Universal Studios, and Disneyland. These were places Kenny usually avoided, even scorned, but he believed that their interest was forgivable, that it came from an innocent wish to please by conforming, not from some witless tourism.

Daphne's phone rang several times before she said, "Yes?" in a distracted, unfriendly way.

He asked if she'd like to buy a magazine subscription to help a degenerate sex fiend through college, and she said, "Who is this?"

"Hey, it's *me*," he protested. "How many sex fiends do you know?"

"Well, you sound different," she said.

So did she. She sounded grudging and dispassionate, in fact, but this was no time for arguments. Instead, he told her where he was and that he missed her badly. "Are they there yet?" she wanted to know, and he realized that he probably couldn't have made the call with Frances and Gus just around the bend, the way Joy and the children were. Cheating on *them* would have a different, more complex moral implication.

Kenny had felt uncomfortable telling Daphne about their visit in the first place. He hardly knew what to call them. He didn't like invoking Joy's name; that seemed like a double betrayal. "My wife" was even worse, with its resounding possessive. So he didn't say "my wife's parents," or even "my in-laws." He finally settled on "the in-laws," with a stand-up comic's disparagement that was suitable, if false. "They show up twice a year," he'd said, shrugging, and even made a face that won him a compassionate smile.

On the phone, though, he sensed that Daphne wasn't smiling. After he told her that the flight was late, he waited, growing more and more uneasy. "I'm going away for a few days," she said at last.

At that moment, Steven rushed up to Kenny, tackling his legs in a fierce embrace. Kenny's knees buckled and he reached down to stroke Steven's hair, a loving gesture and one of restraint.

"They're here!" Steven yelled. Daphne had to have heard him, too. He could probably be heard all the way to Pomona.

"Where? Where are you going?" Kenny said into the phone, his hand sliding down Steven's face, gently covering his mouth. The boy kissed his father's fingers, and Daphne said, "To Seattle. To see my folks."

Kenny's heart leaped and settled, leaped and settled. "That's not a bad idea," he said, as Joy, with Molly in her arms, came into view about thirty feet away. He'd get off fast, tell Joy it was a client. He often called people about business on weekends.

"I think the plane's in," he said to Daphne. "I'll call you tomorrow, okay? Daph?"

"I don't know," she said. "If I can get a flight, I might go out tonight."

"What about school? What about work?" he asked, as

Joy and Molly came slowly toward him, looming closer and closer.

"I'll play hooky," Daphne said. "Like you," she added with soft significance, when Joy was only a couple of feet away.

"Well, thanks," he said mindlessly into the phone. "Why don't you give me a call when you're back in town. Maybe we can get together," and he hung up. Steven was licking Kenny's trembling fingers.

"Jesus, *stop* that!" Kenny said sharply, and tears gathered in Steven's eyes. "I was being a *dog*, Daddy," he explained in a mournful voice.

Joy said, "They've just landed. Let's go to the gate." She marched in front of him like a parade marshal. She never asked who he had been calling.

Now he deliberately looks away from the panic button's light. He watches the gauzy shadows of the bedroom curtains instead. They move in and out of focus and he's lured by sleep and resists. What if Joy had someone else *before* he had Daphne? He would have to have known that, wouldn't he? Wouldn't he? The sand tarts from Greenberg's were different this time, less sandy or something. Maybe they have a new baker. Maybe Daphne's plane is soaring above the house this very minute. There's a thrumming noise that could be a jet, or distant traffic on the freeway, or his own blood circling through his body. Everything is red behind his closed lids.

He wakes to the siren screaming and he *must* get up, *must* go . . . But the siren is still. It's only the same old dream. An inner alarm has roused him to Joy's hand tightly holding his erect prick. She is like a motorman at the throttle of a roaring train. With her other hand, she lifts her nightgown, and then she climbs across his hips, straddling him. His prick is still in the dream, still alerted to the siren that called it to such stiff attention. Joy's eyes are open. Her face has a moonlight pallor as she urges him inside her with that firm assured hand. She impales herself on his obedient sentry, and rides it smoothly, slowly, in the tempo of dreams. He is a common soldier under her brilliant command. He is also oddly female, taken, used, without love or consent. The prick could be *hers*, for all he knows and feels. She rides and rides, clutching his arms, now a marathon dancer in the last frantic hours of dance, soundless until the very end, when she grunts and shudders desperately and rolls away.

6

Daphne slams her small suitcase shut, catching one finger painfully. "Damn him!" she cries, and sucks on her finger to soothe it. It's been two days since she spoke to Kenny and came up with the plan to go to Seattle. Now she has the last available seat on the last evening flight from Los Angeles, and she feels both vengeful and sad.

Before Kenny's call from the airport, she'd had no intentions of taking a trip anywhere. When he had first told her, in bed, about his in-laws' imminent visit, he'd fumbled for diplomatic words. She could keenly sense his discomfort over sharing the news, and had been a model of loving concern. But even then, underneath her acceptance, lay a small, beating rancor. Kenny's family bonds seemed to be growing stronger, rather than weakening. And his relief at her passivity annoyed her. She was playing a part—didn't he notice?—instead of behaving honestly. She hated hearing anything about his life outside their private hectic passion. Yet she'd always smiled when he spoke about the children—their visits to the barber or the zoo—or about the burglar alarm that went off if you touched a lousy window by mistake. Who cared about his children's hair, his windows? How false she was becoming, not just to him, but to herself.

Maybe that falseness was inevitable in a relationship like theirs. Recently, Monica Mann had referred to Daphne as "the other woman" in a mocking, baiting way. What had she said, exactly? "All big eyes and sweetness. Nobody would ever bill you as the other woman, Moss, as the little homewrecker." And Daphne had wept in Kenny's arms until he convinced her that she hadn't wrecked anything; had, in fact, revived his faltering life. His thrusting heart against hers was powerful testimony to that claim.

And she had to give Kenny credit; he tried not to mention Joy to her. But the name itself was so defiantly happy and victorious. Beethoven had written an entire "Ode to Joy." And every Christmas, carolers burst into "*Joy* to the world, the Lord is come!" Oh, boy, Almond Joy. Wife, and children, and now in-laws—a veritable army of victors.

When he called her from the airport, she faced the resentment she'd been denying, and surprised herself with the cool splash of her own voice. Monica would have cheered. As Kenny continued speaking, his omnipresent family reminded Daphne of her own family, of her mother and father in Seattle, of her younger sister Margaret, who was still in high school and had not yet begun making important choices or mistakes. Daphne had instantly made up the story about going to see them. Once she'd said it, it seemed like a sensible idea.

Kenny's control didn't totally mask his fear that she, too, had another life that couldn't be shared, and the new balance of power excited her. It was a little like the liquid thrill of sexual excitement, and it threatened to weaken her new, tougher stance. Oh, she would be sweet again, would let him off the hook. Then she heard the child's voice screaming, *"They're here!"* and she resolved, I *will* go to Seattle.

That afternoon, though, she went to work as planned. It was her turn, which came every four weeks, to go in on Sunday. Daphne knew that it would be hard for them to replace her at the last moment on a weekend, and certain lies didn't come with facility. The telephone rang and rang while she folded her uniform and put it into the knapsack, but she didn't answer it. Let him be the one to wait and worry this time.

The place was pretty sloppy, she noticed as she prepared to leave. Underwear was draped over the chair arms, like a queer set of doilies. A corner of the blue blanket trailed out of the hastily made-up bed. Daphne's lunch dishes were still on the table, and an unmated slipper lay on its side in the center of the room. She thought of how much Kenny liked order, and how she usually tried to tidy things up just to please him. Sometimes she hurriedly threw everything—books and papers, shoes and coffee mugs—into a carton just before his arrival. Now she took spiteful satisfaction in the litter. He doesn't live here, she told herself, closing the door.

Sunday was always a difficult day at the Palomar Arms, with only a skeleton crew on hand. They were easily outnumbered by the visitors, who got in the way even when they tried to be helpful. There were the middle-aged children with their relentlessly cheerful and loud voices; the bored grandchildren; and the assorted minor relatives and friends who came bearing flowers and candy and fruit, as if they were seeing someone off on a cruise. Nobody was going anywhere, at least nowhere that food or flowers were liable to be useful. Yet the ancient Egyptians used to bury their dead with such offerings, just in case.

Pushing a cart of supper trays toward the elevators that Sunday, Daphne remembered the Egyptian exhibit she'd seen in a museum on a class trip when she was a child. Those small, mummified figures—many of them child-sized, too—their awesome repose, their stubborn refusal of worldly treasures. She shivered and knew she was being morbid because of Kenny's phone call (the moment of triumph had passed), and because someone on her floor here had died during the previous night. He'd been a new man, in residence less than a week, and Daphne had hardly known him. Perhaps he was unknowable, reduced to mute despair by senility and the brutal deterioration of his body. While he was still conscious, he began rejecting sustenance, and he ignored the vigorous example of get-well plants.

The Sunday visitors slowed the progress of the elevators even more than usual. Little kids played in them, pressing every button, shoving one another in and out in wheelchairs, for the fun of the ride. While the aides waited, they gossiped about the latest death, and Daphne was surprised to learn that the dead man's place had already been taken. There were seldom any admissions on the weekend.

"Ah, what do you expect?" Feliciana asked. "The beds

here are like parking spaces downtown. They don't get time to cool off. The new guy's a shaker," she added, and Daphne understood that she meant Parkinson's disease, and not the man's religious affiliation. Evita hit the elevator button yet another time. "Come *on*, you bastards," she said, and then knocked her fist against one of the doors.

As Daphne pushed her cart down the corridor of the second floor, visitors came slowly toward her, maneuvering patients in wheelchairs as if they were babies in prams. Daphne knew there was a weight to those chairs that the wasted bodies didn't prepare you for. And an awkwardness to the job that came from being upright and ambulatory. A four-footed animal doing tricks on its hind legs. Occasionally, when she tried to help a patient stuck at a turn of the corridor, or in a corner of a room, she was embarrassed by her own ineptness, and frustrated, the way she was when she tried to push those crazy-wheeled shopping carts at the market. But here the burden was invariably human.

"Oh, look, Pop, dinner!" someone from the outside cried at the first sight of the stacked Styrofoam trays. The microwaves were humming with menace. Daphne tossed a few trays inside and stepped quickly away. The plan to go to Seattle was forming clearly in her head. The odors of the heating food helped her to choose the illness she would pretend in order to get a few days off. A stomach virus. There was one going around, anyway. Daphne actually felt a little queasy then; the merest suggestion could do it, or the reactivated smell of the steamed hamburgers beached in their mysterious gravy.

Au jus, it said on the mimeographed daily meal plan.
Mrs. Shumway is often given to French titling of her in-
stitutional fare—to Carrots Julienne, Chicken Suprème,
and Pears Belle Hélène.

Daphne had a childlike curiosity to see Mr. Axel, the
new man. What did she expect? He would certainly be
elderly, like the others, and there was the further common denominator of a geriatric disease. Parkinson's
wasn't unusual, and she already knew about the rigidity,
the tremors, the drool. There were always fewer men in
residence, giving them slightly more novelty than the
women, who seemed to outlive them through sheer
determination. The ratio between the sexes here, she
realized, was probably close to that in singles' bars. But
there was a greater blurring of gender in old age. The
women, balding, with chin whiskers, and the men growing those soft and useless breasts.

Mr. Axel had the bed nearest the door, and when she
looked inside she witnessed a tableau she had seen a few
times before—the ceremony of the first leave-taking.
The new man was wearing a suit that had outgrown
him, and he sat in a wheelchair that still bore the dead
man's name, stenciled on its back like a movie director's.
Mr. Axel's daughter stood on one side of him, her husband on the other. It was easy to tell who everyone was.
The daughter was aflame with feeling, and the son-in-
law was as superfluous as an usher at a wedding, flanking
the main players with dignified carriage and a sympathetic face.

"Hello," Daphne said. "Welcome to the Palomar
Arms. Here's your supper."

The woman grabbed one tray and laid it down on the

table nearest the window. "Are you a nurse?" she asked Daphne, who shook her head. "A volunteer?" the woman prompted.

Daphne shook her head again, self-consciously. "An aide," she said finally. And foolishly added, "I'm a student, actually. This is only a temporary job."

But that information seemed to feed the woman's intensity. "A college student? That's wonderful! Dad," she said, and paused to squint at Daphne's nameplate. "This is Diane Moss." Her voice would get louder after her father had been there a while, not because of anyone's hearing loss, but out of the knowledge of growing separation, like one person on the shore calling to another one in a rowboat, drifting away. Now her tone was soft and pleading. "This is my father? Joseph Axel, who's going to be staying here?"

"Hello," the man managed, along with a sweet, skewed smile, and his daughter wiped the corners of his mouth with a readied Kleenex.

"He's a . . . he *was* a pharmacist, and he's self-taught in other areas," she said. "In history, the arts; you know, books, music . . ." She trailed off, and looked for assistance to her husband, who only looked away.

"How do you do?" Daphne said to the room in general. "How are you tonight, Mr. Brady?" she called to the other bed, and the legless man there said, "Can't kick," his daily deadpan joke.

The daughter was appalled, but Mr. Axel laughed. Then he said, "Traffic, Sandra. Should start . . . home."

"Soon, soon," she answered. "We want to see that you're really settled in here."

"I'm fine," he said.

"Well, we just want to be with you now," she insisted. But then she followed Daphne out of the room. "Could you . . ." she began, and pulled at her lips as if trying to extract the right words. "Could you look out for him?"

"I only deliver the suppers," Daphne said. "And clean up, later."

"Oh, I know, but if you could make some *conversation* when you do. He's really intelligent, and nice. But we both work and travel a lot. Bud, that's my husband, travels a lot for business, and I like to go with him. We're getting older ourselves . . . everybody is." The woman shrugged and laughed. "Well, maybe not you, yet."

"I'll try," Daphne said. "I really will."

"They treat them all right here, don't they? I mean, given that it's an institution and all. I had to wait over a year to get him in, and it was a special favor, the way apartments used to be during the war. World War II, you wouldn't know about that. We paid supers under the table for the privilege of tiny rooms without a view . . ." Again, her sentence unrolled and came to a stop.

Daphne was eager to get away before she heard too much, before the woman revealed episodes of her childhood, like home movies, and visions of the manly father who had once pointed out the Big Dipper in a summer sky, and who had seemed as tall and powerful as a building against the sky. "I'll come in," Daphne promised. She had a headache and a sudden longing for Kenny. She wished back some of the old innocence that had allowed her to trust without fear or judgment, and knew it was surely gone. His last stilted sentences during that phone call had to mean that Joy was standing right there. She felt indignant for both herself and Joy. The paths of their parallel lives were shifting dangerously toward convergence, and not in the way that Daphne had hoped.

"He isn't always articulate anymore," the woman apologized, "but his mind is perfect. Ask him *anything*. Just give him a little time to answer."

"All *right*," Daphne said, struggling to end this encounter, and helpless to offer comfort. She felt like throwing up by then, and wondered if she were being dealt some ironic justice for the lies about being sick that she had not yet told. "His supper is getting cold," she said, giving the daughter a concrete shape for her flopping, formless guilt. "You'd better help him." That did it, and Daphne was on her way.

The Dream Lady said, "I'm at the foot of a long staircase that goes way, way up into the clouds. There's music—harps and violins—and what's-his-name, Russ Columbo, singing. My father is standing there in his uniform, looking down . . ."

Daphne put the tray in front of her, and the Dream Lady said, "What's this? Hamburgers? Who did they grind up this time?"

The sisters in 225 had no visitors when Daphne got there, but there was evidence that some had come and gone: new kindergarten art, an enduring prickly cactus in a plastic pot. As always, Mrs. Feldman was happy to see Daphne, was generous with greetings and compliments. She asked a few questions about life outside—

"just to keep up," as she said. "What are a dozen eggs going for these days? How much do movie tickets cost?" Her sister was her usual confused and disappointed self. It struck Daphne that her delivery of supper must be the highlight of the old women's day. But Mrs. Bernstein would always be restless with hungers she could no longer grasp or satisfy.

In other rooms, lingering family members cut up the steamed meat, moved it around in the gravy, and fed the patients, and sometimes, almost absently, themselves. Many of the little packets of catsup, mayonnaise, and sugar, the cello-wrapped slices of white bread, and the envelopes of Sanka and Postum disappeared into purses and pockets. Residents without visitors were known to store these and other food items in night-table drawers against emergencies that never arose. After someone died, the cache was always discovered, rotting next to dentures, family snapshots, and ancient gas bills.

Mrs. McBride went on as usual in 227—*her* death would have been bigger news at the elevators, and a major blow to the staff morale. In the kitchen, earlier, there had been comments about the oldest woman's straight spine, her terrific stamina and healthy appetite. Her bowels were admired—"Every day! And firm, but not hard!"—and someone said that there would be live music at the birthday party. Feliciana did a rapid, stamping dance step, and selected the largest hamburger for McBride's tray.

She was sitting up in bed when Daphne got there, and she had a bedside visitor, a young, severe-looking nun. She must have been with one of the older, stricter orders, because her habit was long, black, and voluminous. Maybe she had taken a vow of silence; she didn't even smile back at Daphne. Her hands gripped the crucifix at her waist as if she believed it might be snatched.

The roommate's daughter made up for the nun's silence, addressing Daphne by name, chattering wildly to her stricken mother about the arrival of supper, and whether the bed should be raised and the bread buttered. The mother responded with a single, sustained sound that might have been a shriek of laughter or of pain, or the cry of a jungle bird in a Tarzan movie. It startled everyone, except perhaps the nun, who moved her fingers and lips to bless the food. Too late, Daphne thought as she left.

Most of the visitors, she noticed, had cleared out. She went down the corridor and looked into the new man's room. His daughter or son-in-law had helped him into the issued blue pajamas and green-striped seersucker robe. They fit the slump of his bones much better than the suit had. Its padded shoulders and correct tailoring were meant for the aggressive business of the world, and would never conform to this posture of utter surrender.

Mr. Brady was asleep, snoring loudly, and Mr. Axel looked toward the doorway with expectation. Again, that odd smile.

"Your children gone?" Daphne asked, and he nodded.

His hands, especially the right one, pounded an involuntary tattoo on the wheelchair arms. "Like school," he said. "First day."

"You mean harder on them?" Daphne asked, and he seemed pleased that she had understood him. She picked up his tray and saw that he had eaten very little. "I wish the food was better," she said.

"Late lunch."

The smile was always there, Daphne decided, like a dolphin's smile, and like a dolphin's, it was beguiling but mirthless. She nodded toward Mr. Brady. "And the entertainment," she added.

"He didn't . . . ask for me . . . either," Mr. Axel said.

She guessed that he would always be courteous and uncomplaining like this, would never offer his heart's secrets to anyone. But those flailing hands gave him away, rapping out their protest on the arms of the wheelchair. Unjust! Unjust!

"Well, good night," Daphne said. "I hope you sleep well." While she was stacking the last trays onto the meal cart, she thought that she might have said something better, more personal to him. It was his first night in this strange and final place, and "I hope you sleep well" was as meaningful as "Have a nice day." Yet she wasn't responsible, despite his daughter's need to share the freight of sorrow and guilt. Daphne took the perfume dispenser from her pocket and sprayed a fine rain of fragrance she could walk through. She stopped at a hall window and looked out at the parking lot as the sun was starting to set. The last of the visitors were making their way to their cars. They all had separate and reasonable lives away from this place, and now they hurried off to resume them. A teenage boy went by, carrying one of those suitcase radios. The music was rebelliously loud and lusty, even through the sealed window. Car doors slammed, motors were gunned, and people vanished into the new evening. Then Daphne noticed a figure attached to a lamppost, wrapped around it like a cartoon drunk.

It was Mr. Axel's daughter, and she hung on to the lamp-post as if it kept her from pitching over the edge of a cliff. Daphne watched as the woman's husband emerged from the building and peeled her slowly away and into his arms.

The next day, Daphne called her parents, and their voices were distant and dear. It was raining in Seattle, and although she spoke about the southern sunshine with automatic pride, at that moment she missed the rain. She also poignantly missed her mother and father, from whom she had once longed to escape because they had been so difficult to live with. They were not exactly perfect during the phone call. When she mentioned the possibility of coming home, they were instantly suspicious. Was she ill? In trouble? She assured them that she was fine, that she had a couple of sick days accumulated and just felt like seeing everybody. Didn't they want to see her?

Of *course* they wanted to see her. She knew the inquisition was only part of their old habit of preparing for the very worst, so that something less dreadful might be bravely borne. "What's wrong?" they'd always demanded, and Daphne had learned to adjust her news or hide it when she believed it wouldn't be welcome. For instance, she'd alluded to Kenny without ever mentioning that he was married. She can't even remember the reasons she'd given them for her move to Ventura. They'd come to her easily enough at the time.

On the long bus ride to the airport in Los Angeles, daylight fades and Daphne's reflection is sharpened as the window becomes a dark mirror. She's a pretty woman, even under her own critical examination. And she's still young and relatively free. Her journey home has begun, and it's as if she's being drawn into a safety zone where no harm can possibly befall her; where temporarily, at least, she can take up the dependency of childhood.

7

Sister Maria Gilbert is gone at last. Nora really still thinks of her as her sister Josie's granddaughter, Maureen, that once scrawny, perverse, vain little girl who preened and tap-danced in front of every surface that would give back her own image. The last one in the world to ever go into a convent. Yet she did, at the unholy, or holy, age of sixteen. Nora kept waiting for her to break out of there, or be thrown out, unruly, hungry for the world, and lacking a vocation. But instead she stayed, the most reverential of the flock.

The whole family is loaded with nuns and priests, many of them the ones she'd traveled to help raise after Jack's death. Hadn't she had more influence on them than that? Sometimes Nora wonders if her own unborn children and grandchildren would have also chosen to be black and white and religious in such a heretic, technicolor universe. It's something she'll never know, and part of her is wickedly glad. Her relief is odd, because the absence of children had been so grievous long ago. She was "caught" often enough, as they put it in those days, a strange expression considering her willingness in bed, and her genuine longing for motherhood. But the pregnancies never held more than three or four months. The blood is bright in memory, a warm sticky dream on her nightgown and the sheets, a spilling dream from which she had to wake in horror and then wake Jack. The doctor told him that Nora had a "lazy womb," whatever that was. "God's will," that old fart of a priest—what was his name?—always said. He wasn't that old, she supposes, in his late sixties, maybe. But with an ancient's authority, as if there could be no intermediaries between himself and God. Oh, what did he know! "It's all right, love, it's all right," Jack would croon in his woeful voice, but of course it wasn't all right.

In the meantime, Nora's sisters and her brothers' wives swelled and hatched with the senseless regularity of farm animals. Even two sets of fryer-sized twins survived in incubators, and grew up to be fat and fertile themselves. Her children and Jack's would have been the best of the lot, she'd think during each bitter time of mourning. They'd been smart enough in their tiny gelatin souls to reject this life before the agony of consciousness, hadn't they? A peg to hang on, it was then, because she coveted the downy, born, squirming infants whose godmother she often was. She loved the hot heaviness of their heads against her arm, and the miracle of outcry at the first drizzle of baptismal water.

Maureen has left an old red Sunday missal for Nora's comfort and redemption. It's the kind they haven't used in years, since Pope John the twenty-something started turning things around. Nora opens it and holds it close to her eyes, trying to focus in the opaque, textured light. The print is much too small, and she can't make anything out. But she can guess what it says, the way she used to guess when she was a child and had not yet learned to read. It was a clever trick, encouraged by the grownups—three- or four-year-old Nora "reading" the headlines in *The Herald*. She'd held the paper close then, too, in imitation of adult concentration, and for the delicious, drugging odor of printer's ink. "The sun . . . is . . . big!" she would announce, squinting at the black, mysterious symbols on the page. "Mama . . . is making . . . bread!" Everyone would laugh and love her for being so funny and bright, and she would laugh, too, because it was so easy to please. First lessons in seduction. The real readers in the family hunched over real words in schoolbooks, and scowled in her direction for being the beloved and ignorant baby.

Now she can't read anymore, but she is no longer ignorant, or beloved. The frontispiece of the missal is familiar, though, a miniature of that picture in her childhood dining room, of Christ's Last Supper. There are the same figures, Jesus and His disciples, crowded around the table, ready to break unleavened bread, one of them to break trust, one of them to die. She'd loved that oak-framed picture when she was a small girl looking up at it from another crowded table, from the good smells of supper, one in an infinite number of suppers. And although her sisters and brothers quarreled, and jostled one another for elbow room and larger portions, just as the disciples did in the picture, there was never any question of serious betrayal among them, or of anything ever ending. The words under the illustration in the missal must say, *Take and eat ye all of this; for this is my body*. No juvenile trick now, but the recurring wonder of total recall.

"Do you pray, Auntie Nora?" Maureen had asked a little while ago, and Nora had said yes, although it wasn't true. She didn't believe in anyone or anything to pray to, and without belief there was no burden of sin to her lie. Yet there was a moral question, wasn't there? To tell this Bride of Christ that she still whispered gratitude for favors, and pleas for magic, when she didn't, was immoral, if not sinful. Nora was too weary for any arguments about theology with such a strong-willed child. She knew what Sister Maria Gilbert would say about Nora's immortal soul, about how it was dangling from the wall between this world and the next one, and how it would fall into a dark abyss without warning, and be lost, falling forever and ever. Like Jack's mortal body.

That girl could always argue in a stern, merciless way until she won. Once she'd argued for money and lipstick and freedom, and now for commitment to something she couldn't prove, or even demonstrate. What, Nora thought for a fraction of an instant, if she were right?

As a child, Maureen had had an answer for everything, too. All of the other girls wore lipstick; she *needed* money; why couldn't they let her do what she wanted? She wanted and wanted. Her confounded parents worried, and prayed for guidance, while Nora secretly cheered the independent spirit that was so like her own, and wished it well. Then something happened—a weekend retreat Josie's frantic daughter had shipped the girl off to, and a coming home to God and His reason. How sorry Nora had been when Maureen first came to tell her the great good news. It was right here, wasn't it, or in a room just like this, where the girl sat in an aura of earnest happiness about giving up her ardent quest for boys, all her destructive appetites, the burden of that abundant auburn hair. She was already a smug little saint, and Nora pictured the shorn hair, wafting like feathers past those heaving shoulders and breasts to the floor, and said, "But, Reenie, are you sure?" How could she have doubted it? The child was in a passion of love, swooning for deprivation the way Nora had once swooned with lust.

Nora had still been able to pray in her early teens. She was wild with sinful urges, and wanted to be repentant as long as it didn't interfere with her pleasure. Forgive me, thank you, forgive me, oh, thank you, to Jesus, Mary, and Joseph, to all the statues and icons that shimmered in yellow candlelight at St. Athanasius. Hail Mary, full of grace. The Lord is with thee. And then the melting kisses, the anticipation of more, of something else, of only God knew what. She'd have babies for the church, a *thousand* babies to make up for this recreant heat. Who else but God gave her that quivering breath, the madness that turned her body and brain to candlewax?

Nothing had prepared her for the wedding night, though, not the false piousness of prayer and promise, not the desperate rehearsal of clothed friction in the dark hallway of her house.

In those days, no one told girls anything that was candid or useful about sex. If there were a way to deny its existence, most parents would have. But there was the biological evidence, those consequences of restless pollen and sperm, and the wide marriage beds creaking their message to sleepless children waiting for their own lives to begin.

The cats mated, yowling, under the moon. That dumb hound, Dutch, mounted the boys' legs for want of a bitch, and all of nature bloomed and prospered under the imperious rule of desire.

So the news reached the children, even the girls who were only future victims of it, anyway, and they became excited by the equal horrors of wrong information and the truth. Nora had seen her brothers lined up for the toilet each morning, yawning, and scratching at those crooked little pencils in their underwear. Downtown, in an alley, there were crude wall drawings you were forbidden to look at, but which attracted more visitors than the art museum. One image stayed in Nora's head, although she prayed resolutely for its exorcism. A plump red sausage emerging from a painted cloud of hair, and pointing upward to a scrawled message: *Mr. Henderson's Dick.* Mr. Henderson was a lay teacher of manual training at St. Athanasius, and he was famous for banging boys' heads together like blackboard erasers. The drawing was supposed to be his man's thing, grossly exaggerated, of course, by creative license or ineptitude. But Mr. Henderson's first name was Elmo, after the patron saint of sailors, and intestinal disorders. Who in heaven's name was Dick? And why would he want to be defamed by such association? There were so many puzzling things on this earth that one couldn't speak about to anyone older and more informed. Nora and her friends decided that Dick was probably a boy whose head had been slammed by Mr. Henderson, and that the inscription was a strange kind of artistic signature.

It rained on her wedding day, which was lucky, or unlucky, according to which superstitious neighbor you believed. Nora heard the violent downpour against the high rose windows, louder than Father's voice joining her for eternity to Jack, far louder than their whispered vows, I will, I will.

At the party in the church basement, she took small sips of wine but could not eat any of the splendid food her sisters and aunts had prepared. She stayed among the women and children, her last visit to their stronghold before going away. And for the first time she was truly shy, inhibited by the sudden strangeness of Jack among the other men, all of them flushed and tipsy on their side of the room.

Later, she shivered under his silken length and prayed, a tardy zealot, for the door of her furnace to fly open and pull him inside like paper to be burned. He was too large, and she was barricaded by nature and by fear. No wonder the walleyed cat yowled like that in the yard. No wonder no one would ever speak directly of this. And Jack said, "Darlin', please, my love, oh, easy, darlin'," and bumped blindly against her hard, shuttered self. Mr. Henderson's Dick, whoever he was, had been a genius of anatomy. Even the hair was true, a bristling forest to hide the enemy.

They slept and woke, and Jack labored once more for entry. The kisses, licensed now by God and man, and even his broad lovely carpenter's thumbs circling her naked breasts were wrong. Naked everywhere and punished into waking again and again from the deep warm nest of bedclothes and dreams. Elsewhere, in convents, novitiate cousins and schoolmates knelt at simple cots, earning their rest with a hasty "Our Father," the minor discomfort of cold, bruised knees.

Toward morning, Nora's foot reached out for the solace of Agnes, or Catherine, and found instead his sleeping hand, slowly found all of him, defeated and still in exhausted sleep. This time, she began the kisses, like the old ones in the doorway, and she roused his hand to put it here, and here, and *here!* And her legs finally fell open, two pale trembling heroes to welcome pain.

Nora reaches for the missal, but it's not in her lap anymore. It has slipped away with the vagueness of this day and the one lost before it. What did she have for supper? The tray is gone, her company is gone. She senses Jack somewhere in the dimness, but knows better. She peers strenuously into the peephole of memory as he retreats from her and disappears.

8

It's much too hot to go anywhere. Kenny has taken the whole broiling, stationary day off, and it looms in front of him like a month of days without Daphne. *Western wind, when wilt thou blow, the small rain down can rain?* She'd read that to him a week ago—her favorite verse, she'd said, and her voice had been pitched even lower with emotion. What was the rest of it?

Gus and Frances and Joy halfheartedly suggest excursions as the heat rises with the sun, causing the pool and garden to shimmer like a mirage through the French doors. Inside, in the reliable chill of central air conditioning, they speak without enthusiasm or conviction of Disneyland and the Farmers Market. No one really wants to leave the artificial comfort of the house, except perhaps for a fast swim. But the children are restless a mere hour after waking, and they race around, making too much noise and leaving their milky fingerprints everywhere.

New York, which Kenny misses in occasional sharp spasms of longing, would be worse than L.A. on a day like this. They'd lived in a small East Side apartment, and there hadn't been a swimming pool, or even a mirage of hibiscus and lavender heavy with blossoms and bees. On a day like this, only the streets would be shimmering there, and the *Daily News* would have a front-page shot of some joker frying an egg right on the sizzling pavement. Yet, Kenny thinks, he would have been happy to be hurrying on a heated sidewalk toward some other room, air-conditioned or not, where Daph was waiting for him. New York, with its complex yet practical network of subways and buses, was an easier place for paranoid lovers. He pictures a traffic light changing and the faceless mob crossing the street, each person free in his anonymity, in the convenient chaos of big-city life. Los Angeles is not exactly a small town, but on foot in its spare pedestrian traffic, he feels conspicuous, and, in his car, detectable by model and license plate. Is paranoia always born of earned guilt?

Kenny steps outside in his cotton robe, and is overwhelmed by the heat, as if he's taken a blow to the head. It will be over a hundred before noon, a scorcher, a real record-breaker. He can't quite remember how New York smelled in summer, but it was surely never like this: the sultry perfume of flowers, with the sting of chlorine like an aftertaste. In New York, he would not have been able to shuck off his robe and slice naked into cool green water for instant relief. He doesn't do it here, either. Cautious modesty makes him look up, and Frances is standing at the French doors, sipping coffee, smiling at him and fluttering the fingers of her free hand. On each side of her, one of his children stands with a grotesquely flattened face against the breath-clouded glass. Kenny smiles back at Frances and makes a monster face at the gargoyle children, who scream soundlessly and disappear into the room behind them.

Daphne must be in Seattle, where the small rain down

can rain without stop. He has called her Ventura number over and over. Thank God for push-button phones that allow for quick and quiet dialing. Thank God for Joy's extravagance that has provided a bathroom extension with its own small and steady light. When Daphne didn't answer, in late afternoon, and then in the evening, he imagined other places than Seattle for her to be. He thought of old boyfriends she had casually mentioned in negative ways. He thought of new men everywhere, and how their eyes, and then the rest of them, would gladly follow her—her hair moving in swaying counterpoint to her hips, everything beautifully synchronized, as if she walked to inner music. He moaned in the bathroom, and softly at dinner under the covering blare of Vivaldi's trumpets. He saw Daphne lying in her foldout bed in Ventura, and heard her whisper, "Don't answer it. It's only him. Just let it ring."

His jealous derangement was ridiculous, though, and temporary. She's in Seattle with her family, where she said she would be. He goes inside and is not instantly restored by the cold air. "Jesus," he says, and Gus looks up from the *Times* to ask what's the matter.

"I just remembered something," Kenny says. "Something I have to do at the office."

"Poor Kenneth," Frances clucks. After all her years in social work, she's promptly sympathetic.

"Can't you get someone else to take care of it?" Gus asks. "I'll bet you can fry an egg out there."

Kenny hears water rushing through the pipes of the house. Joy must be taking a shower, and her absence makes his getaway easier. "No, damn it," he says. "It will only take a couple of hours, I think. I'll definitely be back before lunch." He hurries to dress while the water is still running.

Earlier, he'd awakened before Joy, recalling the previous night with confusion and wonder, as if it might have been a dream. Her face was relaxed in sleep, and he clearly remembered her eyes fixed fiercely on his, the deliberate tough rhythm of her body. It wasn't any dream, and he was grateful to be awake first, to escape into the shower, and then into the nonpartisan company of his family. He realized, as he buttered toast for Steven, as Molly's unerring foot found the place Joy's hand had so recently grasped, that he and Joy might never discuss what had taken place, their mutual silence creating a strange conspiracy between them.

In the car, he considers stopping at a florist's. Despite that shyster Larkin's assumptions, he never brings Daphne gifts, except on the formal occasions of holidays. He could buy her something rare and special, something truly exotic that had to be flown in from somewhere, on ice. It would soften the surprise of his unexpected visit. He's prepared to spend a ridiculous amount for a small perishable offering.

But as he approaches Camarillo, he acknowledges that she might indeed not be home, and such an offering left at the door would lose its amorous message as it wilted. If she really is in Seattle for a few days, his gift would rot, and even appear sinister, like the calling card of a madman. And if it turns out that she is home alone, stubbornly shutting out the ringing of the phone, waiting for a more aggressive or original move from him, he could always stop at a florist's later and send enough flowers to turn that dismal room into a Persian garden.

His heart needs the encouragement of his brain's dreamy logic. She *won't* be there; he knows this without doubt during the last miles. He even slows the speed of the car, trying to relax the foot on the gas pedal as he eases its pressure.

Still, he finishes the trip, and knocks on the door when he gets there, softly at first, and then with the brash urgency of a vice-squad dick. He imagines footsteps, or hears them in another apartment, and he puts his hot, thudding ear against the door to listen. The rest of Daphne's poem floods his head. *Christ, if my love were in my arms and I in my bed again!* He shuts his eyes to concentrate all his perception into his sense of hearing. But Daphne's apartment is silent, and he's a green, romantic fool.

How tired he feels now, as if he'd raced all the way to Ventura on foot. There had been a time right after he and Daphne met when Kenny fleetingly considered that he was too old for the hardships of courting. He might be used up too quickly. And other aspects of his life would have to be sacrificed. The quantity and quality of time spent with male friends was already decreasing. He played a few sets of tennis, and a little poker. When he met someone for a drink, the exchange of confidences was more guarded. Was it worth it?

He discovered that he had no choice. Desire propelled him into action, overcoming logic, and his energy was renewed. And of course it was worth it; it was worth anything. Love had been the secret source of his strength then, as it seems to be the draining force now. Love giveth and love taketh away.

Kenny thinks of actually going to his office, to undo

his own foolishness and his pretense as well. But what would he say there to explain his unexpected appearance? He'd told his secretary that he desperately needed a day off, that he didn't even want telephone calls referred to the house. Daphne, at his own bidding, never called him anywhere. He was often as dictatorial as a privileged child, and she was unflaggingly agreeable, like a helplessly indulgent mother. Or had been, until now. There was that new defiant edge to her voice during their last phone call. What had changed her?

He could leave a note now, more durable than flowers. He could write the last line of that poem she loves, its meaning more ardent and accurate than anything he could invent. But she might come home with someone else, and a joint reading of that line is unthinkable. Maybe the exterminator would show up first and have a good laugh before he fogged the roaches. Kenny has a better idea, anyway. He'll go to the public library in Sherman Oaks and find out the poet's name. Then he can look in a bookstore for a handsome volume of the guy's work, and bring it to his reunion with Daphne. The only poetry books she owns are used, marked-up paperbacks, bought for a course she took at U.C.L.A. Having a plan cheers Kenny considerably, and he whistles a little on the way to his car.

He feels like a jerk standing at the reference desk saying, "Western wind, when wilt thou blow, the small rain down can rain?" to the matronly librarian sitting there. And he'll be damned if he'll give her the next line.

She stares up at him and then she rises from her chair, drawing her breath in sharply, and says, "*Christ*, if my

love were in my arms and I in my bed again!" with resonance and feeling.

"That's it," Kenny whispers. It's as if they've just sung
a stirring operatic duet, and he looks around to see if
they've been observed and overheard. But no one seems
to have noticed. "I just wondered who wrote it."

"Anonymous," she says.

"What?" he asks, although he has heard her perfectly
well.

"Anonymous," she repeats. "Sixteenth century."

Kenny is stunned. The words of the poem are so immediate, so suffused with yearning that he can't believe
the poet is unknown. And the sixteenth century! Why,
it might have been written the day before. His shock
and disappointment must be visible, because the librarian
goes to the reference stacks and returns with a weighty
volume. "Here," she says. "See for yourself. They're *all*
anonymous." She pushes the open book into his hands
and he looks down. Daphne's poem is there, among
scores of others. He reads haphazardly to himself, a line
or two from a few of them. *Frankie and Johnnie were
lovers, my gawd, how they could love . . . I sing of a
maiden that is makeless . . . In Dublin's fair city, where
girls are so pretty . . . Now I lay me down to sleep . . .
When Molly smiles beneath her cow, I feel my heart—I
can't tell how . . .* He lowers the book to the desk and
says, "Thank you," before lurching out into the incredible heat of the parking lot.

Anonymous, he thinks, driving the few blocks to his
house. Anonymous and dead. He is aware of everything
he does: his hands turning the steering wheel; his foot

moving from the accelerator to the brake. He opens the car door, shuts it. The careless series of acts that is everyone's life. Tonight he'll try to find the Seattle number. He feels capable of almost anything.

The children storm him as he goes indoors, but their impact is softened by his troubled distraction. He takes only slight notice of their clammy little bodies, the rising odors of chlorine and sunlight. They dance around him as he takes off his clothes and gets into his bathing trunks.

"Daddy's *penis*," Steven instructs Molly, with reverent envy.

She smiles, all-knowing. "Mine!" she screams; and the three of them run through the house toward the pool.

9

The rain is soft this evening, after yesterday's deluge. It's almost a soundless mist, yet Daphne is especially sensitive to the dry warm enclosure of the house. The family is eating dessert, her mother's special bread pudding with hot caramel sauce, and watching the news on television. About five minutes of it can reasonably be called news—Mideast tensions, Polish economic problems, royal wedding plans, the spraying of California's fruit flies—but the program has been extended to a full hour. Most of it is a kind of filler entertainment: interviews with an actress and a political criminal who've written books about themselves; a review, with film clips, of a car-chase movie that's declared "a gas-guzzling gambit"; endless lists of sports scores; and an attenuated look at the weather, using maps and satellite photos, and offering predictions for the entire nation. It will be very hot again in Southern California the next day, when Kenny and his whole family might be fried alive staring into the La Brea tar pits.

"Some news," Daphne's father remarks. He shuts off the television and clears his throat.

He's been clearing his throat all evening, she realizes, and wonders if there's something physically wrong with him. "Do you have a cold, Daddy?" she asks, and he says, brusquely, "No, I never get colds."

This isn't so, but she knows better than to dispute him on a truth he refuses to acknowledge. Working for twenty-nine years in the claims department of an insurance company has made him unnaturally stubborn and defensive. "It's just that you keep doing that, clearing your throat," she says.

He does it again, theatrically this time, like a man choking on a fishbone. "It's the residue," he answers, and Daphne says, "What?"

Margaret sighs, sucking on her spoon the way she's done since she was a baby. "He means the volcanic ash," she explains.

"But there hasn't been an eruption for months, and I thought it *bypassed* Seattle," Daphne says, "and settled miles east of here. I read something about it in the L.A. *Times* a few weeks ago."

"Tell that to the Marines," her father advises, and clears his throat again.

"Daddy," Daphne begins, but her mother interrupts: "This pudding is delicious, even if I do have to say so myself."

Daphne and Margaret glance at one another and smile. How many times have they heard that same phrase from her? It's one in a series of stock inanities she's used for years to quell dangerous conversations. Daphne is moved and irritated at once.

"You don't have to say so yourself, Mom," Margaret says. "Look at my nice clean dish." She holds it up for inspection.

"Piggo," Daphne says lovingly. "Little Meglet."

Not insulted at all, Margaret scrapes what's left at the

bottom of Daphne's dish, too. She has always eaten this greedily, and is still boyishly slender, yet oddly sexy. In just a few months she's changed radically, Daphne thinks, and then isn't sure. She knows that she needs the romance of sameness here—it's one of the reasons she's come home—and there are all the old obliging family ties and rituals, the lukewarm arguments that go back forever in memory. Everyone takes a familiar role. But Margaret is so *womanly* now, so self-assured and sensual. Daphne guesses that her little sister is not a virgin anymore, and has a little moment of surprise and sorrow. Who, she wonders. How?

"My zucchini and cukes just laid down and died this year," her father announces.

Margaret imitates the eerie music of science-fiction movies. "Ooo-eee! Ooo-eee!" She wriggles her fingers right in front of his face.

"That's enough out of you," he says, but without any bite to his rebuke. He has always let her get away with things.

"Daddo blames everything on poor old Mount St. H.," Margaret tells Daphne. "Car trouble, the stock market, his athlete's foot."

"People turned gray overnight," he says.

"Not to mention *gay*," Margaret whispers to Daphne, and they lean together, snickering.

"Oh, Hal," Mrs. Moss says. "That was way over in Idaho, wasn't it? And they didn't actually turn gray, did they? Wasn't it really the ash?"

"I know what I know," he answers, and immediately Daphne sees the two teams that comprise her family, maybe every family. She and her mother are the same, or at least a great deal alike. There is a gentle conciliation in them, a desire for peace that makes them allow stronger, more assertive people to be in control. Her father and Margaret, on the other hand, are like difficult twins, opinionated and tireless in their wrongheaded crusades.

Daphne thinks about the other reason for her homecoming, the wish to resolve her affair with Kenny. She has been here for two days now, and will be going back to Ventura early the next morning. Still, she has not confided in anyone, has not even begun the process of resolution. There had been an opportunity the night before at dinner. Margaret had suddenly asked, "You still seeing that same guy?"

Daphne, unsettled by the question, answered, "Sort of," remembering that it had also been Kenny's evasive answer when she'd asked if he was married.

"What does *that* mean?" her father demanded.

"It means I see him off and on," Daphne said. She gulped some water, heard it gurgling down.

"Oh," her mother sighed. "Well, who wants some more stroganoff?"

"So don't start registering her silver pattern at Friedlander's," Margaret advised.

"Nobody's getting married," Daphne said.

"Lady Di is," her sister said, and Daphne saw, not without relief, that her opportunity had passed.

But who will she turn to when she's ready, when her quick convalescence is over? She imagines telling her father everything, and how hard it would be to present a fair picture, to convince him of Kenny's virtues, and the inevitability of her surrender. It would be like trying to collect on an insurance policy after setting fire to her own house. *Has* she set fire to her own house?

And her mother, what would she make of it all, after the initial shock and disapproval? Daphne is sure that her parents, who married as young sweethearts, have always been faithful to one another, even in their fantasies. In terms of sexual experience, she is probably far older than they are. Her mother would be bewildered, at best; at worst, heartsick that values and life styles have really changed, and aren't merely the make-believe substance of the soap operas she loves.

Perhaps Daphne will have to speak to Margaret, the baby sister to whom she'd once carefully explained, in the dark of their shared bedroom, how a man plants his seed inside the woman he loves. Margaret had burst into contemptuous laughter, as if she had just heard the most ridiculous story. What a little prig I was, Daphne thinks now, remembering that she had managed her entire explanation without one reference to lust, or a direct naming of genitalia. She had been in high school herself then, still intact, but barely, and not for want of curiosity or heat. Her parents' stern morality kept her from complete abandon, but she knew plenty, anyway, especially about tongues and hands, and enough about nether parts.

The telephone rings and Daphne watches as Margaret sprints for it, and is tugged by envy. During those last two nights in Ventura, she'd let her phone ring unanswered while she sipped tea, while she lay drowsing in the bathtub, or disturbingly awake in bed. She knew that she was getting even by her silence, that she was punishing him as she had been punished by his absence. But she was also uncertain of what to say if she did speak to him.

This phone call is for Daphne, and when she mouths "Who?" and Margaret shrugs, Daphne's heart knocks like a faulty radiator. Only Kenny knows that she's here, in Seattle.

"Hello?" Her voice quavers and she's aware of her family's quiet attentiveness. But it's only her old friend Rosemary Hadley calling. She'd met Mrs. Moss at the supermarket the other day and heard that Daphne was going to be in town. Why hadn't she called? What is she doing tonight?

The flow resumes through the valves of Daphne's heart; her voice steadies, and she agrees to visit Rosemary later, after the dishes are done.

It's only a five- or ten-minute walk to Van Horton Street, where Rosemary lives with her husband, David, and their baby girl, Lindsay. Daphne's father insists that she take the car. It's not safe for a woman to walk alone anywhere at night. She remembers how he used to refuse to let her use the car just after she'd gotten her license, and was wild about driving. He would say that walking was a damn sight healthier, that insurance rates were insane because of adolescent maniacs—just read any National Safety Council Survey—that Drivers' Ed ought to be banished from the school curriculum. The sex classes, too, he'd add irrelevantly.

When she's alone in the brown Plymouth wagon, the one they've had for nine years now, she's even more overwhelmed by nostalgia than she was in the house. She used to borrow the keys to this car while her father slept, and then sit in it, inside the garage, with her high-school boyfriend, Jesse Krantz. They didn't ever drive anywhere, she would argue against her conscience, against thoughts of her father's forbidding. They just stayed in the oily darkness to kiss and kiss and paw each other. Their moans were absorbed by the tan upholstery, and mixed with the music from the radio, which they played with the ignition key turned halfway. Jesse worked at a gas station on weekends, and assured her that this wouldn't run down the battery, and that they were also being spared the risk of carbon-monoxide poisoning. He'd insisted on music, the hard-driving acid rock he hoped would make her lose her mind, and consequently her virginity. Often, she almost did. She wonders where Jesse is right now. The last she'd heard, he was living in St. Louis and doing something with computers.

Rosemary and David's house is a miniature Tara. It's lit like a movie set, or a funeral home. There's no doctor's shingle outside. As Daphne parks the station wagon, she remembers that David's practice is downtown, in an office complex called the Dermatology Center. Margaret had mentioned that he does only cosmetic work, helping people to slough off their old skin, like snakes.

David isn't there when Rosemary lets Daphne inside. She makes the appropriate noises of appreciation at the lushness of the house's interior. It was being built, to an architect's specifications, during Daphne's last visit, and Rosemary, who had once been unpredictable, and fun, stood largely pregnant in the raw frame, and went on and on about color schemes and fabrics and period furniture.

Everything is really sumptuous, richer than either of their parents' homes, far better than the digs of Daphne's few other married friends. She thinks of her own place with its foldout bed and phony fireplace, and of the impermanence of all furnished rooms. There is a solid sense of the future here, where Oriental rugs bloom lavishly on the polished teak floors. There is even the important bulk of a grand piano. Does anyone play?

The two women tiptoe, arm in arm, up an elaborate staircase to the nursery, where Lindsay, at three months, is almost hard to find in the skirted, canopied crib. Stuffed animals are propped around her, looking as benign as the lion in that painting of the sleeping gypsy. There is a baby smell of sweet skin and lotions that Daphne inhales as if it were some restorative essence. "She's gorgeous," she whispers, pinching Rosemary's arm, although the dim Cinderella night-light hardly illuminates the tiny breathing form.

They tiptoe out again and go downstairs, into a small paneled room where a fire is burning in a stone hearth. A black woman in a white uniform is setting out a tray of tea. She smiles and backs out as the other two women enter. There have been no introductions, but Rosemary sighs and says, "Janelle has been with us since the baby came. She makes my life possible."

For the first time, Daphne wonders if Kenny and Joy

have household help, too—someone to mix their underwear in the laundry, to strip the secrets of their bed along with the linen. She is a comfortable distance from the hearth, but she feels her face grow hot.

Rosemary pours some tea and, after sipping hers, puts the cup down and stares appraisingly at Daphne. "Tell me about you," she says, but her rings glint distractingly in the firelight, and Daphne feels this is only a courteous overture on Rosemary's part. She really wants to talk about herself, to gather more compliments for her amazing house, husband, child, and servant. Why else would she have the air conditioner and the fireplace going at the same time? At twenty-four, Rosemary is very pretty in the well-tended way of privileged young matrons. She looks older than Daphne, or as if she's trying to look older. In high school, so alike were they in their dress, hairstyle, and mannerisms, that they were often referred to as "the twins." They'd planned to be stewardesses for the same airline someday, and then, after seeing a movie about Margaret Mead in Samoa, to be co-anthropologists instead.

Perhaps it's Daphne who wants to continue talking about Rosemary. When she first saw her old friend tonight and recalled the way they had once urgently exchanged news, she'd had an impulse to blurt it all out, about Kenny and her consuming passion, about his marriage and his stalling. But that moment passed in the ceremony of greetings, and now she ducks her head and says, "Well, I'm still going to school. Can you believe it?" She laughs, eliciting only a weak smile from Rosemary, who'd done four straight years at Washington

State and has a B.A. in art history. Now she's on maternity leave from the art museum, where she assists one of the curators. Daphne drinks some tea, hoping to recapture her earlier poise. It's a smoky, herbal brew that reminds her of witches and spells. "Do you remember," she asks Rosemary, "that creepy girl in eleventh grade who told fortunes?"

"Yes," Rosemary says immediately. "Helen Foswicki. She came from Pennsylvania, and they moved away in the middle of the night, and nobody knows where they went."

"My God, you have a great memory, Rosie. I couldn't even think of her name, just that she had that greasy pack of cards she was always laying out in the cafeteria. The ace of spades meant instant death."

"She said I was going to be rich," Rosemary says. "What did she tell you?"

"Gosh, who can remember? It wasn't that significant, I guess, or maybe I didn't have that much confidence in clairvoyance. You know me; I'm such a hardheaded pragmatist."

"She said I would marry a doctor and have a daughter."

"Did she really? Well, the daughter part wasn't much of a risk. There's always a fifty-fifty chance of being right when you predict the sex of a baby. And all of our mothers were dying for us to snag rich doctors, anyway . . ." Daphne realizes with a start what she's said, and puts her hand over her mouth. "That came out all wrong, Rosie," she says.

"No, no, it's all right," Rosemary insists. "Do you remember how unattractive Helen was, her bad skin and those awful clothes? Yet we tolerated her, let her hang around us, because she told us only what we wanted to hear. It was the secret of her survival in high school."

"But she turned up the ace of spades for somebody once—for Janet Mazur. Who wants to hear a prediction of her own death?"

"Janet would. She probably loved it. It made her important in a way that wasn't possible otherwise. She did have a kind of morbidity, anyway. All that overeating and then throwing up."

"Anorexia."

"No, bulimia, but we didn't know the word for it then. The point is, I wanted to be rich, and . . . *voilà!*"

"So," Daphne says. The bitterness in Rosemary's voice is obvious, and Daphne suspects a revelation about the sadness of granted wishes she doesn't want to hear. And why can't she remember what Helen had predicted for her? Was she so purposeless, even in high school? A few weeks ago, Monica Mann had called her a "California girl," and Daphne had easily perceived the mockery in that phrase. "Why did you call me that?" she'd said. "I'm not a native, I'm not a surfer, I'm not even a *blonde.*"

"Oh," Monica said. "I only mean that you sort of *drift.* You're one of those girls who end up in California, no matter where you start out, as if it's your destiny. And then you never live a serious life. You don't *matriculate.*"

"I am now!" Daphne interjected. "I'll have my associate's degree by the end—"

"Oh, I'm not talking about that," Monica said impatiently. "I'm talking about your *life*. You just do a little bit of everything. A little work for the studios, take a few courses—gemology, psychology, astrology. You get half-assed *associate's* degrees. You see this guy and that guy. You're always in a *relationship*."

"Do you know you're crazy, Monica," Daphne had answered, wondering if she'd ever mentioned being a gofer at Paramount when she'd first arrived in L.A. She looked around the lounge for support from the others, from Mkabi, who was shuffling her mixed-drink flash cards, from Jerry, who stared into space and pretended he wasn't listening. "My God, what's wrong with being in a relationship?" Daphne demanded. "I mean, it would seem to be a sign of maturity, of mental health!" She was almost shouting and her heart hammered.

Monica smiled and she, too, addressed the others. "Do you hear this? Can you believe it's a sign of maturity to work in this death dive and see a married man for quickie matinees?"

Daphne wanted to say that it was none of Monica's business who she saw, and that fat, disgusting, quarrelsome people's opinions didn't interest her. She thought it out in those very words, but her position was still defensive. She had permitted her life to be other people's business by talking freely about it, and name-calling was the most infantile form of argument. Instead, she said, "You work here, too. I don't see you having a serious life, whatever *that* is."

"I guess I'm just a California girl myself," Monica said with infuriating mock innocence, and Jerry laughed and laughed.

"Why haven't you asked me where David is?" Rosemary says. Her tone is challenging, as if Daphne has failed some test and is about to fail another.

"I don't know," Daphne says. "I suppose I thought he was working late or something. I don't know." It is a little strange that she hasn't asked about David, although his conspicuous artifacts make his absence less significant. There are his medical books on the shelves, his pipes and humidor on a table, and his child asleep upstairs in her crib. But nobody would work nights at a place called the Dermatology Center. They probably wouldn't have to. And she has sensed something in this house, without bringing it to the surface of consciousness. Rosemary is so much less playful than Daphne remembers, and it isn't only the sobering process of marriage and motherhood. She's miserable, possibly as miserable as Daphne is. The idea is exciting, like a renewal of their lost camaraderie. Maybe they can go past the materialism of Rosemary's life to its true fabric, and from there right to what's happening in Daphne's life. It will be like the old days in a ruffled teenage bedroom, with the spilling of sacred and profane secrets, and the assurance of an absolute ally. The villains then were parents, teachers, boys who only wanted one thing, conniving girls who gave it freely.

"He has a mistress," Rosemary says.

Mistress! It's such a melodramatic word—something out of a gothic novel—that for a moment Daphne thinks Rosemary is joking.

"He used to pretend that he was working late, and for a while I pretended to believe him. I mean, everybody has an emergency dermabrasion or two, right?"

Daphne hates the threat of hysteria in Rosemary's

voice. She thinks of David at a party last winter, holding up a shadeless lamp in the bedroom as a woman raised her sweater to show him a mole on her back. "Is he going to . . ." Daphne can't finish the question.

Rosemary does it for her. "Leave me? I doubt it. Even David knows there's an expiration date on that kind of heat. It will cool off, become as routine as married sex. But in the meantime, he won't stop."

"Why don't you leave him, then?"

"God, Daph, you're still the same old simplistic kid, aren't you? A plus B always equals C."

"Well, thanks a *lot*."

"I'm sorry. I didn't mean to jump at you. Just guess who I'm really furious with."

"Then I'll repeat myself. Why don't you—"

"Because I don't want to divvy up the Oriental rugs and let him screw his sweetie on his half. Because I don't want everyone to know. I'm *ashamed*, as if *I'm* the one acting like an asshole. Because I don't want Lindsay to have the trauma of a broken home."

As if on cue, the baby starts screaming. There are muffled footsteps overhead, and Rosemary goes to the foot of the stairs. "Janelle?" she calls softly. "Will you bring her down, please?"

The baby sits on Rosemary's lap like a witness for the prosecution. Who wouldn't fall for her story? She *is* gorgeous, with the general loveliness of babies. No dermatologist can give anyone that perfect complexion. Everyone in the world would want to protect her from the foolish crimes of adult behavior. The foreman of the jury rises. Take those adulterers away in chains!

Rosemary continues as if the baby hasn't interrupted

their conversation, almost as if she isn't really there. "Because marriage is difficult and boring, and getting a divorce has to be difficult and boring, too. Because I'd like to kill them in the act rather than do something civil and lawful. I'd like to do something symbolic, like *skin* her."

Mistress, Daphne is thinking, the skin on her own neck itching and tingling. That's what *I* am. Except the connotations are as ridiculous as the word. Kenny hasn't set her up in a lavish apartment. He doesn't buy her expensive gifts. Not that she wants that kind of treatment from him. Aside from sexual fantasies, she mostly dreams about the two of them sitting in the same room, in a kind of timelessness, reading books, and looking up once in a while to read something aloud, and for the pleasure of finding the other still there. But she suspects that everyone would think, Joy would certainly think, that it's a temporary, loveless match based on Daphne's greed and Kenny's natural faithlessness. Rosemary would think the worst of her, too, even if Daphne tried to explain that one can also have a simplistic view of the other woman.

There is a silver thread of drool hanging from Lindsay's lower lip, and Daphne watches, mesmerized, waiting for it to break and fall. "Maybe you don't know the whole story," she suggests.

"What the hell is that supposed to mean?" Rosemary's voice is unforgiving. The baby whimpers, starts a second thread of drool.

"I don't really know what I mean," Daphne says. "I'm just talking to say something."

"Do you see?" Rosemary says. "Even you're embarrassed by the situation." She and the baby seem to be fused together on the sofa. Daphne can imagine David at their side, all of them securely joined, despite his infidelity, in that undeniable unit, the family. Like a small but shining constellation of stars.

"Yes," Daphne says. Mea culpa. Take me away. But wait. Please wait! Just one more moment of happiness!

10

The porch light is on when she gets home. She parks the car carefully, as if her father were watching from behind the living-room drapes, the way he once did.

"Is that you?" Her mother's voice drifts down the stairs.

"Yes," Daphne calls up, and starts to climb. The door to her parents' bedroom is closed. There is no slit of light at the bottom. She remembers wondering about the logistics of their lovemaking. Did they wait for their grown children to go out or fall asleep? Did they ever?

Margaret is sitting up in bed, wearing headphones, swaying voluptuously to the music Daphne can barely hear. They exchange little wrist-flapping waves, and Daphne goes out to the bathroom to brush her teeth and wash her face. Her mother comes in behind her, appears in the mirror.

"You scared me," Daphne says, and knows that she doesn't just mean that she's been startled, but that her mother's reflected face is scary. She looks older than she did during dinner. That ratty bathrobe, soft and achingly familiar, doesn't enhance her looks or promote an illusion of youth. She is barefoot, and in the fluorescent bathroom light, her feet appear yellow and callused.

Daphne's parents are not even fifty yet, but they have stepped out of the magic circle of immortality. Her mother's eyes are faded, squinty. From behind their bedroom door, her father's snoring is like a repeated question, rather than the growling command Daphne remembers. She thinks of Mr. Axel and of his daughter leaving him at the Palomar Arms and then collapsing in the parking lot. Everything in this room—washcloths in their orderly little pile, back-to-back toothbrushes, the deep plastic smell of the shower curtain—is too much to bear. Daphne buries her face in a towel and waits for composure.

"A man called," her mother says.

"What?"

"A telephone call from some man. He wouldn't leave his name."

"Oh," Daphne says.

"I guess I'll turn in," her mother says, but she sounds as if she hopes to be persuaded against it.

"Are you okay?" Daphne asks. "You look a little tired."

"I am," her mother confesses. "You girls can laugh at your father, but since last year, since that first eruption . . ."

"Come *on,* Ma," Daphne says, but her mother sits on the wicker hamper and crosses her ankles. "The laundry won't ever get clean," she says wearily. "I use bleach, blueing."

"It's not likely," Daphne says. "You know that."

"My cakes don't rise the way they used to."

"How did he sound?" Daphne asks.

"Who? Oh, the man on the phone? Disappointed, I think. In a hurry. I hate when people don't leave their name, don't you?"

"Yes," Daphne says. "It drives me crazy." She yawns and her mother stands up. They kiss good night in the hallway between the bedrooms, and separate.

The room Daphne has always shared with Margaret is a mess, even worse than the one she abandoned in Ventura. Clothing, magazines, and records are flung everywhere. It looks like the aftermath of a robbery, or an orgy. The twin beds, painted white when Daphne was fifteen, are flaking and seem too small.

"I feel like Goldilocks," Daphne says.

"What!" Margaret yells. She's still wearing the headphones, and Daphne motions for her to remove them.

"Did you have a good time?" Margaret asks.

"Ummm," Daphne says.

"Fun City, huh? I could never stand Rosemary. She always smiled at herself in the mirror. And she used to use my comb."

"Hey, she was my best friend in high school."

"Well, you wouldn't choose her now, believe me. Or the pimple-squeezer, either."

"You're disgusting," Daphne says, but starts to laugh as she says it.

Margaret laughs, too. "This is just like old times, kiddo," she says. "Except now I'm the older sister."

"It wouldn't surprise me."

"That guy called after you left. Mom wanted to give him the Hadleys' number, but Daddy looked as if he'd shoot her, so she didn't. He's important, isn't he?"

"Ummm," Daphne says again, and feels even worse than she did in the bathroom. "How's *your* love life?"

"Who, me? Not bad." Margaret looks smug, reminiscent. "There are these two boys, Doug and Randy. I can't make up my mind between them."

"You're going out with both of them?"

"Yeah, I guess you could say that."

There is a long pause during which Daphne understands what Margaret wants her to know. "Listen," she says, "do you . . ."

"Daphne, *everybody* does."

Daphne thinks of the stern-faced nun who was visiting Mrs. McBride the other day.

"Except maybe Lady Di," Margaret says. "I guess they can't have these old lords sitting around Parliament in fifty years, bragging about how they once put it to the Queen."

"But Doug and Randy, do you mean *both* of them?"

Margaret giggles. "Not at the same time, dumbass," she says.

What's happening here, Daphne wonders. She sticks her arm out into the space between the beds. "What does this smell like to you?" she asks.

Margaret sniffs, obligingly. "Norell?" she guesses. "Charlie?"

"No, no, not a fragrance. Just what does it *smell* like?"

"Like an arm, like normal sweat. I don't know. What is it supposed to smell like?"

"Nothing. Forget it. Turn off the light, okay?"

It isn't quite dark in the room and Daphne realizes that she's left the porch light on. She's too tired to go down again. And she couldn't face her mother's probable reappearance, the anxious voice trilling, "Everything all right?"

"Do you use protection?" Daphne asks.

"Yeah. Don't worry, I'm not going to make you an aunt before your time."

"I was thinking about *you*. Hey, do you remember when I explained procreation to you?"

"Do I? I nearly died, it was so funny."

"Mags?"

"What?"

"Do you know exactly what you want to do with your life?"

"Sure, exactly what I'm doing right now—living it."

"But don't you want to have a purpose? Or a plan?"

"Do you mean like future goals and things like that?"

"I guess so."

"No. That's all bullshit, anyway. People plan their lives as if they're never going to die. Do you remember what Charlotte said to Wilbur?"

"What? Oh, God, don't tell me."

"She said, 'After all, what's a life, anyway? We're born, we live a little, we die.' "

"Do you think a lot about dying?"

"Not a *lot*. But sometimes right after making it, especially with Doug. Sometimes I feel as if I *am* dying."

"The little death."

"How about you? Do you think about dying?" Margaret asks.

Once, Daphne had confessed in the lounge at work that she thought about it to what might be an obsessive degree.

Mkabi said that she was sure the physical part was not

always terrible. Plenty of people died very suddenly, or in their sleep. "A short circuit," she said, "and the lights go out."

"I just can't stand that my consciousness will leave the earth forever," Daphne explained.

"I just can't stand that my beautiful body will leave," Jerry said.

"Yeah, what if there's a consciousness *after* death?" Monica asked. "A restless, horny consciousness without flesh to satisfy it?"

"I try to keep busy," Daphne tells Margaret. She is close to tears and doesn't exactly know why. Thoughts of death, just before sleep, are inevitable and terrible; but now it's sex that disturbs her. Sex is on a rampage, she thinks, like some uncontrollable epidemic. David and his sweetie, Margaret and her two teenage lovers, Kenny and herself. Perhaps even her parents, consoling one another this minute, right across the hall, about the fallout of volcanic ash. She punches down her pillow, kicks against the tightly pulled sheets, and tries to reduce her oversized body to fit the narrow confinement of the bed.

"Good night, Daffy Duck," Margaret whispers.

"Quack, quack," Daphne answers, growing smaller and smaller, falling away into sleep, knowing with dread and certainty what she must do.

11

Joseph Axel wakes up in the Palomar Arms, aware of an erection and the knowledge that he would like to die. It's not just this place, although the move from Sandra's house has surely reinforced his wish. If he'd had any sense, he would have taken something from the store long ago, and hidden it away for this time. He has always been a realist, especially about the practical matters of life and death. You don't dispense medicine for forty-three years without learning that you can't save everybody, and that finally you can't save anybody.

Adele had invested him with powers he'd never possessed. To her he had been as mighty and mysterious as the alchemists must have seemed to mortal and frightened kings. She had seen him do a few tricks over the years, watching from her side of the counter, the merchandise side. He'd protested at first when she started calling him "Doc," the way the customers did, but the combination of coquetry and genuine awe won him over. And (he can admit this now) he swaggered a little when the simplest emergency measures saved the day, the life. Ipecac for the croupy child, the new antibiotics that cured bacterial pneumonia. The very illness that had taken Adele's young father, a man born in the wrong century. So what if Joe hadn't invented the stuff? At least he was able to break the cipher of the doctor's hand-writing and, wearing his white coat, grind the powders, hum an incantation, and come up with the winning formula.

Adele sold the bathing caps and the shampoo, the ear-plugs, and the Modess. She gift-wrapped perfume and baby toys and Russell Stover candy. She was very hard-working, and her lively personality encouraged business. Who didn't love Adele? But he was the deity in that store, the one to roll back eyelids and find the irritating fleck of dust. The hero of the mortar and pestle.

To the end, to the very end of her own life, she believed that he would save her, too. And he was glad she had not outlived him. He hates to be here now, not himself, not in his rightful body, but here nevertheless. He has a cold and sane longing to be dead. But if he had deserted Adele by dying first, and she had landed in this place, she would have been terrified, confused, and tor-tured. She would have looked for substitute saviors, prob-ably anyone in white—even the man who moves the dust around the floor now and sings a song about laying his baby down.

Joe feels the tension of his erection and hopes the bedclothes hide it. He has no baby to lay down, no desire to lay *anyone* down. His tumescence is an ironic side effect of the medication, a priapism that comes without true lust, without purpose. He can only hope it's gone before the woman comes in to sponge him. Must he pray to Priapus for his release?

In her last days, Adele, who had been religious, never seemed to pray. She looked past the helpless doctors, her eyes terribly alive above the oxygen mask, pleading with Joe, depending only on him. And when the doctors left the room, he removed the mask long enough to slip the tablets in—sugar only—but she made the face of a child tasting something bitter, the bitter taste of medicine that would work, that would stem the rising tide of water in her lungs. She trusted him right to the last minute. He thought of hurrying her along, the way Schur had hurried Freud when living became impossible. Joe had so many opportunities—extra digitalis, a few quinidines, even an injection of adrenaline. She would have smiled at him as the needle slipped in, but he couldn't be her murderer and her redeemer at once. The morality of it was too confusing; the act was beyond him. I'm only a druggist, he'd think. I'm only human. And finally she was gone.

And the erection he would like to hammer down with his fist, if he could make a proper fist, is dying on its own, too. He looks toward the door whenever a shadow crosses it, hoping, now that he'll be presentable, for Sandra, or for the pretty young woman who brought supper the other night and was so distressed by her own pity. A different woman, who chattered musically to him in Spanish, brought the food last night. While he tried to eat, he distracted himself by thinking about the store, on Meserole Street in Brooklyn. Between the window displays of suntan oil and patent cold remedies, he'd kept a pyramid of old apothecary jars, their inscriptions in gold leaf: *Spirits of Aethyl Nitrate, Tincture of Ferric Chloride, Aluminum Hydroxide.* Sunlight was gold on gold, and the blue and amber glass shone like jewels.

After Adele died, and he retired and came to live with Sandra and Bud, she paused one evening in the middle of stirring something at the stove, and said, "Dad, I wish you'd kept a few of those jars when you sold the store. They were so beautiful, and they're really valuable now." There was more grief in her posture and the heaviness of her tone than a couple of old jars could ever arouse, no matter how handsome they were. He guessed that she was lonely for her mother, and for the past.

He believed that his own loneliness was more constant and more profound. He missed everything about his old life, in spite of the comforts of that new home. The dear presence of his grandchildren was the only strong consolation. Deborah, the oldest, and the only girl, was as dark and radiant as a biblical queen. She would come up behind him and cover his eyes. "Guess who, Poppy?"

Daniel was gentle and ambitious. He read his homework aloud after supper, and invited Joe into his room to watch *Star Trek* and *Get Smart*.

Joe favored the youngest, Kevin, who was cursed with a kind of intensity that made him unpopular and unhappy. Only his grandfather could get close enough for touching.

All three of them liked to hear Joe talk about the store, but they weren't interested in its practical or nostalgic aspects. They wanted him to tell about the holdups during the last years, especially the time the junkie shot up right there in the telephone booth while his friend kept a trembling gun against Joe's head. Again and again, they wanted him to say how he sensed when he was about to be robbed, by the way a man walked into the store, absently fingered counter displays, and then looked directly into Joe's eyes, delivering a reckless message.

The grandchildren were half grown when he came to California to stay, and soon they moved away, one by one, to school and marriage. There was a great-grandchild, then another. The first symptoms of the Parkinson's had already begun. He knew what they were and chose not to acknowledge them. His cockeyed gait. "Daddy, don't run, you're *lurching*," Sandra said. And he'd answered. "Right. What's my hurry? Where am I going?" His steps became carefully small and he often felt he was only moving in place. In the room he'd inherited from Daniel, a room that still had rock star posters and a stolen red *Stop* sign on its walls, he observed his hands in the pill-rolling motion that was once deliberate but was now involuntary—thumb against forefinger, with nothing between them—an early, absolute sign of Parkinson's.

The disease is progressive; he knows that. Is everyone born in the wrong century? He knows what the medication can and cannot do. Sandra would pick it up at a twenty-four-hour discount place that sold everything from cocktail snacks to bikinis. The world is coming to an end, he'd thought, the first time he walked into one of those all-night stores with its numbered and lettered aisles, the young, indifferent checkers jerking around to the incessant Muzak. But the world was only changing —nothing serious.

He locked his bedroom door and looked up his disease in Daniel's encyclopedia, desperate for promising news he might have missed. The language of the short article was both direct and lyrical. It said that the victim moves forward with small mincing steps as if he were trying to "catch up to his center of gravity." The mind remains clear, it said, but eventually the patient is confined to bed. How careless he'd been, or what a coward, not to have prepared for this possibility. Jacobs, a gentle pinochle player, whose pharmacy was a few blocks away, on Marcy, downed half his inventory as soon as he learned that he had cancer. Before he lost the courage to command his fate, and the ability to swallow.

After breakfast, two aides arrive to take Joe and his roommate, Brady, off to the recreation room for a talent show. Brady, in fact, will be part of the show, and tries to get Joe to do something, too. His shaking head shakes more violently to indicate that he can't. "No talent," he tells Brady, who says, "Awww," in mock disgust.

The recreation room is filled when they get there, and other wheelchairs are maneuvered to make room for theirs. This is obviously a popular event, a rare instance of democracy between inmates and staff. A nurse, wearing a black paper mustache, serves as the announcer. She says a few words of welcome before introducing "our own Jeanette MacDonald, Mrs. Rose Barstow!"

There is a thunderclap of applause, and then a pretty, elderly woman in a lavender dress sings "Buttercup" from *H.M.S. Pinafore*. Her voice is quavering, but sweet, like a voice on an old phonograph record, and she knows all the words without faltering. She is accompanied on the piano by a cadaverous-looking male patient, who uses the pedals with unexpected force and energy.

Next to Joe, another man in a wheelchair cries, "Oh,

God, oh, God," and Joe looks at him in alarm, thinking the fellow is having a stroke, or at least a vision. But everyone else ignores him, including Rose Barstow, who keeps singing without a break until the end of her song.

The nurse emcee is up again, clapping vigorously and saying, "Let's hear it for Rose!"

Then a maintenance man, a black fellow who could be a descendant of one of the Nicholas Brothers, does a wild and impressive tap dance; and he's followed by a woman in a green bathrobe, like Joe's, who stands with her walker and solemnly recites "In Flanders Fields." Joe notices another woman across the room, who looks older than Methuselah, and is fast asleep, or pretends to be. She must be the birthday girl, the one approaching her first century.

There are a few other performers, including a man wearing a T-shirt with a woman's face on it, who does some gymnastics. In this place, where walking unassisted is an accomplishment of note, his contortions seem extraordinary.

Brady is on last, and he turns out to be a comedian of sorts. Anyway, he wheels himself to the front of the room, where he tells a few jokes, most of them borrowed from television comics, and told in borrowed voices. He sings bits of various songs, altering some of them so they relate to his own double amputation. A line from "All of Me" becomes "Take my legs, I want to lose them!" No one in the room appears to be offended or embarrassed, as surely most people would have been in an ordinary performance elsewhere. And when Brady finishes with the beautiful Beatles song "Yesterday" and comes to the line "Suddenly, I'm not half the man I used to be," there is raucous laughter and cheering. This is the brave side of things, Joe understands, the toughing out of tragedy. The idea is to be darker than the darkness, and then you can hope to endure it. When the man next to him starts saying, "Oh, God, oh, God," again, Joe knows that it's only *his* routine, his response to the demons that have come and taken away autonomy and freedom. His litany is tolerated by the others the way Brady's tasteless jokes are, and the boring recitation of "In Flanders Fields."

Joe imagines getting up there himself and announcing that for his opening number he's going to take his own life. There could be a long drumroll, a dramatic bow . . . and then what? No digitalis, no quinidines, not even a cyanide capsule like the ones Hitler had stashed in the bunker for his big act. And Joe has the fumbling fingers of an amateur now. Even if he had the right stuff, he'd probably drop it, let it roll out of sight under the piano. The crowd would hiss. They'd have to take him off with a vaudeville hook. His real talent, he knows, is for continuation, not much of a crowd-pleaser anywhere.

There are prizes for all the participants in the talent show. Brady gets a ball-point pen. He asks the nurse with the paper mustache if she'd like his autograph. The woman who sang "Buttercup" is given a clear plastic rain hat with a design of pink and blue polka dots. "Oh," she says. "I haven't been out in the rain for years." But then she opens its accordion pleats and ties it under her chin.

12

Ah, the numbers, the blessed numbers. For a while they flush everything else out of Kenny's head. His fingers move over the calculator with virtuoso speed and precision, and he hardly ever makes a mistake. In another life he might have been a church organist, or a jazz musician.

The client on the other side of the desk waits with almost breathless apprehension for the final tax figures. When the waiting becomes unendurable, he shuffles his feet in a little sit-down soft-shoe dance. Kenny flashes a fast, reassuring smile without losing a beat in his computations. He notices the other man's telltale pallor, the patina of perspiration. People have passed out in this office, sliding suddenly and quietly out of sight, and Kenny keeps a vial of smelling salts in a handy drawer. He feels that the man's fate is in his charge, that he's about to deliver something almost as important as a biopsy report. The malignancy, though, is the client's wish to defraud the government and get away with it, to make Kenny the knowing criminal and himself just a lucky dope.

But the smile and his expertise are the only things Kenny will offer. He knows all the angles—the various deductions and dodges—and he gently indicates what is legal and what isn't. He doesn't proselytize or sit in judgment. Instead, he gives shrewd and suitable advice. That's what he's paid for, and he's very good at his job. But it's not the part he loves.

Even when he was a little kid, Kenny was a whiz at arithmetic, although he never distinguished himself in other subjects. The thing was that numbers worked out, no matter what you did with them. You could depend absolutely on their pure truth. The introduction of more difficult concepts like fractions and percentages delighted Kenny, while most students struggled to grasp them. He did his friends' math homework and they wrote his book reports in return. But he would have done his part without reward, simply for the pleasure of doing it.

Occasionally, he thinks with vague uneasiness about those artists who contribute something of value to the culture of their time. Even the commercial moviemakers whose taxes he handles talk excitedly about "lasting social documents." Kenny's ability with numbers is a kind of gift, too, he supposes. Anyway, an honest and ungrudging commitment is what really matters. You do what you have to do and then it has value. Kenny's younger brother, Robert, who loved drawing maps for Geography, coloring in each state with a fresh bright crayon, and who was voted Class Rembrandt in junior high, is an electrical engineer back East. Useful, yet unfulfilled. He keeps taking evening courses in pottery and weaving, but they don't give him the satisfaction he needs. From the first, Kenny knew that his own future would involve those remarkable numbers that distracted him from unhappiness, that even worked as a soporific.

Their parents were embattled way before the boys were old enough for school. They kept Kenny awake at night with their yelling, and the punctuation of banging doors. Robert slept through everything, open-mouthed and dream-bound. And after nothing else helped Kenny, not humming, not covering his head with his pillow, or stuffing the ends of the blanket into his ears, he would count—one two three four five six—he wanted to reach a trillion, but somewhere in the hundreds the crashing voices on the other side of the wall would start to recede, and Kenny would grow deliciously heavy with sleep. He never counted sheep, or needed any image but the physical numbers themselves: the handsome upright 1, the humble round-shouldered 2. What a fine counter he was for such a small boy. What a smug, performing little brat. The butcher his mother went to would give him pennies if he counted them aloud for the entertainment of the other customers. Kenny didn't mind being the floor show in the circus sawdust of the butcher shop. He liked it when the customers declared him a baby Einstein and he could go home, his pockets jingling with bounty, the numbers still resounding in his head like a beloved song.

Later, when he was older and had discovered the easy friendship of his own body, he helped himself to sleep by touching. At first, he didn't give up his habit of counting. It simply became the accompaniment to his new work—the counting of strokes, faster and faster, the numbers going by in a blur!

When he began to notice other bodies, and hear mystifying numerical jokes, about men with three or four testicles, about the number of sexual positions, about the number 69, he fixed his mind on something or someone else at night, and trained his willing hand to give him slower and more narcotic pleasure, and he didn't have to count at all.

Despite her looseness with money, Joy is clever at math. She balances her own checkbook, and chooses to do it without the aid of a calculator. Before the children were born, she worked for a philanthropic organization, and she always read their financial reports with professional interest and acumen.

Daphne, on the other hand, says that math eluded her in school, that she'd break out in a sweat at problems that required calculations of the mileage of speeding trains, or the conversion from gallons to pints. "Oh, why didn't I know you then!" she once asked Kenny. Her helplessness with numbers doesn't amuse him; still, it's only a small flaw among her numerous great virtues, and they often look over her bank statements in bed. But Daphne won't even attempt to solve the little puzzlers he likes, those slightly more complicated versions of the math problems she's always hated. "Please," she'd beg him. "Stop! I don't care how many times the missionaries row the cannibals across the river. I don't care if they all drown, or get eaten by piranhas!"

Both of Kenny's children demonstrate an early talent for numbers. Molly keeps anxious tabs on her toys with a mysterious mathematical system of her own. And at four, Steven will do his multiplication tables for anyone who'll listen. Kenny was like that, too, but out of a more compelling need.

When he and Robert were little, Robert, the favored

child, was overwhelmed by attention because he was frail and asthmatic. Or maybe he was frail and asthmatic because of the attention. Whenever Kenny began to feel deprived of his share, or when his parents became dangerously belligerent with one another, he would ask, "Hey, who wants to hear me count to a million?" Hardly anybody did, but it was a way of affecting the environment, of having some power at an otherwise powerless age. In a few years he expanded his repertoire to include riddles and mathematical card tricks.

"So?" the client asks now. "Will I have to hock my kids?" A vice-president of Creative Development at a major studio, he's also a gallows humorist. Others in his seat have made shaky jokes about jumping off cliffs or selling their blood, but they, too, were obviously grieving over impending loss. Like most people, they instantly convert numbers into dollars and cents, into sports cars and beachfront property, and they don't appreciate the logic and beauty of simple addition and subtraction. They want miracles.

Well, who doesn't? Kenny could use one himself. His fingers go slack on the calculator as he recalls how horny he was that morning, and how sad. Frances made blueberry pancakes for breakfast, while Gus dandled and nuzzled his grandchildren. Joy, in a powder-blue bathrobe, was like a pretty teenager who is looking forward to the day, to her whole life. She set the table with a dreamy lack of attention. She called her parents Mommy and Daddy. Steven drank his milk in breathless gulps, and Molly put her delicate foot in Kenny's lap. He imagined tapping his orange-juice glass with a spoon, for silence, and then making an announcement. "Listen, everybody. This wonderful family scene is a lousy fraud. I'm in love with someone else, and it can't be helped. It's as inevitable as—as a progression of whole numbers!"

The spatula Frances held would have trembled on the griddle, spattering batter and grease, and Gus might have keeled over in disbelief. Molly would probably have wriggled her little foot and then kicked Kenny, hard. And Joy would have looked at him with adolescent contempt, and at her own reflection in the toaster with vanity. All the boys who'd loved her once would be tickled pink to have the chance to love her again. Steven would have yelled in his loudest voice: *"Two times three is six! Two times four is eight! Two times five is ten!"*

It was another hot day, but this time Kenny was going to escape to the office for a few hours. He could try calling Daphne's apartment, and if she was there he'd make an impassioned and eloquent case for himself. They would meet; things would go on as before. He looked again at the scene in his kitchen, marveling at its unbroken peace. He raised his cup and it was filled with steaming fragrant coffee. Butter slid and melted over the pancakes, and Kenny squeezed Molly's foot. "What's on today's agenda?" he asked.

The client has one hand over his nose and he's making snuffling noises. He'd never looked like a crybaby to Kenny. Besides, his eyes are dry and furtive. Jesus, *movie* people. They have such a weird lack of propriety. "Are you snorting *coke*, Mr. P.?" Kenny asks.

The man opens his hand to reveal a Vicks inhalator. "Nah, I've just got a little cold. Anyway, can *I* afford coke?" His question has the whining inflection of a plea.

"I'll let you know in a few more minutes," Kenny says.

When he has the total, he leans across the desk and the client backs away slightly from the news, before leaning forward, too. Kenny writes the figures on a pad and pushes it across the desktop.

"Oh, fuck," the man says. They always say that, or something like it.

It's time for Kenny to do his stuff. He suggests other possible allowances and shelters. "We need bigger write-offs," he says, "and we want to avoid preference items. Let's see if we can convert some of this income into capital gains."

The client is less rigid now, is almost ready to smile.

Kenny feels exhilarated. He explains it all carefully, his fingers playing with the calculator at the same time. Now he'd like to show the guy a couple of card tricks that would knock him on his ear. But he has to move him out of the office quickly, so he can start calling Daphne.

The client makes a brave crack about getting off the breadline, and Kenny relaxes him further by saying that he wouldn't have to pay such big taxes if he didn't earn so much money in the first place. "Yeah," the man concedes, and his smile breaks.

Kenny looks at his watch, remembering that Daphne has a class starting in a few minutes. If she's back from Seattle, that's where she'll be. By the time the class is over, he can be in the parking lot at the college, waiting for her.

13

It amazes Daphne that she is able to behave as if her life is not about to be radically changed. Feeling only a little silly and self-conscious, she stands near the blackboard, where Mr. Steinmetz has instructed her to stand. She glances at the mimeographed script in her hand and sees that many of its lines have been marked with a yellow highlighter. She has the lead in this reading, the part of Jacqueline Saunders, a heroine Daphne herself has created.

On the other side of the classroom, the heavyset man who always wears a Dodgers cap, and who still has the kind of sideburns that were popular in the sixties, is ready to play opposite her in the role of Jake Monroe. When Daphne wrote this teleplay, she had pictured Jake as looking something like Cary Grant in *To Catch a Thief*. When she'd indicated, in her original treatment, that he was an "older" man, she'd meant it in the sophisticated sense, meant someone worldly and experienced, sexually attractive, but without youthful superficiality. Mitchell? Marty? She can't remember the name of the man in the baseball cap, but he's hardly right for the part of Jake. This is just a reading, but Mr. Steinmetz has put unfair pressure on the script by casting one of the leads so poorly. Any of the younger women in the class might have played Jacqueline with credibility, although Daphne realizes that her description of the heroine, whose hair is waist-length and brown, and whose voice is throaty, could also be a description of herself. Is the likeness limited to physical characteristics? Plays are a little like dreams. And dreams rise up from the unconscious, heavy with clues to the real concerns of the dreamer. Daphne is suddenly afraid that personal feelings will overtake her in the middle of the drama, and that she won't be able to continue. Her decision to break with Kenny is an ache in her body that travels from head to belly to fingertips. She is not immobilized by it, but surely that could happen at any time. Perhaps, if she's lucky, the full force of her resolution won't strike her until she has spoken to him. It's an occasion she dreads, and yet one she must pass through.

Daphne has come directly from the airport to school. Her suitcase is under her seat across the room. Again, she imagines the telephone ringing in her apartment, and is grateful for this delay in her confrontation with Kenny. She twists a lock of hair around one finger, and looks at the lines of the script, silently mouthing some of the words.

Oh, Jake, honey. Sometimes I worry that we'll always be this intense. Or that someday we won't be.

She can't even remember writing that. It sounds so artificial and dumb. The man about to play Jake has a paunch that he taps with one hand, making it quiver. His breath is audible. My God, what if she starts to laugh? She does that sometimes, when she's nervous or unhappy.

"Okay, okay," Steinmetz says. "We don't have sets or costumes, so for all intents and purposes this is a *radio* play. When I was a little kid, they had this great new invention called the radio. It was a little box, and they squeezed all these little people inside: the Lone Ranger and Tonto, Jack Benny, the Green Hornet, the Singing Lady . . . All I had to do was hear them speak their lines and I was *transported*. I could picture everything. The horses, the dust they kicked up when the sound man knocked two coconut shells together, everything. So we have to forget about Daphne and Marshall here, and concentrate on Jacqueline and Jake, on the magic of the *words* they speak, and see if we're persuaded. Okay, stand by. Action!"

Daphne begins. "Oh Jake honey," she mumbles as quickly as she can. "Sometimes I worry that we'll always be this intense or that someday we won't be." She glances around the room apologetically, but everyone is attending to the script.

Marshall clears his throat, something Jake wouldn't do in a million years. He lifts his eyebrows and grins at Daphne, as if asking to be forgiven for this foolishness. Then he reads: "Baby, I want you to move in with me." His voice is high-pitched, his eyes dart like a shoplifter's.

Baby, I want you to move in with me! She remembers writing that all right, the words she would have had Kenny speak at any time. Now they are as trite as the lyrics to a fifties hit. Bay-bee, I want you to move in with me-ee, we could be so ha-a-a-pee! And her own next lines are positively ludicrous.

It's funny. I've longed for you to say that, but now I'm kind of scared . . .

She's been nagging the guy for three scenes to make a move toward commitment, and now she's *scared*. What is she supposed to be scared of? That she can't live with his furniture? That his landlady won't approve? Daphne says her lines, looking at Steinmetz and praying for an interruption. He should be yelling "Cut!" or something by now. But his eyes are shut and his face is peaceful and expectant. He actually seems convinced, even trans ported. How little people settle for, Daphne thinks. No wonder everything on television is so bad. No wonder the quality of life isn't much better.

Marshall, as Jake, reads: "Scared of what, my love?"

"Of nothing," Daphne says firmly. "I'm just being an idiot. I'll pack my things and be at your place in thirty minutes."

Marshall peers at his script, turns a page, perplexed.

Steinmetz opens his eyes. "That's not in the script, is it?"

"I'm improvising," Daphne says. "For the sake of verisimilitude."

"You can't do that," Marshall says. "What am I supposed to say?"

"What's in your heart," Daphne advises, and is astonished when his face blazes with color.

"That would be swell if this was a theater class," Mr. Steinmetz says. "Then we could do improvisation, psychodrama, method acting, anything you want. You could get to be a table, or a rosebud opening. But in television you've got to stick to the script. And so far, so good, I'd say. Any comments?"

Mrs. Spurgeon, a woman in her sixties who's working on a children's fantasy about George Washington returned from the dead, raises her hand. "What about morals?" she asks.

"What about them?" Steinmetz says irritably.

"Well, doesn't somebody have to take responsibility for all this looseness? Doesn't somebody have to say, why don't they just get married if they're so crazy about each other, and make it legal?"

"What is she, a lawyer?" another woman asks.

"Oh, Christ," Steinmetz moans.

The man who did the treatment about the aborted fetus waves his hand frantically, as if he's trying to flag down a train. "Get with it, lady," he says. "This is the *twentieth* century!"

"Well, I think it's disgusting," she tells him.

"Yeah, but the question is, does it play?" Steinmetz insists.

"Listen, everybody, I'm sorry," Daphne says. "But I just got back from a trip. I'm tired and a little on edge."

"Is *that* in the script?" Marshall asks.

"Oh, why don't you take off that stupid cap!" she cries, and instantly regrets it. He's probably profoundly bald—hence the cap in the first place, and the compensation of those overgrown sideburns. "Don't!" she says, a moment too late.

But he's not bald at all. In fact, he has a luxuriant

head of dark hair that springs into shape as soon as the cap is removed. Someone rowdy whistles and applauds. Daphne feels embarrassed, as if it were an erection Marshall has exposed. Without the cap, and if he could lose some weight . . . He's really a very nice-looking man, and probably a decent one. Look at his range of emotions in this short, excruciating session: the appeal of his smile before saying his first line; the way he blushed when she suggested he speak his heart; his humiliation at the revelation of his own good looks. He might have had a crush on her all term, and now she's spoken harshly to him without due cause. Her ache has become centralized, and it's radiating. She longs for Kenny, while Marshall longs for her, and maybe Mrs. Spurgeon longs for Marshall, in a hapless chain of unrequited longing. She has been so selfish and self-centered, so stonily elite in this roomful of people she had privately considered losers. Course takers, idlers, lost California souls. Even Steinmetz, the so-called authority here. What is he doing in Ventura, when Hollywood is so close? And what did he ever have produced, anyway? A few soap episodes. A couple of rewrites for that old sitcom, *I Married Joan.*

But what makes Daphne think that she's different, only a tourist slumming in purgatory? Monica may be creepy and crazy, but she's right about the direction of Daphne's life. It must change if anything worthwhile is to become of her. This knowledge is fortifying. It will give her the strength to be firm and articulate with Kenny, and to survive the dread of their meeting until it finally takes place. "Forgive me, Marshall. Please," she says, "can we just continue?"

He nods, crushing the ebullience of his hair under the Dodgers cap. There is a ruffling noise as everyone looks at the script again.

"Scared of what, my love?" Jake asks.

"Of . . . oh, of everything!" Jacqueline answers. And it plays.

14

There are so many pretty women in Ventura. And their clothing is wonderful, full of color and movement. Those ridiculous high-fashion styles in the *Times* look fine on real bodies. Tight, faded jeans do, too.

Kenny sits in the Toyota, the raised tinted windows isolating him in unnatural dimness from the dazzling scene outside, making him a voyeur when he'd rather be a participant. He'll be able to open the windows soon, but now the sealed car holds the last few blasts of air-conditioned relief. A tape of Mahler's Fifth slightly tempers Kenny's insane bliss. The fourth movement will probably make him wild again, but it's worth it.

He's a little early; Daphne won't be out for about ten more minutes, if she's coming at all. Her car isn't in the lot, but she could have taken the bus today, or come straight from the airport in a taxi. Kenny believes she's inside the building he's facing; he feels it in a rare tremor of clairvoyance. He'll have to ride around again a few more times to cool off, but he doesn't mind. He doesn't mind anything right now. It's one of those moments of well-being in which he is indestructibly robust and hopeful. Perhaps the women walking by would not be so pretty if his spirits were lower. But now they look perfect. How lucky he is to be alive in an era when life is extended by science, and sexuality is celebrated by just about everyone. Jesus, he's tempted to roll down the window now and shout something to that pair of athletic beauties jogging past like madwomen in the heat. Nothing macho or obscene. Just "Hello!" or "Great day!" or something else as innocuous as that. Better not. In the rearview mirror, he sees his excited eyes and thinks that he looks like a sex maniac in a schoolyard. He could get a faceful of Mace for his friendliness, or Daphne could show up as the campus police drag him off. Oh, where the hell is she?

He opens the window because he's sweating and starting to feel uncomfortably alone. The air is appallingly hot, and he quickly rolls the window shut. He turns on the ignition and begins riding in a slow, small circle, the air conditioner on low, the music brilliantly loud. And then, at the very peak of the fourth movement, he sees her come through the center doorway of the building. Even from a distance, her stature and beauty don't seem reduced. He puts the car into neutral and leaves the motor running, wanting to watch her walk toward him, and wanting to delay the exact moment of reunion a little longer. He is aware that he often holds back this way in lovemaking, for the same exquisite sensation of harnessed pleasure.

Other students come through the doorway and walk behind Daphne—stragglers from her class, he supposes. Several classes must have broken at once, because now other doors open and more people wander out. But he can focus only on Daphne, as if she's crossing a broad stage under the faithful beam of a spotlight, carrying a suitcase. He is about to open the door and run to her, when a man just behind her catches up and, after a brief exchange, takes the suitcase from her hand. She protests, but not enough, and then they veer off, heading away from Kenny.

"Hey!" he yells, and he opens the door of the Toyota. Mahler pours out in a torrent, and several people stop to listen and stare. Daphne doesn't hear anything; she's too far away. Christ, she's getting into that joker's car. He's wearing a baseball cap, and he's putting her suitcase into the backseat. Then he holds the passenger door open for Daphne and touches her arm. Is she smiling? They look like they're about to go off on a fucking honeymoon. Kenny wants to drive right up to them, but there's a small flurry of traffic around him, and he might get stuck. Instead, he leaves his car door open, the motor and music still on, and starts to run across the parking lot. "Hey!" he yells again, and bumps into somebody, spilling books to the ground. But he doesn't pause or turn around, even when curses are called after him.

He gets there just in time. He has to tap on the window, and she looks up in absolute amazement, as if she never expected to see him again in this life.

She doesn't get out, which infuriates him. He's breathless and plastered with sweat, standing there with his hands on his hips and heaving like an asshole, while she turns away to say something to the guy in the car with her.

Then both doors open at once. Kenny wants to embrace her, but it's too awkward. The man is out first and rushes up, extending his hand. "Marshall Haber," he says, and Kenny assesses him with some relief. He mumbles his own name and they shake hands while Daphne waits.

"Hello, puss," Kenny says, turning to her. His voice is too loud and possessive.

"What are you doing here?" she asks, and wishes that she didn't tremble so easily.

He opens his hands. "I was just driving through," he says, "and there you were." That doesn't even earn him a smile. What was she smiling about so much before he got here?

"Come on, I'll take your bag," Kenny says. She hesitates, and he knows immediately that he'll play that moment of hesitation over and over again in his head later. Someday, when they're quarreling about something else, he might even bring it up. It scares him to see himself hoarding such ammunition for future discord. He had planned to come to her unarmed, except for the argument of love.

She turns to the man in the baseball cap and says, "Kenny's an old friend, Marshall. But I didn't know he'd be here. Thanks for offering the ride, anyway."

Marshall looks as if he's used to defeat, as if he expects it. "Sure thing," he says, and pulls her suitcase out of the car. He gives it to Kenny in a gesture that seems unnecessarily formal. Still, Kenny thanks him, and they shake hands again, like a couple of Frenchmen. He supposes he's lucky not to get kissed. He and Daphne have not kissed yet, either. They haven't even shaken hands. "Old friend," she'd called him. Meanly, he stores that phrase next to her hesitation, and they start to walk in silence across the parking lot.

Daphne looks behind them. "So long, Jake!" she bellows, and Kenny turns to see the guy in the baseball cap grin at her and cup his hands around his mouth. "Au revoir, Jacqueline!" he answers, and they wave gaily at each other.

"What's that?" Kenny asks, struggling to lighten his tone. "A code or something?"

It's difficult for Daphne to make eye contact with him. In the powerful sunlight, he appears golden and illusory, like a field of wheat. After all her preparation, she's unprepared for this meeting. "It's only a little joke," she says.

Nothing seems funny to Kenny. His plans have been spoiled and it's Daphne's fault. But he doesn't want to quarrel; he wants to establish the mood he'd anticipated, to recall his own manic happiness and arouse hers. He shifts the suitcase to his other hand and puts his arm around her waist. She allows herself to be drawn close enough for a glancing kiss. "I missed you very much," he whispers.

"We have to talk, Kenny," she says. It could be another rotten line in her teleplay.

"Among other things." He puts his mouth against her warm hair.

He's taking over. It's what he does. In bed his aggression is a healthy challenge she loves to meet. Here, now, she feels repressed by it, and impotent. She stops walking and stamps her foot. "No!" she says.

"No, what?" he asks pleasantly, teasing, bluffing.

She's spoken in the brittle and stubborn voice of the airport phone call. She sounds like Molly, trying to fight bedtime forever.

"I want us to stop, Kenny," Daphne says. "I decided while I was in Seattle. This makes me too unhappy."

"Would you be happier alone?"

"No," she answers truthfully. "At least, not for a while."

"Oh, come *on*, Daph," he says. "This is a hell of a reunion."

"That's because we're not together anymore."

"Yeah, I noticed that."

"Sarcasm won't help, Kenny."

"Okay, what will, then? Just tell me, and I'll do it."

"No, you won't," she says softly, but she knows he's heard her.

"Listen," he says. "Did you get my message in Seattle? I think I spoke to your mother. She sounded a little like you. My heart was clunking like a kid's."

"You didn't leave a message. You didn't even leave your *name*."

"That's because there really wasn't any message. I was only dying for the sound of your voice. I called you a hundred times back here first." He hesitates and then says, "I even went to the apartment once."

"Why? Why did you do that? I told you I was going away, didn't I?"

"*Why?* I'm in love, that's why! I'm irrational! I brought you flowers, but they died." The last doesn't seem like a lie after he's said it. He had seriously considered bringing them, anyway. And they would have died. When they reach the Toyota, he wishes that he'd filled it with orchids, like a Mafia chief's hearse. He's surprised by the chugging engine, the music still playing. He's surprised the car wasn't stolen, with an open invitation like this. Maybe his luck is about to change. He looks at Daphne, hoping she'll seem impressed by this display of recklessness, but her face tells him nothing. He puts her suitcase into the trunk and then fumbles with the handle on her side, made clumsy by her lack of response. When the door is open, he says, "Get in," incapable of more graciousness than that.

She obeys, without speaking, a passive rebel, and now she reminds him of Joy, of all the times they've entered cars, rooms, even their bed, in controlled and furious silence. How unwelcome these comparisons to his wife and daughter would be to Daphne right now. He hates himself for thinking of them, and is glad, at least, that she can't read his mind. Sitting close to her like this, he is rushed by tenderness. It is much better than the scalding lust he's felt for days. This requires no effort on his part, no act of conclusion. He has only to experience it.

All the pretty women in Ventura, in California, in the *world*, and he wants and loves only this one. It's a miracle, not the kind he'd hoped for earlier in his office, that would have untangled the intricate knots of his life, but the simpler, more available miracle of selection and desire. He would like to say something about this to Daphne, but he knows it's too soon. She wouldn't believe him or really listen. Someone has brainwashed her about the dangers of her own need, and she's frightened and grieving. He risks putting his hand briefly against her face, and then he starts to drive her home.

15

Well, what did she expect—that she could end it with
a fast phone call, the way you cancel a dental appointment? That it was possible to avoid a scene simply because she didn't want to suffer one? She gets out of the
car quickly before he can open the door for her, that old
trick of chivalry to gain advantage.

Kenny follows Daphne through the narrow lobby,
carrying her suitcase. He's reassured by the dim light of
the hallway, the familiar dank and slightly spicy odor.
His heart moves swiftly with hope, as it always does
here. He knows that soon it will all be better, that the
moment they lie down together, they'll also lay everything else aside.

Daphne thinks that it will be over before very long,
and then she remembers other afternoons, his moving
shadow on her back as she unlocked the door, and she
has to steady the hand holding the keys.

The apartment is stifling and dark. After she draws
one of the blinds halfway up, Daphne sees the debris
she'd deliberately left before her trip, and decides to
ignore it. The hell with it, she tells herself as she sits in
the straight-backed chair, exhausted, and determined to
begin.

Kenny is disconcerted: there was no instant magic as

they crossed the threshold. Daphne's sitting there like a hanging judge. And, Jesus, what a mess.

She registers his survey of the sloppy room, that thoughtful frown. He looks around as if he's checking for evidence of intruders. A robber would have to be pretty hard up, or totally lost, to choose this place. She's aware that Kenny is reserving comment and that he's playing at being man of the house. He picks up the single slipper in the middle of the floor—a pitiful clue—and lets it drop back down. It sounds a muted thump. He turns on the air conditioner to its whirlwind maximum level, and pulls the other blind open with a clatter. Then he kneels at the fireplace to start the idiot fan rotating. In contrast to his noisy puttering, her own quietude gives her unexpected confidence. She folds her hands in her lap, completing the picture of serenity. But when he sits on the sofa, with the orange light flickering across his dear face, her confidence is threatened. What if he proclaims his love again?

"Now," Kenny says. "Tell me what's happened."

"Nothing. Nothing's happened." He's caught her off guard, and she can only come up with a defensive, sullen answer. Anyway, nothing really has happened, in the way he probably means. An old lover hasn't swept back into her life. And she hasn't had a reeling epiphany. Does anyone ever have one, except for heroes in books? And is heroism only a lie we read about? "*Nothing's* happened," she repeats, "and that's the whole point. I feel cheated, Kenny, really ripped off." He doesn't ambush her with arguments. He doesn't leap from his seat to take her into his arms, and she's relieved and disappointed at once. And because he hasn't interrupted her, she feels compelled to go on. "I keep thinking of you with your family, and that you won't ever leave them, no matter what you say."

His family! Kenny has a nightmare vision of having literally left them somewhere, intending to return in a few minutes and then forgetting his intention. By mentioning them in this room, Daphne has violated an unspoken pact. She's ruined the order of things, and he'd like to wring her neck. Instead, he's doggedly patient, as he was earlier in the parking lot, where he'd been the one to break faith by his errant thoughts. "But we had a schedule, Daph. We agreed on it, didn't we? You understand how complicated everything is."

He's being too reasonable, as if she's a child who needs the rules of a simple game explained once more, and he's the magnanimous uncle. Her anger is building, but she can handle it. It even gives her a bloodburst of energy, like a sugar high. And she won't justify his condescension by acting like a baby. She, too, is a reasonable adult, and can match his patient manner, word for careful word. "It makes me foolish, you know," she says. "The kind of woman who writes to Ann Landers for advice she doesn't really need. Vexed in Ventura. I hate being like that. I'm *not* like that." She hopes she sounds assured, that the quiver in her voice only attests to the power of her conviction. "When you're not here," Daphne continues, "sometimes I daydream about where you are and what you're doing."

"I do the same about you," he says.

"That's not what I mean. I imagine you talking about

dinner and wallpaper, and shutting off all the lights in your house, one after the other. I see you kissing your children good night, and then making love to your . . . to Joy." She waits for him to deny that last, but he only smiles sadly and leans forward a little, encouraging her to go on. "It makes me heartsick with envy," she says. "It makes me cruel in my thoughts."

What does she know about cruelty? His wife and children, abandoned in a cloud of highway fumes, dumped in an alley, or on the treacherous peak of a glass mountain.

"In my parents' house," Daphne says, "I looked at all the things they've accumulated over the years—pots, colanders, photographs, canceled checks, place mats, tax returns, plants, the things in the medicine chest and the kitchen cupboards, the marked boxes in the garage and the attic . . . clothing and tools and yearbooks and letters. I realized that you're bound to your family by things, by possessions and experience, even by the bad times. You and I were good together, Kenny, but we hardly have any history between us. And history always wins out in the end."

Place mats. Pots. His whole fucking life will be strewn with household objects. He'll be Atlas with a moving van on his shoulders. A domestic animal when he wants only to be animal. "I said it would take time," he says, trying to ease the clench of his jaw. "And you've been great so far. You know it isn't just a stall. You know that I love you very much."

"Sure. And you love your children. And you love family life."

"Some of it," he admits. "In a way. I'm *used* to it. But I'm not happy there. If you imagined me happy there, Daph, you've made a big mistake. I shut off all the lights in all the rooms, and I kiss my children in their sleep. But I don't make love to my wife anymore."

Daphne has strayed from the argument. She wonders why she recited that incredible inventory of her parents' belongings. Does she want the torpid peace of their life? The word "rooms" that Kenny spoke evoked an image of her childhood home, and then one of the Palomar Arms. She sees an empty stretch of corridor broken only by the bars of light falling from each separate room. "Do you think we deserve to be happy, Kenny?" she asks. "I don't mean just you and me. Do you remember in Philosophy when that guy with the shaved head said that it wasn't our purpose on earth, that we weren't put here to be happy?"

He nods, still wandering in the strange gloom of his house, where he's just shut off the lights, just kissed his children while they slept.

"Well, he was a liar, or a lunatic. When I go to work every day, I see that everything ends in despair. Even with happiness, life is tragic. But without it, it's . . . absurd! So I want to be happy now."

"I thought we were."

"In a way. For a while. But we have too many restrictions, too many limits. Oh, you know what I mean, Kenny."

He stands and goes to the fireplace, with his hands open in front of him. He could be warming them at the paper flames. It *is* chilly, Daphne realizes. The flesh on her arms has risen in visible bumps from the chill, and the fine hairs are up with emotion. She and Kenny are moving toward a separation, and yet there's a perverse delight in this encounter. We're merely talking, she marvels. Why is it thrilling?

It occurs to Kenny that they've never spent so much time here without physical contact; that's the trouble. He turns and walks to the side of Daphne's chair, where he lowers himself, cross-legged, to the floor. With one finger he traces the curve of her ankle. "This is time in which we could be loving one another," he says. "This is lost happiness." He slips off her shoe and holds her foot in his palm, the way he holds Molly's.

She pulls it away. "Don't," she says, and remembers saying, "Don't, don't," to Jesse Krantz, her hand guiding his with crazed indecision.

"I only want us to comfort one another, puss," Kenny tells her.

"That's not what you want, Kenny. You want to rip open the bed so we can fuck like rabbits, and then you can go back to L.A. and I can go to work."

"Okay!" he says. "Okay! I want that, too! Don't you?" He moves quickly to the arm of her chair, before she can stand, and kisses her fiercely.

She endures the kiss and then releases herself by shoving hard against his chest. She gets up as he sinks sideways into the chair. "Keep your tongue to yourself!" she shouts.

"Come on," he says, getting up, too, and holding out his arms.

"Keep back!" she warns him.

He wants to laugh, but doesn't. "Come on," he says again, softly now, taking a few steps toward her.

She reaches behind her for support and finds the neck of a table lamp. She yanks the lamp up and holds it over her head. She'll hit him with it if he comes any closer. A headline flashes by: MISTRESS SLAYS MARRIED LOVER IN TRYST.

Jesus! When she pulled the lamp up like that, the plug came out of the socket, trailing sparks. She looks insane. Yet how beautiful she is, how terrific! He loves her the way he loved statues of women in museums when he was a boy—ideally—and in the astounding way he's learned to love flesh-and-blood women. The lamp trembles in her fist, its shade rocking. She looks like the Statue of Liberty, raising her flaming torch. All at once he's the tired and the poor, and deeply yearning. "Oh, Daph," he says.

"I just can't live like this anymore," she explains, slowly lowering the lamp.

He takes it from her and sets it back on the table, its shade drunkenly askew. "I know that," he says. "It's only temporary." But she doesn't seem to have heard him. She's crying a little and has started to walk around the room. The fake firelight dances on her legs when she passes it. "It's not only things, either. I want mornings and the middle of the night," she says, marking her demands off on her fingers. "I want days when we're not in bed together, but can look forward to it. I want to make love like it's not an emergency—two firemen putting out a fire and then going their separate ways. Do you know what I mean?"

"Yes," he says. "I think I know what you mean."

"So it's no good pretending I have any of it if I don't, is it? It's not *lasting* comfort."

"No, no, it isn't."

Daphne puts her hands to her face and he thinks she's resumed crying, but she hasn't. "I don't want to smell like this anymore," she declares.

"You smell lovely," he says. "You smell lovely everywhere. I'd like to keep your smell on me all day."

"I don't!" she says. "And I can't really wash it off, I can't get rid of it. I think I'm starting to rot, like them. Only it's too soon!" She waves her hands at him, two panic-stricken birds.

"Shhh," he cautions. "Don't do that, puss." He catches her hands and holds them to his mouth. "Lovely," he says, kissing each folded finger.

"I deserve to be happy!" she cries, drawing her hands away to the solace of her own lips.

"You do," he agrees. "Listen to me, sweetheart. I'll do it. Oh, come here."

The room is too cold and too bright. Daphne wants to be wrapped in blankets, to burrow into their warmth. She also wants to keep talking, only partly for the lulling pleasure of voices. It's as if they're interested strangers again—just meeting—eager for the newness of unknown stories, and willing to keep lust waiting, breathing heavily in the wings. But Kenny is unbuttoning her shirt, slipping her jeans down, and her underpants. How quickly and deftly he does it. Her arms go around his neck of their own dumb accord. His shirt smells of laundry soap and sweat.

"*When?*" she insists, and he misses her meaning for only an instant.

"Right away," he says. "I promise you that. I solemnly promise you everything." God. He means it. After she helps him undress, hampering him, really, with fumbling bursts of passion, they move apart, each to a window to shut the blind.

Then they open the bed, but not in the old frenzied way, as if something living were trapped inside. Daphne recognizes a married languor in their gestures, and as she lies down, she thinks giddily that they're officially engaged now. Fiancé. Nuptials. Bonds of matrimony. The ceiling stars glitter like tinsel. "Kenny, the stars," she begins, and he says sternly, "Shhh! No more now," so she closes her eyes. It's all right; they'll talk for years and years.

For the first time, making love to Daphne seems to be a challenging, possibly dangerous assignment. Like a demolitions expert, he needs absolute silence, perfect concentration. With the bed open, the room is claustrophobically small. And crowded. He's been followed here by the living ghosts of his family, and they surround him, bumping against each other. Who said that when two people lie down together they're never alone? Here's Joy and the kids, her folks and his. They lounge across the pillows, test the thin mattress with their fingertips. "Go away," Kenny whispers roughly, tossing bedclothes into the shadows, flinging himself down.

"What?" Daphne whispers back. And then Kenny is over her, and soon he's inside her, nectar and cream. He has so many hands and mouths. She loses track of them, and of herself turning on the bed, the bed spinning in the room. Yet she can't come, although she labors forever at the edge of it. And he tries to wait for her, but is unable to. Well, it's been days.

They rest awhile and begin from the beginning, as if they already have all the time they need. And finally she cries out louder than she ever has, a shout of triumph, really, and of wonder.

They have to get up soon. She's due at the Palomar Arms, and Kenny has an appointment with a client. They can lie still only long enough for their galloping hearts to slow to a canter.

While they're getting dressed, he tells her that it will take a little while longer, just until his in-laws go home. Will she grant him that much?

"Yes," she says, with cold satisfaction and a terrible underlying excitement. When he buckles his belt, she has a fantasy that he's putting on a holster. It's as if she's arranged with a hit man to do a murderous job.

16

The lounge is crowded tonight, and filled with smoke and tension. When Daphne was living in Los Angeles, she worked in the campaign of a man running for the city council, and this room reminds her of headquarters on the eve of Election Day. The candidate was a born loser, yet there was a charged atmosphere created by the hard-core gambler's optimism and the sadist's excitement.

Jerry is smoking a big cigar. It looks like the kind that explodes. "If McBride croaks before the sixth," he says, "I'm out fifty bucks."

"You always going in over your head, man," one of the maintenance crew scolds.

"Ah, it's just a cold," Feliciana says. "Don't get so uptight."

"Just a cold, huh?" Jerry says. "Then how come they got her hooked up like a monkey in a lab?"

"Yeah, where they sending her, to Mars?"

A male aide says that they have to turn the old lady all day and night, like a goddamn hourglass.

"Just wait until you're old," Mkabi tells him.

"Yeah, I can hardly wait," he says. "It looks like a laugh a century."

Daphne sits next to Mkabi on the orange couch. She is possessed by her own news and wants to announce it.

But she sees that it might be difficult for the others to understand that a major change has taken place in her life. Mkabi would say that Kenny's promised Daphne the sun and the moon before, and she'll believe him when the divorce papers are filed, not a minute sooner. Monica wouldn't give Daphne's tidings more than a cursory smirk. Daphne longs to share everything now, while she's still stunned with success. She could also use some fresh assurance that she's not a bad person. She'll just have to wait until the evidence is entirely and clearly in. They're all so preoccupied, anyway.

"Your dance card filled for the big day, babe?" Jerry asks Daphne. "You'd better save me a waltz."

No one mentions her recent absence, or asks if she was ill or only playing truant.

"I saw Mrs. McBride," Daphne says to Mkabi. "She didn't get a tray tonight."

"Save her life, probably," Feliciana remarks.

"But she looked awful."

"I don't think it's quite as bad as it looks," Mkabi says. "It's a nasty cold and a fever, that's all. Of course she's so old, and Rauscher's covering himself, against bronchitis, pneumonia, uremia. He doesn't want to take any chances. Doctors get sued these days if they cut your toenails crooked."

Daphne remembers the poor man in *Madame Bovary* who loses his leg because of a bumbled operation on his foot.

"And there's the party," Mkabi continues. "He wants to make sure she keeps going until then."

"It will keep Rauscher cool with the authorities, help them overlook the violations."

"Yeah, inspectors don't notice mice and roaches wearing party hats."

"Listen, a reporter came yesterday. They may be doing a feature. We'll all be famous!"

"So why doesn't Rauscher send her to Community Memorial or Ventura General?" Daphne asks.

Monica squeezes between them on the couch. " 'Cause that's where they bump them off, Moss," she says. "How many do you think come back, once they leave?"

"And the families start worrying they'll lose the beds here, if they do pull through," Mkabi adds.

"Hey, maybe I ought to reserve one now," the youngest aide says, but nobody laughs. "Well, it's like low-cost housing, right? You've got to get on the waiting list."

"It's like buying a grave," Monica says. And there is a long, troubled, smoky silence.

Mr. Brady, who's watching *Hogan's Heroes,* salutes Daphne when she comes to collect the trays. He's cleaned his, but Mr. Axel still seems to eat barely enough for survival. Earlier, she'd offered to help him with his food, but he declined. Now he's the first one to remark on her absence. "Missed you," he says. "You all right?"

"Yes, I went home for a few days, to Seattle, to visit my family." How long ago that seems now. She might have imagined the whole trip.

"Done you . . . good," he says. "You seem happy."

His observation delights her. If visible changes are taking place, it must all be right somehow. Should she tell Mr. Axel, an impartial stranger, about herself and Kenny? It's not the most appropriate moment. The canned laughter from the television set is loud; Mr. Brady is joining in. And Daphne knows she is ready to reveal only the parts of her story that are guaranteed to win approval. Again, she decides to contain her news. Happiness is a much more general subject. "Mr. Axel," she says, "do you believe in happiness as a human right?" His tremors are rampantly active tonight, and she hopes he doesn't think it's a savage or stupid question. "I mean," she emends, "do you think that's why we were all put on earth, to experience pleasure?"

"Oh, no!" he answers, so quickly and fluently that she's surprised, and unaccountably let down.

"Then why *are* we here?" she demands.

He shrugs. "Same . . . reason . . . as cockroaches," he says, ". . . dinosaurs."

"Oh, but our *brains!*" she protests.

He makes a rattling sound that resembles laughter. "The . . . fancy brain . . . thumb . . . the noble . . . heart. Just dirty tricks."

He's drooling, and without self-consciousness Daphne takes a tissue from his bedside table and wipes his mouth, the way his daughter did that first day. He swallows convulsively a few times, and she's scared that she's stimulated him too much, that something bad is about to happen. But after a while she notices that the tremors have abated slightly, and that his eyes are glossy with animation.

"We eat . . . brains of other . . . animals," he says, "and . . . don't get . . . smarter."

"We eat their hearts, too," Daphne says, prompting him.

"And are we . . . more . . . loving?"

It is a comment, not a question, and one against which she feels hopelessly weak. She can't even make a subjective argument: you are loving, I am loving, Mr. Brady is loving, Mkabi is loving, my mother and father are loving. It's the world he's talking about, and how can she come to its defense in a nursing home, and in the aftermath of her own treacherous happiness?

17

"I won't!" Nora says, and opens her eyes. No one is there now, but a moment ago a group of small boys circled her bed and urged her to get up, to stop faking, or else. She's dreaming too much, that's the trouble. The medicine they're giving her for the cold brings dreams before she's fully asleep, and worse ones after.

"It's only a cold," she told the nurse that morning, or yesterday. "Just let me sleep."

But they didn't. They touched her forehead and her feet. They pulled the sheets and plucked her from sleep as if it were a Boston morning and she was late for school. "I'm finished with all that," she told them, and they pricked her fingers and wrists for spite, and blew chalk dust into her face until she had to shut her eyes.

The television set is playing, and she can't make the picture out clearly, but there's grand funereal music. Someone important must have died. Who is left?

Her roommate's daughter turns the sound up and waves at Nora. "Did you have a good nap?" she hollers. "This doesn't bother you, does it? Mother and I just want to get a look at the bride."

What is that girl blathering about now? Brides in funerals, and the mother propped in a chair with pillows and made to watch, even though she's crying, "Wah! Wah! Wah!"

Nora's nose hurts, and her hand. Things in them. Everyone's cheering. "Here they come!" her roommate's daughter cries. "Oh, she's beautiful, isn't she?"

A flock of aides and nurses rushes in. "Hurry up, it's the Princess," one of them says. "Lady Di!" another one squeals.

Did a princess die? Is that all the fuss? They even die on television now. There is no privacy left for anything.

"Do you know how much that gown cost?" somebody asks.

"Lower the volume a little, will you?"

"She's not sleeping. You sleeping, Mama? Man, look at all those crazy people."

"It's their custom. You know, it's their thing, like we have about our Presidents."

"Huh! We *shoot* 'em."

"Not enough, if you ask me."

"Shame on you, girl. Oooh, look at the Prince!"

"Wah, wah!"

"I heard he's a fairy. How old is he, he's just getting married?"

"I wish I had a chance at him. I never even had a single lousy chance."

"Is she contagious, do you think? Should I have my mother moved?"

"Princey don't play polo in Ventura."

"You want that mother-in-law wears a crown to bed?"

"Have to shoot foxes."

"Have to curtsy."

"But that girl's going to be *Queen!*"

"Me, I'd rather be Dolly Parton."

"Mother, can you see?"

Nora closes her eyes, and when she opens them again, everyone is gone, and Jack's funeral is on television, just like a ball game. Where is Father Michaels? He'd boot their fannies for this, and excommunicate the lot of them. It's a disgrace, but she's too weary to protest. There's the long, long center aisle of St. Athanasius, and she must walk the whole way. The coffin is like a small polished jewel box in the distance. Her brothers say she can look—all the damage is underneath, out of sight. Agnes's older boys lift Nora's elbows, hurrying her along, making her float a little. She doesn't want to be on television. She doesn't want to look at Jack in the blue suit she's chosen for him, and the starched white shirt and the crimson tie. They'll have rouged his cheeks because the ruddy blaze of blood is gone, and she doesn't want to see the clown's rouge or the tallowed flesh it covers or the quiet breast of snow with its crimson Christmas tie.

So she says, "I won't!" so loud she wakes herself up, and she's in bed with broth running up her nose, and a man she doesn't know at all leaning too close and peering at her. He smells like buttered bread. Under the dark circle of his hat, he has ringlets like an angel, and a deep beard of curls. Nora has an instant of absolute terror.

"Mrs. Mankowitz?" he asks. "From the Sisterhood?"

She is so drenched with relief by his human voice that she doesn't quite comprehend what he's said. "It's only a little cold," she tells him, and he says, "Ahhh," and sits on the chair next to her bed.

"My own mother, too," he begins, shaking his head,

and then he smiles so sweetly at Nora that she wishes she could remember who he is.

It doesn't matter, really. He takes her hand, and his is warm and leathery soft like the muff she carried on her wedding day. "Prayers are being said," he advises her. Special Mi Sheberachs sent up by her loved ones, for a Refuoh Shlemoh, and she is mentioned daily during regular services as well. "Your daughter makes sure of it. She's a wonderful, wonderful girl," he says, and Nora can't think how to deny that. If she had had a daughter, she *would* be a wonderful girl, so his confusion is innocent and inoffensive. "And she'll be blessed by your speedy recovery," he continues. "We know that the Almighty is merciful and does not wish us to suffer."

She can't argue with that, either. If there was a God, He probably would be merciful and not wish for anyone to suffer. Nora nods, attempts to smile.

"Everybody sends their regards. Do you know who asks for you?" he inquires, and before she can speak, he begins a mysterious and melodic litany: "Rabbi Singer, Cantor Zweig, Mrs. Rubin, Shmulke Rivkind, all the Goldens, Dr. Pinsky, Mr. Diamond . . ."

In addition to being human, his voice has a soothing lilt He sings the names of all these unsolicited benefactors like a lullaby, and Nora drifts safely and buoyantly away.

"So!" he says briskly, bringing her back. "Zei gesundt. Take care and be well." As he stands, he lays her hand down as if it were a fragile teacup, and like that ring of rowdy boys, he's gone.

18

It's Kenny's turn to leave town. For the last two days of his in-laws' visit, they're all going to San Francisco. It will be cooler there, and the coastal drive is very beautiful.

Before Gus went into the hospital to have his lung removed, he made a list of all the things he wanted to do, if there was time enough when he got out, if he survived. Sobbing, Frances had read the list to Kenny over the phone. Gus wanted to start a window herb garden in their New York City apartment. He wanted to get season tickets for the Met, extravagant seats in the grand tier, and wear formal clothes to all the performances. He wanted to go to Evanston, Illinois, and visit his parents' graves; he wanted to spend more time with his family, and drive the lovely distance from Los Angeles to San Francisco at least once again. This is his last unfulfilled desire, but he has already started a new, urgent list. "How many times does a man come back from the dead?" he asks.

They take Joy's roomier Oldsmobile, and she's decided to drive the first stretch, with Molly in the car seat between Kenny and herself. Kenny is grateful for the distraction this trip might provide. Since his last visit with Daphne, he has been unable to think of anything except what he is about to do. Even the faithful numbers fail to comfort him. At the office, he looks out the window most of the day, and sighs much too often. Yesterday, a petrified client interpreted Kenny's brooding as a prelude to disastrous news for himself. "It's really bad, isn't it?" he kept saying. "I can tell by your face, by your eyes."

Frances has packed a picnic lunch of cold chicken and deviled eggs, and brownies made that morning. They have a thermos of iced tea for the grownups, and apple juice for the children. The stereo speakers surround them with music. The car is equipped with every conceivable comfort, Kenny thinks, except a bathroom, and something to ease the heart.

Gus is indeed like a man newly restored to life. His wonder and appreciation are boundless. "Look at that!" he exclaims, over and over, at the rushing landscape.

Joy has always been a good, confident driver. On other, longer trips, Kenny has felt comfortable enough to sleep a little while she drove. But today her foot seems to move erratically from gas pedal to brake, and he finds himself stiffly braced and watchful. "You're not accelerating enough when you pass," he says.

"Relax," she answers. "Enjoy the scenery."

"Why? Won't I ever see it again?" As soon as he can do so casually, he'll offer to spell her.

Their first rest stop has a spectacular water view. Kenny had once been sophomoric enough, and enough in love, to compare Joy's eyes to the color of the ocean. Glancing covertly at her now, he sees that at least he was not inaccurate. Her eyes are still a vibrant Pacific blue.

She is as miserable as he is—he knows the signs: her

insomnia, the raw-bitten cuticles, a restored moratorium in their bedroom—and perhaps the outrage he expects will turn out to be mere relief. At last, one of them is going to make the required move. With uncanny luck, she might even beat him to it.

She performs a different role, as he does, for the benefit of her parents. When they're around, Joy talks to Kenny, mostly about domestic things, but her tone is chatty and convincing. They plan menus and outings, discuss the children and the laundry, as if their life together has and always will have this civilized tranquil dailiness. Their common deceit is unplanned and unspoken. Neither of them wants to cause Gus and Frances discomfort or sorrow during this vacation. Kenny thinks that his bomb will soon travel long-distance, and find them in what had seemed the safety of their own beds.

But now they're sitting on a redwood bench in dappled California sunlight, coaxing nourishment into their well-nourished grandchildren. Joy finds a chicken thigh, the part Kenny likes best, and hands it to him. "Tea?" she asks. "Lemon?"

Gus says, "Next time, I want to go to Hawaii, maybe even on to Japan." He pulls Molly onto his lap. "We'll get you a hula skirt, missy, a little grass skirt."

"Me!" Steven cries.

"We'll get you a nice Hawaiian shirt, Stevie, and a couple of hairy coconuts. We'll hit 'em with a hammer —bang!—and we'll drink the milk."

What about me, Kenny wants to say, and for the first time he envies his children, in a childish, heartbroken way, as he'd envied Robert long ago. They'll all go to

Hawaii without him—or perhaps, because of him, no-body will go at all.

Gus sings "I've Got a Lovely Bunch of Coconuts" in a zany accent, and soon Joy is laughing. "Oh, Daddy," she says, and leans across Kenny to hug her father. Tears fill Kenny's eyes and he must jump up and stand at the railing, pretending to stare at the view until he's more collected.

He takes the wheel when they leave the rest area, and drives more than a hundred miles without stopping. When he's beginning to feel cramped and cranky, the others, at Joy's instigation, start to sing rounds, something he hates in the best of times.

"Down by the old, not the new but the o-o-old mill stream!"

To avoid discussion and conflict, Kenny moves his lips once in a while and hums a little.

"That's where I first, not the second but the first, met youuu!"

Steven, who has changed places with his sister, catches Kenny out and reports him immediately. "Daddy's not singing."

"Sing, Daddy!" Molly commands, and when he doesn't comply, their chorus dies in a discordant whine, as if the needle has been rudely snatched from a phonograph record.

"Oh, be a sport, Kenny," Joy says.

A sport! He looks at her and she smiles, showing her dimples and all her teeth.

"I can't concentrate on that stuff while I'm driving. I can only do one thing at a time."

"Hmmm," she says, ostensibly to the children. "Maybe Daddy should run for President."

It's all good-natured, and everyone laughs, except for Kenny.

They start "Row, row, row your boat" without him, their voices stronger and more determined than before.

Kenny hunches over the wheel as if he's peering through a heavy fog. Why do people always feel compelled to sing in cars? It's nerve-racking and probably causes plenty of accidents. And then he remembers himself soaring from Ventura on the freeway one day, singing his fool head off along with the Supremes.

They stay at the Fairmont, because they did the last time and liked it. And as they did then, Frances and Gus order rollaway cots brought to their room for the children. Molly and Steven, who both napped in the car, are still slightly crazed from the long confinement of the ride. Kenny can hear the television playing in the next room—a noisy kiddie show—and occasional shrieks as his children chase one another and jump on and off the beds. Joy is using the bathroom, and Kenny slips out to knock on the door of his in-laws' room. "Hey, listen!" he says brightly when Frances lets him in. "I've decided you guys deserve a break. After all, it's *your* vacation. So why don't Joy and I keep the kids with us this time?"

Of course it's useless. Frances and Gus insist. It would be a deprivation, they say. How often do they get to do this? And Kenny and Joy are the ones who deserve the break. The traitorous, clamorous children back them up. They like Nana and Poppy's identical room much better.

Kenny has to trudge back next door and hope that no one mentions his offer later, because Joy will instantly know his true motive: he doesn't want to be alone with her.

They have dinner on the wharf, and then walk in the fine air of the evening on Ghirardelli Square, where Gus buys balloons for the children. They all look into shop windows, and once in a while Joy and Frances disappear into one of the shops and come out with packages. Gus and Frances stroll with their arms entwined, and Kenny is paired with Molly, who rides his shoulders like a queen on a howdah. She makes his separateness from Joy seem less noticeable.

Molly's heart-shaped helium balloon is pierced by a metal canopy they pass, and Steven's leaves his fist to soar up and away from all their reaching hands. They run a little, shouting at it, until it disappears into the darkening sky near the water. Its loss signals bedtime, their return to the hotel.

Kenny stays under the beating stream of the shower for a long time, adjusting the water every few minutes until it's as hot as he can bear it, and he feels pounded and steamed into sleepiness. He can't help thinking that he's like a cartoon bride who fearfully avoids the fatal encounter of her wedding night.

Joy is sitting up in her bed when he comes out, and there is a large flat box on the pillow of his. "What's this?" he asks, not touching it.

"A present," she says.

"What's the occasion?" He tries to keep his tone friendly and inquiring, but it comes out wrong. He sounds the way he feels, anxious and suspicious. The shower's anesthetic is quickly wearing off.

Joy's hair has been freshly and vigorously brushed, and is not yet fully settled against her scalp. He might have chosen to continue loving her.

"No occasion," she says. "I saw it. You've been very good with my mother and father."

"That doesn't require a reward," he says. "You know I love them."

"I know," Joy says. "It gives you great redemption. Oh, go ahead and open it, Kenny. It won't bite you."

He goes to the bed and sits down to open the box. Under many layers of tissue paper, there's a coppery-red cashmere sweater. At first he's relieved. It's obviously an expensive gift, but not a particularly inspired one. He doesn't care that much about clothes—certainly not the way she does. But then he sees that it's an out-of-season color, the color of the deciduous trees in their early autumn days together in New York, a fashionable color for the coming season here in California. The sweater stirs him with reminders of the past, and threatens him with intimations of the future. "It's beautiful," he says. "It's really great." He knows that he hasn't said anything she's waiting to hear. It is the most agonizing moment of their entire marriage, worse than all the quarrels, the spiteful silences. "Thank you," he adds helplessly, as if he's just remembered his manners.

She doesn't answer, and he won't look at her. He stares into the box on his lap and hears the familiar sounds of nightly ritual as Joy shakes a sleeping capsule from the vial on the nightstand, and then another. He hears the click of the light switch an instant before it's dark, and then the soft wheeze of the bed when she lies down. He could go the few steps to get in with her, and risk one last time of intimacy. He wouldn't consider it a serious breach of his promise to Daphne. She seems much further away now than the journey's distance between them. He has never been so married. And he even feels unafraid of sexual failure, for once. Other modern couples do it, he knows, in a conscious mutual gesture of farewell. More suitable, really, than the impersonal, less perilous handshake or kiss.

But Joy has offered him a truce, not a gift for leave-taking. And he chooses to stay on his side of the room. The tissue paper whispers noisily as he sets the box on the floor between the beds. "Good night," he says into the darkness.

At three or four o'clock, when he's still unable to sleep, Kenny, like Gus, decides to make a list to ensure his own continuation. He thinks about it for a very long time, but discovers that there is nothing reasonable he really wants.

19

Brady had lived and worked most of his life in the China Bay area of San Francisco. He'd been a dock-worker and still has the arms to show for it. Perhaps maneuvering the wheels of his chair helps to keep his muscles toned. His only, onetime visitor since Joe's arrival has been his ex-wife, an aluminum blonde with a painted death's-head and a youthful figure. She pulled the curtain around his bed that day, and Joe heard their low voices, her flinty laugh.

If both men are awake after Brady's evening television programs are over, he usually tells Joe about the days when ships were essential to the commercial life of the country. Some of the stories, about disturbed sailors and gang wars and smuggling rings and murders, sound apocryphal. They could have come straight from recent episodes of Brady's favorite shows. But Joe has lived long enough and has read enough history to know that these things might have happened. And Brady has such a lively, ironic, Runyonesque style that he keeps Joe from thinking too much about himself, his greatest preoccupation since he's come to the Palomar Arms.

Sandra and Bud are leaving for a trip to the Orient in a few days and, although he hates himself for it, Joe is beginning to feel like a deserted child. They need a vacation, he reasons; they're entitled to their own independent lives, but still he feels ill-treated and abandoned. Do the old always get like this?

His own father had been the same way toward the end. He'd become enraged if he visited, without invitation or warning, and didn't find them at home. And after he came to live with them, Adele said one night that she couldn't help it, but his shuffling footsteps behind her from the moment she walked in the door until she went to bed drove her crazy. She said that the old man was like a dog you'd forgotten to feed.

Brady is a fine raconteur, but Joe has good stories of his own. That fellow fifty years ago who staggered into the store like a drunk looking for a saloon, and who turned out to have a bullet in his gut he wanted Joe to remove, as if it were an eye cinder! The man's wife had shot him during a supper argument, and he didn't want to go to the hospital, for fear she would get into trouble. And the addicts. All these poor punctured kids today think they've invented drugs. Only some of the names are new, and sound glamorous: angel dust, crystal, snow. There were always doctors who wrote prescriptions, in a deteriorating hand, for fictitious patients, and then drove from pharmacy to pharmacy to get them filled. And the dead-eyed housewife who offered to kneel behind Joe's counter in exchange for a quarter grain of morphine. He could tell Brady tales that are far better, and far worse, than that junk he watches on television. Except he couldn't tell it in a straight compelling narrative, without slobbering and gulping and drowning half the words.

So far, Brady has not talked about his failed marriage

or the amputation of his legs. Maybe they won't live together long enough for such intimate revelation. One night after supper, though, he turned to Joe and said, "I'll bet you never dreamed you'd end up with somebody like me," as if one of them were a mail-order bride.

He's watching *The Incredible Hulk* tonight, an incredible choice for a grown man, Joe thinks. The fantasy isn't complicated enough, and the makeup is preposterous. With all his tough experience, how can Brady succumb to such nonsense, look so absorbed and entertained?

A different girl brought their supper in before, and then took the trays away. Daphne is off for the weekend. Joe regrets his unkindness to her a few days ago. In his astonishment at being old, he had forgotten how difficult it is to be young. He owes her something now, some comfort to dispel the discomfort his bitter honesty obviously caused her. When the opportunity arrives, he'll pay up.

Brady watches the commercials with the same rapt attention he gives to the shows. He actually seems to enjoy those mini-dramas of clogged drains and coffee nerves. He's been inside for so many years; there are things advertised that he probably has never seen off that small screen. Can he imagine how a Chicken McNugget tastes? And what does he make of all the new "feminine hygiene" products they allude to so seductively but never really identify? If they'd been developed when Joe still had the store, he'd have had to keep them behind the counter along with the old-fashioned syringes and the inadequate contraceptives. Recently, in a Hollywood drugstore, he saw a woman casually throw a package of condoms into her basket, along with the mouthwash and Band-Aids.

Sandra, who tried to dig her way to China when she was a child, will be walking in Peking soon.

Why don't they put old men like Brady on television and let them just relate what happened in their lives? What Studs Terkel puts in his books. The sponsors could sell aerosol cans of the *real* smell of women. Why not? Joe's heard they've already got some with the odor of new cars. But they can't can the thrill of first possession, of brand-new chrome and upholstery, the freedom of driving down a street toward some place you have not yet been. And even Donahue probably wouldn't want to hear Brady's stories, much less the rest of America.

Daphne offered to feed Joe the other day. It may come to that eventually, but not yet, although he likes to look at her, to hear her voice.

Today a troop of Girl Scouts came to distribute crafts they'd made to the patients. Their leader explained that the girls were earning proficiency badges this way. What useless, wonderful things they brought! Pen wipers, piggy banks, tea towels, key holders. The leader said that most of the materials they'd used were salvaged household goods: scraps of cloth and felt; wrinkled pieces of tinfoil; empty Clorox bottles. The girls said, "Hope you feel better soon!" and were gone in a green streak through the door.

Once Joe made love to Adele in the back of the store, half-lying against cartons he'd cushioned first with towels and clumps of excelsior. He put the BE BACK

SOON sign up, but someone hammered at the door anyway, and rattled the knob. Gasping, nearly strangling
him, Adele said, "Maybe we should go. Maybe it's an
emergency." But she only said it so it would be said.

Oh, to be in China!

There is a woman down the hall who is almost a
hundred years old. She has a cold or la grippe, and
everyone is talking about her as if the *Titanic* is going
down, and they keep rushing in and out of the room.
Why can't they just let her go?

Twice a week the physical therapist says, "Grip my
hand. Harder! Come on, *harder!*"

Brady shuts off the set and tells Joe about the enormous rats that used to come out of the holds of the ships.
"Cat chasers," he calls them. Rats with fists and fangs,
and eyes like loading bosses. Somehow, he and a couple
of other workers caught two of them and put them in a
cage. The men were careless and young and didn't think
about the plague or anything like that. At night they
brought their girlfriends down to the dock and made the
rats snarl by poking them with sticks through the bars.
The girls would scream and shut their eyes, but it always
put them in the mood, Brady says.

20

On Saturday morning, Daphne calls her friend Louise Weber in Los Angeles. Louise manages a bookstore in Beverly Hills where Daphne once had a part-time job, and they've hardly seen each other since her move to Ventura. They agree to meet at the Saks Fifth Avenue parking lot off Wilshire Boulevard at noon.

Their subcompact cars look conspicuous there among the sleek Mercedes and Rolls-Royces, like grubby children at an elegant grownup party.

"They might tow us away in a sudden antipoverty drive," Louise says. She has her small daughter with her, although her former husband had promised to baby-sit so the women could really talk. "What could I do?" Louise asks. "That shithead always leaves me hanging at the last minute." She glances down at Peyton, who is three. "But you're going to be a good little girl and let Mommy talk to Aunt Daphne, aren't you?"

Peyton is noncommittal, or perhaps nonverbal. She also appears to be antisocial, and refuses to acknowledge Daphne's presence as well as any supposed kinship between them. She lurks behind Louise's legs and looks as if she's trying to swallow her thumb.

They go to a restaurant where shrimp salad is served in giant Lucite shells. Peyton crawls under the table and won't be coaxed or ordered out. "It's okay," Louise says, dropping the tablecloth over her child. "She always freaks out a little when Don doesn't show. She'll get over it."

After the food arrives, Daphne tells Louise about the commitment Kenny has made to her, and that they plan to be married as soon as his divorce is final. It is such a relief to talk about it that she spills over with details.

Louise is an excellent listener. She manages to feed Peyton tidbits under the table without diverting her attention from Daphne.

"He's on an overnight trip with them now," Daphne explains. "And then her parents are going back to New York. As soon as they're gone, he's going to speak to his wife. They'll start proceedings."

"What if she fights him on it?"

"I don't think she will. They're both so miserable, and they've been that way for ages, before I even knew him. She probably wants to end it as much as he does. I guess it's very hard to make the first move."

"Oh, I don't know. Don left a note on the refrigerator with a fruit magnet."

"God."

"Does his wife have somebody, too?"

"No. He doesn't think so, anyway."

"Mmm, better if she did. They have children, don't they?"

"That may be the only major problem," Daphne says, poking at her salad. "Kenny's a marvelous father. He wants to keep things very amiable, so that he gets shared custody. The only thing that scares him is losing his kids."

"That woman doesn't know how lucky she is. You just have to pick the right wrong man, I guess." Louise pauses, and then she says, "You'll be sharing that custody, too, you know."

"I know," Daphne says. "Kenny says that they're great kids. They really *look* like great kids."

"Yeah, and Auschwitz looked like Disneyland."

"That's not very funny."

"No, it's not. I'm sorry, Daphy, I'll be good. Listen, hey, congratulations!" She leans across the table and kisses Daphne's forehead. "You're a bride-to-be, as my mother used to say."

"I haven't even told *my* mother yet. I haven't really told anyone until now."

"Smart move." And when Daphne flinches, Louise says, "Let's celebrate. We'll have some wine, on me."

Daphne glances around the restaurant, which is mostly filled with well-dressed, chatting women, shopping bags at their sides. She wonders if Joy ever has lunch here. Peyton moves restlessly against her legs. "Not today, thanks. We'll do it when it's official. It will be more of a celebration then."

"Do you want to go shopping or anything, while you're in town?"

"That's what she does."

"Who?"

"Joy. Kenny's wife. He says she spends half her life on Rodeo Drive."

"A compulsive shopper. I've never had the pleasure, or the money. The shops are a real kick, though."

"I've looked in windows, but I haven't ever been inside the fancy places."

"You haven't? My God, Daphne, we'll have to expand your experience. Come on, we'll start your trousseau."

"Forget it, Louise. I can't afford those shops, either. Kenny says it's like setting fire to money."

"So we won't buy anything. We'll just browse."

"Like this?" Daphne indicates their similar jeans and T-shirts, her own clogs that she now sees are badly scuffed.

"Oh, sure. They'll think we're millionaires. The real rich always wear disguises. Did you think they wear their old tiaras when they go shopping for new tiaras?" She leans under the table, lures Peyton out with a bread-stick.

As they enter the first boutique, so many of Daphne's senses are assaulted at once that it takes a few minutes before she can sort everything out.

It's cave-cool, of course, and darker than the sun-bleached street. Muted music, a punk-rock group singing the same undecipherable phrase over and over again, sounds as if it's coming from everywhere: ceiling, walls, floor. There's a wonderful scent that reminds Daphne of hotel soaps and greenhouses. She inhales it deeply, as if it might make her high. Her own perfume seems as blatant as an air-freshener. She takes another hit of the fragrant room and looks around. The clothing glimmers and winks, shivers and purrs. Pewter and bronze and silver predominate. There are sequins and jet beads; velvets, silks, and suedes; and brocaded fabrics that look like medieval museum hangings. There are vulgar belts —twisted satin ribbons snarled with seashells and rhinestones, and feathers that must have been plucked from living, screaming birds.

Everything demands to be touched, and yet is forbiddingly untouchable. When Daphne finally works up the nerve, and puts her fingertips to a smoke-colored leather pouch, its texture is shocking, like the powdery-soft skin of the old women at the Palomar Arms. "What if they wait on us?" she whispers to Louise, who shrugs and touches everything in sight.

But the shop is active and they don't draw attention. Rich women, not disguised at all, are being cared for by saleswomen who look rich themselves. Everyone seems vaguely familiar or famous to Daphne, as if each woman is a composite of Barbra Streisand, Barbara Walters, and Cher. When she realizes that she and Louise are being ignored, she relaxes a little. The music has a rocking, hypnotic beat. What are they singing? Gotcha baby on the ram run? Watcha gimme for my man, son? Whatever it is, Daphne finds herself humming and moving with it, gaining confidence. She gently handles the sleeve of a perishable pale shirt, looking for the price tag. She wants to read some prices; for some insane reason, the idea excites her. But she can't find the tag. It's not dangling from the other sleeve, either, and it's not inside the collar. Where do they hide them? Maybe you have to ask, so someone can say what what's-his-name—Vanderbilt? Morgan?—said about the cost of a yacht: "If you have to ask, you can't afford it."

Peyton starts to touch the clothing, too, without Daphne's reverent regard. She simply wallows and winds herself in a row of skirts, making a cloth mother-substitute while Louise is occupied. She gains them the attention they've been avoiding, and soon they're in another shop, with different music—the Waitresses, this time, singing "I Know What Boys Like"—and a different, but related, scent. This boutique serves chilled white wine to its customers. Louise takes the proffered glass, but Daphne is already drunk with sensation. She discovers the prices of things hidden deeply and discreetly *inside* sleeves, and under hems, and is pleased to see that they are as astronomical as she'd suspected. She spends such a long time looking at one delicately iridescent sweater that a saleswoman pulls it from the rack on its gilded hanger and leads Daphne to a dressing room before she can protest. "I'm Millicent. Call me when you're ready," the saleswoman says, a provocative command, and then she leaves, flinging the curtains shut. The three walls of the enclosure are mirrored, and the lighting is subtly different here. Daphne's skin looks peachier, the sweater the color of raw sugar. She is braless, and after she takes off her T-shirt, she looks at herself for a long time. She is not usually this vain. Now she can't get enough of her own reflection, reflections. She spreads and raises her arms so that her breasts are rounder and the nipples flattened. So this is what Joy does, Daphne thinks. She puts the sweater on then, because Millicent might come back and ask her what she's doing, and why she hasn't called yet. It is almost weightless against her skin, and is a flawless fit. She has never worn anything like it, has never been so conscious of a piece of clothing before. Does Joy feel this sensual in the dressing rooms of these shops? And does she become frigid only when she has to leave those multiple rhapsodic visions of herself? I'm losing my mind, Daphne decides. Something in the fragrance or in the air conditioning intoxicates and causes delusions. Using only minor contortions, she finds the price tag on the sweater. Three hundred and twenty dollars! It doesn't even have long sleeves. In ordinary light, it's probably an ordinary beige.

The curtains of the dressing room are pulled open, and Daphne begins preparing her defense against a sales pitch. The sweater is too tight, too loose, the wrong color, and it itches.

But Louise is standing there, with Peyton tucked under one arm, like a parcel. "Oh, wow," Louise exclaims.

"I was just going to take it off," Daphne says. She giggles. "Three hundred dollars," she whispers. "Three *twenty.*"

"Criminal," Louise says. "My mother could go to Yarn City and make it for ten bucks."

"They're crazy. That's more than a month's rent for my place in Ventura. Oh, Louise, I want it."

"Then take it."

"Are you kidding? I can't afford—"

"I didn't say *buy* it, dummy. I said *take* it."

Daphne pulls the sweater off quickly, and puts her own T-shirt on. She is so upset she stutters. "N-n-never! I c-couldn't." It's freezing in the dressing room and she starts to tremble.

Louise shifts Peyton a little and takes the sweater from the wall hook where Daphne has tossed it, inside out. Without ceremony, she shoves it into her shoulder purse and opens the dressing-room curtains.

Daphne dances after her, hissing, and poking at Louise's shoulders and back.

When they're in the center of the busy shop, Daphne, even in her distraction, notices that her saleswoman is turned away, waiting on someone else.

Louise hands her purse to Daphne, saying, "Hold this a minute." Then she sets Peyton down suddenly and pinches the little girl's arm, hard. "*Beat* it," Louise tells Daphne, who walks swiftly forward and out the door as Peyton starts to scream.

Daphne still feels faint as they stand together in the Saks parking lot. She wonders how she'll be able to drive back to Ventura. "We could have been arrested," she says. "We might still be." She looks all around her. "Poor Peyton." Poor Steven and Molly. She reaches her hand out to touch Peyton's damp cheek. The child has stopped sobbing. She just shudders occasionally and fingers the roll of Life Savers Louise has given her.

Louise opens her purse and hands the sweater to Daphne.

"I can't keep this, you know. I'll mail it back to them," Daphne says. "Tell them it was a mistake, a crazy impulse. What's the name of that place, anyway? I'll take the money out of the bank and pay for it. How much is it with the tax?"

Louise smiles. "Wear it in good health," she says. "Be happy."

21

He has never liked airports. There is so much re-
strained panic, so much denial. People who don't truly
believe that planes can go up in the air and stay there
ask eagerly about the in-flight movie in the nonsmoking
section, and if they can have window seats. When flights
are delayed, passengers wander into gift shops looking
for something they can convince themselves they want
or need. Some of that stuff could never be sold anywhere
else, except maybe in hospitals.

Today the place is especially difficult and chaotic.
That morning the air-traffic controllers agreed to go out
on strike. Many flights have been canceled, and all of
them are late. Gus and Frances are still scheduled to go,
but Kenny knows that anything can happen. If they
have to stay in L.A. longer, it would be a kind of re-
prieve. Would Daph hold him responsible in some way?

A crated dog yelps and yelps for freedom, and there
are too many people milling around, and too many excited children, including Kenny's own. Only foreign-
speaking adults seem to be having earnest and important
conversations. Because he can't understand them, Kenny
feels cheated of the diversion of eavesdropping. He
wants to hear the enlightening secrets of other, unknown
lives. Those who speak English reveal only their worry

about canceled planes, or say inane things like "Do you have your boarding passes?" and "Don't forget to call tonight." The travelers are overloaded with hand luggage, like refugees fleeing a besieged city. Those here to see them off are empty-handed, ready to wave goodbye.

Although a delay was guaranteed, Joy had insisted on being early—she always insists on being early—and that adds to the restless period of waiting. They all stare up at the Arrivals and Departures board, watching the deletion of other flights, listening to the groaning response of the crowd.

Kenny has bought Frances a mixed bouquet of long-stemmed flowers at an airport stand. They lie across her lap now, their heads drooping, their stems moistening her skirt through the soaked green paper. He sees how cumbersome they'll be during the five-hour flight, and imagines them wilting in the darkness of an overhead bin. What kind of amateurs will be trying to guide the planes safely out and in?

He has already taken Steven to the men's room twice, where the boy sat on the toilet asking shrill irrelevant questions and doing nothing else. On their third trip, Kenny is impatient and irritable. "Come on, Steven," he says. "If you're not doing anything, let's go!" As if they're late instead of early. As if he would rather be outside with the others, fostering his own anxiety. As always, Steven picks up on his father's mood. He complains of a stomachache. But he plays with the paper dispenser while he sits there swinging his legs, and then with the electric hand dryers after Kenny pulls him up and out of the stall. Another little boy, with his father, fools with the soap dispenser. The two men exchange rueful smiles, and Kenny has an intuition that the other man is divorced or separated. Back in the main waiting room, Steven wails loudly and piteously, "Daddy, you didn't let me finish! I have to move my *bowels!*" Fucking nursery school, Kenny thinks as an elderly woman glares at him.

He approaches his wife and her parents, and even his small daughter, as if they're strangers he might sit next to without attracting notice. Fat chance. Molly claims him the way he's seen people greet their luggage as it moves slowly toward them on a carousel—with the glee of recognition and possession. And Gus stands and puts one arm firmly around Kenny's shoulders. It's his usual wordless prelude to departure. At the boarding gate, he'll probably embrace them all and then tearfully advise them to lay off the sweets. He is such a demonstrative man. Joy has said that he never left the house without kissing her and her mother goodbye, even if he was only walking to the corner to buy a newspaper.

Frances asks Joy if she's thinking of going back to work soon, and Joy answers vaguely: "Maybe. I don't know. After Molly's in school." Then Frances asks when they're coming to New York again.

Kenny looks at her, alerted. Their fondness for one another has often allowed for a kind of shorthand communication. And her professional experience has surely developed her instinct for domestic trouble. Now he tries to assess what she might have perceived or guessed, in spite of his, and Joy's, little dance of deception. "Who knows?" he says with caution.

"Don't you want to see the trees in October, dear?" she asks, sweetly wheedling. Neither Kenny nor Joy answer, and they look away from one another.

Then Joy takes Molly to the women's room, and they're gone for what seems like ages. Kenny turns to Steven, hoping he'll use some of that nervous energy to occupy and entertain his grandparents. The boy is silent and clings to his father, as though he has some uncanny premonition of the future. "Come to Grandma," Frances says, holding her arms open, and as soon as Steven feels Kenny's slight push in her direction, he holds back.

"Fair-weather friend," Kenny tells Frances, and they smile. Gus pats Steven's head. Kenny has a sudden impulse to tell them everything while Joy isn't there, and is horrified. It's not like the idle notion he'd had at breakfast the other day, but more of a compulsion, something he might do against all reasonable judgment. His belly starts to cramp. "Be right back," he says, practically flinging Steven away from him. He sprints toward the men's room, rushing past Joy and Molly without speaking to them, although Molly calls angrily after him.

Sitting on the toilet where Steven had played, Kenny trembles and tries to release his clenched gut. "Shit," he mutters, "oh, shit," not without noting the irony, but he can't free himself from the spasm's grasp. Over the loudspeakers, messages for strangers invade his privacy. "Will Mr. Ralph Arnold please pick up a white service phone?" "Will Ms. Carolyn Green please meet her party at the insurance counter?" Why do they use the word "party"? Who the fuck still buys flight insurance?

He's sweating now and worries that he'll pass out,

trousers down, on an airport john. Fucking coward. Why am I so afraid, he wonders, and then admits that it isn't fear but loss that has gripped him. He is about to lose Frances and Gus as surely as if their plane is destined to crash on takeoff. Dearly departed. They'll never forgive him for the grief he's going to cause them.

As soon as this is all clear in Kenny's mind, his belly relaxes a little. He wipes his forehead and upper lip with toilet paper and starts to feel even better. He can't really understand this easing. Nothing has changed, except his acknowledgment of what must happen, his acceptance of responsibility. He wishes, as one wishes at a deathbed watch, that he had been better, more loving, although he knows he's been good. This wish doesn't come from a false hope of pardon and grace. There's no possible plea he can make for himself that will alter the outcome of things. Joy's parents will be as resolutely unforgiving as they have been passionately loyal. And he doesn't forgive himself either, not yet.

Finally he's able to rise, fairly steady on his feet. He washes his hands and goes back to his family.

22

They come in the middle of the night, as she's always known they would, with flashlights, like a search party. Nora lies as still as a bird dog in long grasses, waiting. Playing dead. No, that can't be right.

But they go right past her, their lights blinking, to the other side of the room. One of them says, "Put the sheet on her," and the other one says, "You got the feet? Okay, now *lift*!"

Has the poor wretched thing died at last? And now they're taking her away. They'll call the daughter and she'll shriek and carry on. She will have to look for something else to do with her days. At least Nora won't have to listen to that voice anymore, asking questions which will never get a satisfactory answer.

Nora's head hurts—the lights passing briefly over her were somehow painful—and she aches so deeply in her bones that she imagines something willful has entered and wormed its way to the very center of her, into the marrow. The new ghost?

She wants to be rude and tell them to be quiet and work fast and just let her sleep. But her voice won't come out of her throat. The words are all there, piled up in a clotted heap, along with a mad jumble of names: Jack, Mother, Catherine, Jesus, Reenie. The passage has become too narrow for them to escape. She's not frightened, though. It's not her they've come for.

Who will they bring in next, after this one's gone? Ah, she doesn't care, as long as they're quiet about it. And this time she won't look when they take the body by, covered from head to foot. They strap them down, too, heaven knows why. She doesn't need to see that. Bad luck. Bad dreams.

She does look, anyway, at the last moment. Why, they haven't even covered the face! And the daughter's right there, helping them push! "Mother, are you comfortable?" she asks. What's wrong with that girl? Will she be calling down into the grave, asking, "Mother, are you comfortable? Do you want the Jell-O tonight?" Now they've all gone mad, or Nora has.

But then the corpse struggles in the straps and says, "Wah!" So she isn't dead after all. Maybe it isn't the middle of the night, either. When the door opens, Nora can hear the meal carts rolling, and morning banter, before it shuts again. It's just those dark shades making an artificial night. Her father did that for the measles, hanging blankets at the windows to protect her eyes. She lost track, somehow, something she'd vowed never to do. But when has she last had a calendar, or a clock?

She wants water suddenly and says so. The word comes out, as if it's liquid itself, trickling through the narrow space. Someone brings it, and lifts her head so she can drink. "Easy, Mama, slow." When they try to take the cup away too soon, her hand comes up to grab it back.

23

Mrs. Shumway is at the cauldron, stirring something dense and forbidding, when Daphne comes to work on Monday. Bats' toes and gnats' ears. Yet it doesn't smell that bad. It hardly smells at all.

There's good news in the kitchen, and everywhere. Mrs. McBride has passed through the crisis. They were ready to give up and send her away, when she began to get better. Now she's starting to sit up a little, and take nourishment eagerly by mouth. She's very weak, of course, but that's certainly natural, considering her great age. Her survival is a miracle of sorts, one that makes the long-shot bettors feel religious and hopeful. They'll feed the old lady up, and move her around to get the blood swirling. They have five weeks until the party. She won't have to dance or anything, just sit there and reign. They'll dance for her, and around her. She'll be the Queen of the May in September.

Daphne smiles at all the easy celebration, but she can't concentrate on it for long. Kenny's in-laws flew back to New York today. At least she thinks they have. But Kenny would have let her know if the strike had detained them. And he promised to speak to Joy as soon as possible, as soon as they were alone. That could be tonight. This moment. All day, Daphne's been obsessed with her mental schedule of Kenny's hours: now they're driving away from the airport; now he's in his office, trying to work; now he's on the way home, opening the door, stepping inside . . .

She ladles food into the trays and wishes for him that it's over, that it has gone well. She's not sure what she means by that, except that the suffering will not be too enormous, or enduring. She wishes his marriage to have an easy death.

Will good news bring more good news? She hasn't been superstitious since childhood, when she turned playing cards up on the kitchen table—red for yes, black for no. Or pulled a thread from her skirt so she could drop it and watch it form the first letter of the name of the boy who would love her. She looks down at her uniform and there are no loose threads visible. But there is one on Feliciana's sleeve, and Daphne plucks it without attracting anyone's notice. Then she drops it casually to the floor, not following its descent. That's part of the magic. When she does glance down, she can't find it at first. Maybe it's fallen under the assembly table, out of sight. Then Feliciana moves her foot a little and there's the thread. Daphne sees that it's curled into a convoluted and mysterious shape, like no recognizable letter of the English alphabet. Certainly not a K. Or a B, for his last name. Not even with the license of imagination.

Of course, Feliciana has stepped on it, altering its destined form, invalidating its meaning, or lack of it. Oh, stupid adolescent game. As if you can control the world with cards or threads or wishes. Still, she bends quickly to retrieve the thread and put it in her pocket, feeling the heat darken her face as she rises.

Later, Daphne stands at the elevator bank with the

others. They've exhausted the subject of Mrs. McBride's recovery, and even their own capacity for jubilation, and still the elevators haven't come. Daphne scouts desperately for something neutral to talk about, so she won't start thinking about Kenny again.

It occurs to her to take her turn at telling a horror story, and because she can't invent one, she decides to borrow Faulkner's "A Rose for Emily." It was her first reading assignment for the World Literature class, and it has all the components needed to be successful here: love, suspense, and plenty of ghoulish details. Naturally, she can't remember it verbatim; this will have to be a loose interpretation, revised and condensed for the sake of liveliness. Updated, too. She's about to begin the way they used to begin oral book reports in high school, with the title and the author's name. Instead, she simply plunges in and says, "Something strange happened on our street in Seattle once." She's surprised by her own ingenuity and by the immediate attention she receives.

"There was an old woman named Emily Grierson who died." The silence is very gratifying; it's always good to begin with a death. "She'd lived with a devoted elderly servant." Daphne decides not to say the servant is black, as he is in Faulkner's story. Most of the women in her audience must be sick to death of devoted black servants, in fiction and in life.

"There was insanity in Emily's family," Daphne continues, "and her father drove away any young men who might have married her anyway." She remembers that in the original story Emily is still single and past thirty when her father dies. That doesn't seem so remarkable in the new Seattle version, so she says that Emily was over forty and had never gone out with anyone. There are exclamations of sympathy. When she describes Emily's refusal to acknowledge her father's death, Evita says, "Loco," and makes a spiraling motion near her ear. Daphne goes on, encouraged by audience response. She rechristens Homer, Emily's lover, Hank, and refers to him as a "hard hat." The word, like his nickname, sounds ruggedly modern and sexual. Then she tells about the arrival of Emily's busybody cousins, whose purpose is to derail romance. They're booed and derided for their villainy. Love is the proper hero.

"One day," Daphne says, "Emily went to the hardware store and bought some rat poison."

"Don't start with rats!" Ruthann cries.

"Here it comes," Feliciana warns.

"Get rid of those cousins."

It's the sort of tale that doesn't hurtle toward its climax, and yet everyone is still attentive. No one has even pushed the button for the elevators since Daphne's begun. She tells it all, with increasing confidence: Homer/Hank's disappearance; the peculiar odor from Emily's house; her thirty-year seclusion, during which she becomes fat and ugly, her hair turning iron-gray; the discovery, after her death, of the locked, dusty, rose-colored bridal chamber.

Then Daphne is close to the end. "The man himself lay in the bed," she says, and knows that sentence is exactly as it was written. It pleases her greatly to speak it. She remembers that in the book the single line had its own paragraph, giving it added impact. She wishes she could recall the rest of the story as it was written, too, or could read it aloud. It was the best part. There was something about the long sleep that outlasts love, and about being cuckolded. But the actual words elude her. And she's committed to finishing this irreverent revision.

"Everyone just stood and stared down at him," she says, "at his smiling skull. What was left of him looked as if it had been lying in an embrace. Then they noticed the pillow next to his, and the indentation of a head on it. One of them leaned forward and picked something up, trying hard not to breathe the stale air and dust. He held up what he'd found, so the others could see. It was a long strand of iron-gray hair."

There's a significant pause, and then Daphne is praised and congratulated. The story is a wonderful success. The ending, the whole thing, seemed so obvious in her slipshod retelling, but no one had objected. Her listeners had generously let her relate what they already knew or suspected.

The elevators come and Evita laughs, rolling the first cart in. "They're like to be starved to death up there," she says.

"Lots of gray hairs on those pillows."

Daphne is extremely uneasy. There's a weight of pressure near her heart, and her breath is shallow and quick. What a variety of stealing she's managed to do in such a short while. A husband, a sweater, a famous story.

"It's not really true, you know," she says as the elevator rises, with Lucille and Evita beside her.

"That's okay," Evita says.

"It's actually a work of fiction, a short story I read in

a book for school. It's called 'A Rose for Emily.' " The heaviness in her chest lifts only slightly.

"It doesn't matter," Lucille says. The elevator stops and the doors open.

"Of course it matters," Daphne answers. "Someone made it up and it wasn't me. I didn't even tell it right. The servant was black. Hank's name was Homer. And it isn't true. It didn't actually *happen.*"

"Who cares for that kind of true," Lucille says coldly, and glides away.

Daphne stands there, puzzled and hurt. Why is she being deprived of her right to confession? And why is Lucille so hostile?

"We get enough of what happens," Evita says.

The plane doesn't crash on takeoff. It soars beautifully upward, against all possible influence of disbelief and fear. Kenny and Joy and the children stand at a window to watch the ascent. They stay there until there is nothing to see but a fading jet stream against the hanging blue sky. "All gone!" Molly says.

The flight finally left at noon and now Kenny's family is hungry for lunch. At least, the children are, and they head for Steven's favorite fast-food place, a taco stand midway between the airport and Sherman Oaks. Kenny hates eating in the car, or at one of those sticky fly-bombed tables outside. And he doesn't trust the underage chefs or the cheap spicy ingredients they assemble. But he suggests going to Mister Taco's anyway, because he wants to please Steven, to make up for being so grouchy at the airport.

Once Joy said that women can always tell when their husbands are having affairs. This was long before Kenny's own fall from innocence, and the remark entertained him and made him curious. When he asked her how women knew, Joy said with authority that men give themselves away by erratic changes in their behavior. They're very mean at times, without provocation, and much too good at others. Guilt is what drives them, of course, she said, first to rage, then to repentance, and back to rage again, etc., etc. It was so transparent, and boring. "Where did you read *that*?" he'd asked. Joy was always reading in those days, with a rather catholic appetite. She zipped through every new novel, books by Theodor Reik and Wilhelm Reich, glossy fashion magazines with their articles heralded on the covers: "The You He Never Sees," "An Exotic Oriental Palette for Spring," "Why Men Fear Intimacy."

"I didn't read it anywhere," she said. "I just know."

"Oh, yeah? Not by observing me, kiddo," he'd answered.

"No," she admitted. "Not you."

By then his curiosity became less general and more stimulated. Which one of their friends was screwing around? "Nobody," she said. "Do you think I'm a fink?" He nagged at her, cajoling and threatening for a whole day before she would tell him, making him swear first not to tell anyone else. It was Gene Warner, a tax colleague and tennis buddy, with whom Kenny had thought he had a pretty close friendship. He was genuinely surprised, a little thrilled, and envious. The Warners were separated a few months later, and then divorced—the first in their social circle to fall, to fail.

Kenny looked at Joy, at all women, after that with new respect for their witch-like intuition. Sometimes he thought, why *do* men fear intimacy?

Now, watching bits of shredded lettuce escape from his taco and disappear into the car's upholstery, he wonders if he, too, has been giving himself away all along. He's hardly had any unprovoked flare-ups, just frequent irritable moments. Anyone could have those, for any number of reasons other than infidelity. The usual tension between Joy and himself was enough to make them both more radical in their ways, and a lot less civil when they were unobserved by others. One night, after a bitter bedtime quarrel, she cut all his ties in half with her cuticle scissors. The next day she went shopping and replaced them, but she never apologized.

He tries to sort things out in his head, to recall how he was before Daphne, how he's been ever since. A few weeks ago he and Joy had attended an open house at a new nursery school they were considering for Steven. Kenny perched on one of the tiny chairs, sipping the watered punch and eating cookies, while a teacher showed them the doll corner with its miniature facsimiles of domestic life, its jumbled box of grownup clothes. Kenny realized how far he'd come from this Lilliputian world of artless play. The sight of the tiny iron, cordless, resting on the toy ironing board, made him feel gravely aware of what he'd done with his life.

He wandered among the teachers and other parents later, talking too much and too fast, with the desperate patter of a salesman at a closing door.

Joy nudged him. "Hey, relax," she said. "This isn't Eton, you know. And *we're* looking *them* over."

He held up his paper cup of punch. "The Crayola juice," he said. "It's gone to my head."

He might be a little strung out at times, but he certainly hadn't been too *good,* at least not with Joy. And yet he did have an occasional urge to be more decent at home after a splendid afternoon with Daphne. Had he been, without knowing it? And was he ever conspicuously so?

Lately, when he kisses and hugs the children, he believes that some of his old spontaneity is lost, that he isn't simply demonstrating how much he loves them; he is also false and calculating. It's as if he's buying their favor, stockpiling affection against future bitterness. And Steven and Molly, who like most children know everything but cannot say so, sometimes squirm in his embrace.

Joy rattles the ice in her paper cup of Coke, crunches a chip of it noisily between her teeth. Long ago, in New York, they'd once passed an ice cube between their mouths, back and forth, until it melted.

He'd been so careful of his actions, working like the CIA to cover all his movements without leaving an incriminating mark. How clever he'd felt at times, how safe, stashing poor Daph in Ventura, straddling both lives like a cowboy on a fence.

He looks at Joy's familiar profile, once beloved, once despised, and wishes he had been less clever. If she already knew, he wouldn't have to tell her. He doesn't believe in her natural intuition now, any more than he believes that men fear intimacy. "Anybody want anything else?" he asks. No one does and he drives them home.

He parks Joy's car and takes his own Toyota to the office. He has only one appointment, and some paper work that occupies him for less than an hour. After that, he sits at his desk, leaning back with his hands locked behind his head. It's after three; Daphne will be leaving for work soon. He thinks of calling her and continues to sit there in the same position. Then, without really focusing his eyes or his thoughts, he folds a sheet of paper into an airplane and sends it sailing across the room. It swoops nicely before crashing into the far wall and dropping to the floor. He goes over to pick it up and notices that there's something typed on the tail. It seems he's made the plane out of a letter his secretary had left on the desk for his signature. Miss Oberon is a very stern and efficient young woman who would not be amused by his mistake, even if he said something playful about sending the letter airmail. Oh, well, he can always retype it himself later, at home. The thought of home staggers him. He doesn't want to go there at all, and certainly not before he has to. He shoves the plane into his pocket, looks at the clock on his desk and then at his watch for confirmation. There are a couple of hours left to kill, but he's incapable of killing them here in the cage his office has become.

Daphne has probably left for work by now. Kenny has never been to the Palomar Arms Senior Home. From what she's told him, he's sure it's depressing. It would be pointless for him to seek her out there, or anywhere, for that matter. That's why he didn't call her before, hasn't called her since his return from San Francisco. She's waiting to be given notice of a mission accomplished, not of his chickenhearted misery in carrying it out.

He hears Miss Oberon in the next room, typing like a woodpecker, and he senses her disapproval of his silent indolence in here. He pulls the door open and announces briskly that he's leaving for the day. She asks if he can be reached, and he says no and goes out.

There are any number of things he can do, he thinks, as he walks to his car, squeezing the keys in his fist until they leave their imprint on his palm. He can go to the beach, for instance, or to a movie. Neither idea has the least appeal; they were only ideas. He can just drive around for a while with no destination. From the look of the freeway, plenty of people do that. But he's too restless to sit still while the scenery speeds past him. He needs to *do* something, to *go* someplace. All of his friends are at work. His unexpected appearance at someone else's office at this time of day would be considered strange. He doesn't want to talk to anyone, anyway, except maybe Gene Warner, and Kenny hasn't seen him in four years.

He ends up at a bar in Hollywood, a place that's cooled to an extreme and is doing a lively business for this time of day. Men and women move with absolute purpose toward one another, and gently collide. There's lots of touching and almost-touching that looks casual, but will certainly lead to some shared beds before the afternoon's over. All around Kenny there's the reassuring rumble of easy, come-on conversation. Yet he feels peculiar here, in social limbo, not really married or single, not really up to the game or completely out of it. He pities the players for the loneliness that's drawing them together, and is jealous of their potential for adventure.

The bartender shows up and Kenny orders vodka on the rocks. At the end of the bar, the television set is on without the sound. Mary Tyler Moore is throwing her tam into the air, and for a few minutes he stares without concentration up at the screen. The jukebox provides an incongruous country-western number.

After Kenny's drink comes, a woman sits on the stool next to his and says, "Hello, there," with a slight, charming stammer. He swivels to face her, raising his glass in an automatic gesture of greeting. She's very beautiful in a glossy and obvious way. Compared to Daphne, or even to Joy, she seems to have spent too much time and too much controlled effort on her makeup and hair. Is she a prostitute? She'd certainly taken the initiative with him, although her manner was modest, almost shy. And her clothes, a green linen sundress and low-heeled sandals, are tasteful and simple. Of course, it's hard to tell from appearance alone what anybody does these days. A plumber Joy called recently arrived to replace a faucet wearing a dinner jacket. Joy thought he might have been doubling as a movie extra, or was on his way to a wedding. And last summer Kenny was introduced to a nun at a beach party who was wearing shorts, and a T-shirt that said *Here Come De Judge*.

Other people are laughing, and the woman is looking at Kenny in a pleasant, inquisitive way. Is she waiting for him to buy her a drink? He glances at her glass and it's full.

"I'm Mary," she says.

"Kenny," he offers, and that's that. If she *is* a prostitute, he supposes she'll let him know sooner or later. He doesn't have to think about that right now, or about anything else.

"Do you work around here?" she asks.

"Not exactly," he answers, wondering if he seems too cryptic or wary. He notices that she's hardly dimmed the considerable wattage of her smile.

"I do," she says. "Next door. I'm in the newsroom." *The* newsroom, not *a* newsroom. This place must be close to a television or radio studio. It's probably a regular hangout for the people who work there.

He smiles back, drinks, careful not to generate a further exchange of personal information. Some friendly anonymity is all he needs. He just wants to get a little buzz on and feel good. He swirls the remaining ice and vodka in his glass.

"I'm an associate producer," Mary says. "Lou Grant is my boss."

Kenny looks up, ready to go along with the gag, but she's quite earnest. Her face is bright with innocence and she has too many teeth. His eyes skim the television screen and go back to her. There's definitely a resemblance, he sees now, a clever mimicry of expression.

"He's a wonderful man," she says.

"You bet," Kenny agrees, and finishes his drink quickly, turning away. Jesus. He's shocked and shamed at mistaking a poor deluded woman for a working prostitute. "Well, Mary," he says, sliding from the stool. "It was very nice to meet you."

She clears her throat. "You're in a hurry. I didn't think you were. I thought you might want to, you know, spend some time."

In Minneapolis, did she mean? With Ted and Georgette and Rhoda?

"Fifty dollars," she says. "A hundred for the evening, and it's early."

Kenny is too stunned to answer.

"Do you prefer Cheryl Tiegs?" she asks softly. "Brooke Shields? Blondie? Nancy Reagan?" Her inquiring voice follows him out into the white and shimmering street.

Joe doesn't expect a visitor this evening and then at 7:30, when visiting hours are almost over, his grandson Kevin appears at the door. "Poppy?" he says, hesitating before entering, as if he doesn't recognize Joe, or as if Joe might not recognize him. The boy has surely grown since Joe last saw him, almost a year ago. Do boys still grow at that age? He is the youngest of Sandra and Bud's children, but is already an adult. Twenty? Twenty-one? The child Joe loved best because his parents loved him least. They would be indignant at his assessment. If anything, they'd say they loved Kevin more than the others, gave him more of their time and energy and money. He was the child that surprised them in their thirties, after their ideal family of one girl and one boy was already established. There was never any question of abortion, which Sandra claims is proof that Kevin was a wanted child.

No one can deny that he was a difficult one. Getting stuck midway in the birth canal (turning to look behind him, like Lot's wife), and requiring Sandra to undergo a Caesarian section after hours of labor. And then the months of colic and fretting. The other two thrived, while Kevin developed allergies to dust, grass, wheat, eggs, milk, and animals. He had frequent nightmares and wet his bed. His hair grew in willful spikes, and his teeth in a fearful overbite. In school he earned the nickname of Chink and then Metal Mouth, and suffered as well from dyslexia.

His sister and brother went to college and now they're married and have children of their own. A few months ago, after dropping out of a remote forestry school in Oregon, Kevin had joined the army. He's stationed at Fort Sill in Oklahoma, where he's studying heavy-armament repair.

He's wearing his uniform now, and appears to have outgrown it during his trip west. The untamable hair has been shaved, and his skull looks stretched, the way it did right after he was born.

Am I dying, Joe thinks. But no, the others, who are loving and conventional children, would also have come. They don't even live that far away. Kevin is simply here, and Joe will not question his own good fortune. "My grandson," he tells Brady, and feels the old riotous pride. He remembers the musky sweetness of Deborah's hands across his eyes; Daniel's serious and handsome face.

Brady has no children or grandchildren, and his interest in Kevin is friendly and peripheral. He lowers the volume on the television set out of courtesy to them, but Kevin wheels his grandfather to the lounge near the elevators, where a few other patients sit in a frieze of apathy.

The boy volunteers that his parents sent him money for this journey home. They wanted to see him before they leave on their long trip. He has just come from their house, and will be going back to the base tomorrow. "So, how are you doing?" he asks. He's lit a cigarette and inhales so deeply with each drag it's a wonder he doesn't hyperventilate.

"All right," Joe tells him. "You?"

Kevin laughs, chokes, and mashes the cigarette out, making the standing ashtray wobble and clatter.

"Friends?" Joe asks, wanting lies. Kevin has always been a loner, and what could a peacetime army be but mostly a collection of loners? Men who avoid civilian danger by waiting around for a real war. Joe has a vision of the barracks at Fort Sill, in which there is no camaraderie, no conversation. A radio plays some alien, whining music. Each man is on his bed cleaning a gun or a shoe.

"Oh, yeah, plenty of guys," Kevin says, after he's stopped coughing.

"Girl?" Joe persists.

"*Girls*, Poppy," Kevin boasts, downing Joe's last hope.

He knows that there are worse things than this boy's troubled life, but now he cannot call them to mind. Someone else's grandson who comes here in the toga and paint of a religious cult seems contented, at least, even serene. Any delusion would be better than none at all, wouldn't it?

Kevin does quick takes around the room, at the people sitting there, revealing with only a few flickers of his eyelids his fear of what he sees.

Joe's instinct, as always, is to be protective. At horror movies, when Kevin was a child, Joe would force the boy's head against his own chest during the scariest parts, warning him not to look. Now he watches those restless eyes and tries to trap them with his gaze. They are like small feral animals he cannot grasp or stay. He remembers how they'd once widened and focused at the stories of the drugstore holdups. But so did Daniel's, and even Deborah's. Joe refrains from saying many things. Don't look. Don't smoke. Be careful. Keep in touch. Don't shoot.

As if Kevin can discern these thoughts, he taps Joe lightly on the arm, and smiles. Those costly straightened teeth don't belong in his face.

"Want to hear a joke, Poppy?" Kevin asks.

"Sure," Joe says.

"Okay. How come there are no ice cubes in Poland?"

Ethnic jokes have always made Joe uncomfortable, but he says, "I'll bite."

"Because the lady with the recipe died!"

Joe suppresses a groan. Just as he'd suspected, the joke is childishly corny, yet mean at its core. What if the boy tells it some night at the wrong bar? I can't protect him forever, Joe decides, and manages to crank out his strange new whinny. Kevin looks at him doubtfully for a moment and then joins in. He whoops and cackles the way he did when he was little. What a pair they make with their barnyard noises! Everyone stares at them, and Joe feels embarrassed and quickly enervated. Still, their laughter provides a grace note for the visit. It extends the fantasy that everything's all right.

When they go back to the room, Joe makes Kevin wait while he struggles among the things in his nightstand drawer. The money is in the back, where it's least likely to be stolen. Sandra gives him an allowance, only what he might need for the week. The bills won't separate the way they should, the way they used to. When he made change at the store, he'd snap each one between two fingers, and then hold it up to the light to be sure. Old money is easier. These dollar bills are like leaves of crisp lettuce, the pages of a new book, like freshly minted counterfeit money. His hands fly and fishtail and he has to give Kevin all of it.

"No, no," the boy says.

"Yes!" Joe insists, and Brady shuts off the TV and says, "Hey, listen to your grandpa, sonny."

Kevin finally stuffs the money into his pocket. It is stupid to quarrel over what neither of them needs. Then he bends, blocking the light for an instant, and kisses Joe almost on the mouth.

26

Kenny is a little late. The children have been fed and bathed when he gets home, and are waiting for him to put them to bed. Joy doesn't ask where he's been, and Kenny doesn't tell her. It would be difficult to explain why he went to a bar, and then to a bowling alley, during a workday. He's not much of a drinker and he's never liked to bowl.

Molly and Steven go to bed with uncharacteristic surrender. First, Kenny takes the paper airplane from his pocket and lets them take turns launching it from the high perch of his shoulders. Molly murmurs sleepily about the big airplane in the sky as Kenny tucks her in, and he guesses that she will dream of flying.

The table is set for dinner, two places once more. He's hungry, in spite of everything, and has the idea that they should both be fortified with food before they talk. Now, putting out the platter of chicken, watching Joy toss the salad, he says nothing. They're back to their old silence, and he doesn't mind. It's much less tiring than keeping up that flow of jabber to fool and satisfy someone else. If he had not met Daphne, if neither he nor Joy had ever fallen in love again, would they have stayed like this? It's a sorry compromise that Kenny knows people make, out of habit and convention.

When they've finished eating, he helps with the dishes, as he's always done. As always, she rises from the table first, and carries the large empty platter to the kitchen. He follows, and waits only until she's set the platter on the counter. After all his procrastination, he wants to get it over with quickly. "Joy," he says.

She sits down immediately, and her attention is absolute. He's caught her with the sound of her own name. When did he use it last?

"Is it serious?" she asks. She might be consulting a doctor for a diagnosis, after a long secret illness.

"Yes, very," he says. "I've been seeing someone."

"Ah."

"I'm afraid that I love her."

She taps her fingers on the tabletop. "So."

"And we've been so terrible together, you and I." He says this pleadingly instead of as the fact it is.

Joy looks past him to the window, as if her thoughts are elsewhere, as if she can't concentrate. Will she demand another opinion?

"Didn't you guess?"

"I suppose." She doesn't sound sure of herself. He remembers again her bravado when discussing Gene and Marilyn Warner. *Transparent. Boring.* Because it wasn't happening to her then, to them.

He wishes she would speak again now, but she doesn't. So he continues. "I think I should leave. That I should move out." He wants to shake her, tell her to wake up. His news isn't having enough impact, and he wonders if she believes him. "Would you please say something?" he asks.

"Like what?"

Jesus. "Like what you're thinking, what you want to do." He's been careful not to mention the children yet, and hopes that she won't, either.

She looks directly into his eyes. "I hate you," she says. "Joy."

But she no longer acknowledges the name. She stands and rinses the platter under water that must be too hot for her fingers.

"I'm truly sorry. For everything," he whispers.

The steam rises from the sink, obscuring her face.

Kenny leaves the kitchen, goes into the dining room and then to the den, trying to decide what to do next. In all his imaginings of this scene, there was always the uproar of combat. He was prepared for that, if he was prepared for anything at all. She should be smashing dishes instead of rinsing them. He should be shouting instead of choking on all the unsaid words.

Maybe he ought to go upstairs now, take a few things, and go to a motel. Would it be a strategic mistake? A moral one? He could never sleep there anyway, never tolerate the confinement of a single strange room. And he can't go to Daphne's either. His mission is not accomplished. He and Joy are not done with it.

He wanders back into the kitchen, but she's no longer there. The faucet is dripping. Otherwise, the house has an ominous silence, different from the one they had silently agreed upon. Kenny feels unaccountably nervous. He goes from room to room, looking for her. He won't call her name, though, certain for some reason that she should not know his whereabouts before he knows hers.

Their bathroom door is closed and he stands before it, listening. Nothing. "Joy?" He knocks and slowly turns the handle. The door opens without resistance, but she isn't in there.

Then he hears footsteps, downstairs, and the drone of the garage door, lifting. He runs, taking a few steps at a time, but the car is pulling out of the garage when he gets there, the headlights dazzling before the electronic door lowers again.

She doesn't like to drive at night, claims that she suffers from night blindness and must follow the tail-lights of another car or she loses the road. She'll be back soon. She's only avoiding the confrontation, delaying it, the way he's been doing for days.

In the shadows of the garage, Kenny sees the outlines of beach chairs, rakes, bags of gravel and charcoal, and he recalls Daphne's litany of coveted things. He goes back into the house and upstairs, where he checks on the sleeping children.

Then he goes downstairs once more, to the kitchen, and loads the dishwasher. He scrubs the pots and wipes all the counters with the yellow sponge. Househusband.

Most of this day has been spent in the company and contemplation of women. In the bowling alley, there were only a few other men playing—teenagers, really. The other lanes were busy with women's leagues, competing. They wore uniforms, bright satin shirts with the team names bold on their backs, and their own names embroidered over the various curves of their left breasts. *Linda*, broken precisely at the *n* by a pointed peak; *Sandy*, gently rising and falling; *Paulette*, stretched across a broad, nearly flat plain.

Kenny bowled terribly; three gutter balls in the first five frames. He looked around him in an agony of self-consciousness. The teams of women on each side appeared to be too busy with their own games to have noticed his failure. They razzed and cheered one another, and were as raucously noisy as a flock of tropical birds. But when it was her turn, each player rose and went to the edge of the lane and paused there, purposeful and sober, before letting go. The pins exploded. Most of the women racked up scores he would have had tattooed on his chest.

He was reminded of Miss Oberon and her flawless typing; of Joy intent on the work of childbirth; and of Daphne in bed, sweetly yielding, yet authorizing their pleasure.

It was hard to bowl by himself. Aside from being solitary and tedious, it was also physically exhausting. When he stopped long enough to drink a beer, his shoulder muscles ached and his legs trembled. The thunder of the balls and the repeated crash of falling pins got on his nerves. Yet, once he started again, he kept at it. He played like a maniac: strikes, spares, splits, gutter balls. His chest pounded and his back hurt. I'll feel this later, he told himself, although he was already feeling it. He kept score as if he were playing against an opponent; they were both lousy. When one of the women on the team to his right strayed too close, he gathered up his score sheet and crumpled it before she could read it.

Kenny goes into the den and watches a British drama on Channel 28. He can hardly understand what anyone is saying. At ten o'clock he watches the news, most of which is bad. The air-traffic controllers continue their strike. In Warsaw, the Solidarity union threatens one. James Brady suffers a major seizure. There's a shooting on Wilshire Boulevard. The commentators, a man and a woman, shuffle their papers and make brave, ironic asides about all the bad news. They are like a married couple, muddling through.

At ten-thirty, the garage door whines open. Kenny jumps from the sofa to shut off the television set, as if he's been caught in a disgraceful act. He listens hard, and hears her come in and go upstairs. When her footsteps are overhead, soft in their carpeted bedroom, he climbs the steps, too. All of his muscles ache, from the bowling, he supposes, from the tension. He wants to finish. He wants to console her and receive consolation in return.

She is standing nude near her closet when he gets to the door of the bedroom. It is a shocking, spectacular sight. Her body is very lovely, girlishly slender, as he once preferred women's bodies to be. He is not aroused, except by sorrow and a loathsome pity.

She must have torn the clothing from her to have undressed this quickly. Now, with dreamlike slowness, she lowers the white veil of a nightgown until the light of her skin is doused. She gets into bed and takes a magazine from the table and opens it.

"Won't you talk?" he asks, and she shakes her head, looking down, turning the pages.

It is like visiting a sickroom to which he has come without medicine or gifts or the proper words of encouragement. "In the morning, then," he says. The pages turn.

Kenny lies down in the guest room just down the hall. He's afraid to shut off the light. The air conditioning is constant, maddening. He gets out of bed, adjusts the thermostat, and then opens a window. The air is heavy and natural, and summer insects are singing close by. When he's back in bed, counting, the burglar alarm begins its high-pitched scream.

27

Daphne is determined to be very good with Kenny's children, to dispel the wicked myths about stepmothers. As she goes in and out of the rooms collecting trays, she thinks seriously for the first time that she and Kenny must also have children together, a new family that won't depose the old one. The drowsing patients, returned to childhood by their captivity, the soft food, and early bedtime, awaken maternal feelings in her she didn't know she had. All of Kenny's children will eventually be friends. A picture of a large bountiful table, in some as yet unknown kitchen, comes to mind. There is sunlight, and the overlapping talk and laughter of an animated family. Daphne swears never to use plastic forks or spoons, paper cups, or anything made of Styrofoam. Their meals, even picnics, will ring and chime with the resonance of silver on china and glass.

"Everything is made of down," Miss Nettleson says. "You can't imagine how gentle—the walls, the chairs, my downy arms and legs. It's very pleasant. Nothing bumps or jars . . ."

Daphne helps her to lie down, pulling the covers up to make her comfortable. She disappears under them, becomes a flat, invisible terrain. Last week, Lucille said, "If I ever get like that, I hope they take me out back and shoot me. Like a horse." "Just think," Daphne tells Miss

Nettleson as she tucks her in, "the dream is the reality. *This* is only a dream."

As Kenny is a wonderful father, she can become a perfect mother. After practicing on these elderly children, how can she not be prepared for the real thing?

Once she'd had a dream herself, just after making love with Kenny, and before coming to work. She lost its content as soon as she woke, but some of its essence stayed with her. It had to do with mothering, and was sad. In her pragmatic way, Daphne concluded that Kenny, hungry at her breasts, and then the warm flood of semen inside her were the forces that had triggered an unconscious wish or fear. All day she kept thinking about the life process, its inexorable advance toward aging and death. By evening she'd worked something out, in a bemused fashion. When she saw Mkabi in the lounge, Daphne said, "I had the craziest dream today. Life was completely reversed—you know, people were born old and they died young. They moved *downward*, from being hopeless, to fulfillment, and then to innocence." She was a little ashamed of pretending this was the substance of a dream, but she would have been more ashamed to admit to it as a conscious thought. "Weird," she said, covering herself further.

"That's almost the way it is," Mkabi said.

"Well, sort of," Daphne allowed, smelling a wisp of her hair, then her hands. She took out the flask of perfume and moistened her pulsating wrists. "Refreshing," she said, offering the perfume to Mkabi, who shook her head. Daphne went on. "Except that infants are appealing in their helplessness. Their dirty diapers are okay, somehow. You don't mind the smell and you know they'll outgrow it, anyway. *You* become helpless in the way you feel about them. Otherwise, who would ever survive to grow up? It should be that way when you're dying. Someone should want to hold you in their arms, to nurse you out the way your mother nursed you in. And just like a baby, the one dying shouldn't have a drop of memory. I mean no longings, no regrets, not even language." She became very embarrassed then. Her recitation sounded too theoretical to be the stuff of dreams. "Stupid, right?" she asked, and Mkabi said, "Yeah," but not unkindly.

The sisters are sitting on the edge of one bed. Mrs. Feldman is combing Mrs. Bernstein's hair. Theirs is the recovered nursery, a grotesque realization of Daphne's dream/idea. She stays and talks with them a little longer tonight, and Mrs. Feldman says, "I detect something. I see stars in your eyes, honey. She's in love, Pearl!"

Mrs. Bernstein, limp and drifting under the strokes of the comb, smiles her half-smile. The notion of love still triggers her approval.

"Getting married?" Mrs. Feldman inquires cozily, and Daphne nods, smitten with pleasure. She can tell her news to everybody now, one by one.

"I'm glad and I'm sad," Mrs. Feldman admits. "I always wanted you to meet my nephew, Richard. He's some handsome fellow. He looks like what's-his-name, on the news." She snaps her fingers, soundlessly, and tries to remember.

"Dan Rather?" Daphne asks. "Tom Brokaw? Frank Reynolds?"

"It will come to me," Mrs. Feldman promises. "But what's the good? You're taken! Congratulations!"

"Thank you," Daphne says.

Taken. It's a lovely romantic and sexual word. She carries it like a gift along the hallway. It carries her from room to room as she collects the trays and says good night, rehearsing her new maternalism.

Only Mr. Axel resists.

She looks at his scarcely disturbed dinner and makes clucking noises. "But you have to eat," she says.

"Not hungry," he answers, ducking his head, something Kenny's daughter might do. When Daphne herself was a baby, she had to be coaxed with the promise of Buffalo Bob's likeness at the bottom of her cereal dish. She also thinks of Peyton Weber under the table in that restaurant, snatching bits of crust from her mother's hand, and she smiles.

The meat course and the vegetables are cold and congealed, but the tapioca pudding doesn't look much worse for the waiting. Its bumpy surface is still intact. She breaks it with the side of a spoon, scooping some up, and holds it to Mr. Axel's mouth. The mouth shuts in a hard steady line, while his hands quiver and jerk.

"Just a little," she urges in a motherly singsong. "Just a tiny taste."

"Don't want," he says, throwing his voice.

"Let's *go*," Daphne says, sounding like a drill sergeant to her own ears.

His mouth opens slightly, and he drools. Going in, the spoon catches the spittle and tries to return it. His teeth close in a sudden vicious chomp. They seize the spoon and it cracks in two with the decisive snap of a mousetrap. Daphne is so startled she lets both pieces drop into his lap, tapioca and all.

"I guess he don't want it," Mr. Brady says.

Mr. Axel's eyes are alight with victory. There is a man behind them. Daphne mops delicately at his soiled lap, aware of the man in there, too.

She is virtually childless by the time she gets to 227. Who can possibly love them the way she meant to?

Mrs. McBride's room is a private one now. Unlike Mr. Axel, she chooses to eat, to live. Another aide has assisted her, and she's been fed, sponged, and put to bed. She sleeps easily, and breathes like a dependable machine.

She'll outlast us all, Daphne thinks. She'll have her party. A reporter from the newspaper will come and ask her how she accounts for her longevity. Daphne has seen other interviews like that. A turkey farmer in Texas, claiming to be 116 years old, said that a diet of fried giblets and corn bread was solely responsible for his survival. The newspaper published one of his recipes. It sounded revolting, and his printed age looked more like a record temperature. Another man, in another paper, was photographed with his enormous family. He coyly alluded to an active sex life at 101. His unsmiling wife was in her eighties.

Some of the patients at the Palomar Arms make nocturnal visits to one another's beds, and not always in a state of confusion. Staff members are ordered to scold them severely and accompany them back to their own beds. In stubborn, recurrent cases, the use of bed straps is advised. Feliciana has asked what Rauscher's so worried about: pregnancy? VD? She draws curtains, closes doors, and turns her back.

Mrs. McBride sleeps untethered. Is the lusting consciousness gone before the body? Oh, let it.

Daphne reaches into her pocket and finds the thread from Feliciana's sleeve. She shuts her eyes and drops it to the floor at the foot of the bed. She drops it and picks it up at least twenty times, until she gets a satisfactory facsimile of the letter K. "Ahhh," she says, touching the footboard of the bed for balance.

Mrs. McBride opens her eyes. "Who is it?" she asks. "Is it for me?"

28

It's only one of the girls, a flitting white shadow, mumbling something, joggling the bed.

Nora calls, "Who is it?" and the girl is gone from the room. They're always going somewhere. Well, let them. She's wide awake now, and no mistake. There used to be days for waking and nights to sleep, a safe and orderly life. Now there's only bits of moon and sunlight as random as birds.

She tries her breath and it whistles clean. Her voice works again, too, but she's her own listener. It's not an old woman's crazy habit. She talked to herself as a child, too, in those rare sweet moments of solitude. And later, after Jack was gone. Hello? Hello?

That one's daughter was forever answering. "Were you calling? Do you want the bedpan?" Who ever wanted a bedpan?

There's no one in the other bed. It's bent in half and stripped naked. Today, or yesterday, Nora asked the girl with the spoon like a steam shovel, "Is she dead, then?" And the girl laughed and said, "How can you be eating pudding, dead?" If they won't pay attention, there's no use talking to them.

Anyway, Jack is dead, as dead as cats and kings. She doesn't think of him enough, that's the trouble, or she thinks of him falling.

Once, a boy and girl came from a school to put her voice in a machine. They said, "Please talk into this. Tell us everything you can remember." The machine hummed at first and the boy said, "Shit," and hit it with his fist until it was right. Then Nora spoke of the gas lamps in the Boston house, and the church school near the stables, and beer carried home in sloshing wooden pails. They asked, and she told them, about her slow, zigzagging journey west, about all the houses where she was needed and went, where the cries of nieces' children dragged her upright from sleep into unknown rooms. She once thought of all those moves as her own Stations of the Cross. "Oh, wow, great," the boy said, and "Wait, wait!" as he opened and shut the machine a few times. The years slipped and shifted while Nora waited. When she began again, with Jack making a pine table, with the saw's harsh steady whisper and golden sawdust snowing, the girl stopped the machine and said, "No. Please. *Women's* history."

They played it back for her later, but that wasn't her voice in there; it was someone else, in a deep tunnel, or inside a cupboard, talking about Nora's life. And she never said about Jack.

If Nora forgets him, who will remember? When people used to say "A fate worse than death," maybe that's what they meant. But there isn't any worse.

He fell from a building under construction, from the glassless open frame that would be a window. It was that easy. He must have become dizzy, they said, or careless. He was sitting on the ledge, one leg in and one out. It was a brilliant March day. Spring was promised and the sky passed right through the open rooms. Perhaps the sun glinted too much off the head of his hammer and dazed him. His hand still held the hammer as he fell; the tenpenny nail was still poised, slanted on its point, to be hammered in place.

Someone hammered it. The window glass was put in, and walls made bedrooms and kitchens. People moved into the building with pianos and children and chairs. For months, Nora could not look into any large distant space without a falling body appearing on the threshold of her vision. In summer, she would not pass the building with its open windows, and piano music flying out.

The terrified men came to tell her, to catch her when she fell, their arms weaving a net under her fainting falling self.

Her brothers were summoned and went in their work clothes. Henry said, "All the damage is in the back, underneath." He meant Jack's soft perished head, like the fruit of the crooked peddler.

William fingered her brown lace cuff, pleating and releasing it. "He's the same, Norry," William said. "You can look at him if you want to."

So she did. The hands were turned in at his sides, and someone had closed his eyes. His hair was rumpled and dusty. Tiny crumbs of plaster in his lashes and in the curl of his ear. If his eyes had been left open, would she see the blurred scene of his falling, everything upside down and rushing past? Would she see the shock of joy that was in them that other morning, when her knees gave way like the edge of the world?

29

Stewart Bench is, thank God, as unlike that prick Larkin as possible. Kenny has been referred to Bench by a corporate lawyer he knows, to whom he briefly mentioned his marital problems. Bench has important political connections, and serious aspirations of his own. Everything about him—his dark paneled office, his grim expression, his impeccably tailored clothing—seems serious.

When Kenny mentions that Joy knows about his love affair with Daphne, Bench becomes very upset. "Never, *never* admit to adultery at this stage of the proceedings," he says, as if this is only the first in a series of divorces Kenny intends to initiate.

"The courts are growing more lenient toward men in terms of custody," Bench advises. "But there are still some mother-loving judges who'll give children to hookers with child-abuse records. They're hung up on some cockeyed vision of their own American Moms."

"Well, Joy's not unfit, you know," Kenny says. "In fact, she's a pretty good—"

Bench holds up one hand. "Please. Don't be too civilized, Mr. Bannister, all right? Dustin Hoffman's not going to play you in the movie. And we won't need your testimony to your wife's virtue and beauty. Her attorney will take care of that. It's your own credentials we're concerned with here."

The man is obsessively cautious; he must have been toilet-trained with a gun. He's sharp, single-minded, and possibly unfeeling. Kenny had hoped for his formidable professional reputation in someone softer, a lawyer with whom he might have discussed the nuances, whose sharpness would be leavened by humor and a spirit of conciliation. Yet, if Kenny were choosing up sides in a stickball game, he knows he would even pick an arch-enemy who could hit.

Bench suggests that he continue to live at home. Moving out at this point would be as legally dangerous as his confession to Joy. And he should not be in contact with the woman in question.

"Daphne Moss," Kenny says, and Bench waves his hand as if to strike her name from the record.

"If you leave now," he says, "you can be accused of abandonment, an added complication to your confessed infidelity. I assume you can remain in residence with your family?"

"I guess so," Kenny says.

When he's back in his own office, looking through the ledgers of a notorious tax evader, it occurs to Kenny that he didn't ask Bench how long he has to stay at home, how long before he can resume contact with Daphne. He'll have to call him and find out.

That morning, Kenny had awakened very early in the guest room, without the usual assistance of his alarm clock, or the first stirrings of Joy's body in the same bed. He was able to make his bed and be downstairs in the kitchen, dressed, before the children were up and could question the new sleeping arrangements. Eventually, he would have to explain things to them, but they didn't have to witness every aspect of the estrangement. He wanted to spare them what he and Robert had not been spared. It seemed, at breakfast, that Joy would cooperate. She was passive, almost a sleepwalker who went from refrigerator to stove to table without unnecessary comment to anyone. Molly's foot in Kenny's lap, under the table, was like a secret handclasp of encouragement. He remembered how happy he'd been the day she was born, thinking that he would have a woman's ideal love from the beginning of her life until the end of his own. This morning, he wasn't feeling so secure. He'd braced himself for battle, and when it didn't come he couldn't relax.

When he was a boy, his mother would grow inexplicably quiet and calm in the middle of a raging quarrel with his father. And his father couldn't rouse an appropriate response no matter what he said or did. Finally, he would give up, dropping his guard and wandering away. Then she would attack him without warning and with such ferocity that Kenny felt his father's bewildered alarm enter his own body.

Kenny closes the ledger and reaches for the telephone. He discovers that Bench is gone for the day. Well, he'll make one phone call to Daphne, just to explain what has happened and why they must temporarily keep their distance. He becomes aware of the mechanics of the instrument as he holds it. The dial tone is like a warning hum. He thinks of phone taps, and hidden tape recorders. His secretary is not making a sound on her side of the partition. Kenny has unbidden images of Nixon and J. Edgar Hoover, and an absurd one of Miss Oberon, her ear pressed to a drinking glass that's held against the wall.

He waits until noon, and then excuses himself from the client he's taken to lunch, and goes to the pay phone on the wall between the rest rooms. Here, too, the Muzak continues its relentless melody.

"Hello, puss," he says when he hears Daphne's groggy greeting. "Did I wake you?" He feels better just picturing her, wound naked in bedclothes, heavy-lidded and slow with sleep.

She comes awake quickly to his news, though, and makes welcome offerings of sympathy. "My poor sweetheart," she says. And, "Oh, oh."

A toilet flushes and the door to the women's room opens. A large woman squeezes past Kenny, holding his elbows as she goes by. "Excuse me," she says.

"Who's that?" Daphne asks.

He tells her that he's using a pay phone in a restaurant, and she says she was wondering about the music.

"This is actually an undercover phone call," Kenny says with forced levity. "In fact, my lawyer warned me not to contact you at all."

"Are you serious?" Daphne says.

He explains that it's all stupid, but necessary. The whole business of custody will depend on a particular code of behavior for a while. He has to live at home. They can't see one another. "Like Romeo and Juliet," he adds, before remembering their tragic fate.

"For how long?"

He has to acknowledge that he's not sure, that he didn't have a chance to ask. When she doesn't say anything, he covers the silence by telling her that even if they can't see one another, he'll continue to call her like this, against his lawyer's orders. "That's the best I can do right now, puss," he says. "It's very hard."

Now she withholds her sympathy. He hopes she's reserving judgment as well. He is acting for both of them —she must surely recognize the minor heroism of that.

Someone comes out of the men's room and then stands there, jiggling coins in his hand, looking elsewhere, but listening.

"I have to go now," Kenny says. "I love you. Everything will work out." Why does that sound like a recorded message?

"Yes," Daphne says. He wants more, but the eavesdropper's eyes are on his back. Kenny would like to turn and confront the man with a hostile look. Instead, he whispers a hurried goodbye and slinks back to his table.

That night, Joy doesn't seem surprised by his punctual appearance.

Molly and Steven cheer his homecoming with their usual excess. I can live through this, he thinks. The house is fragrant with dinner cooking. The furniture is standing in familiar places.

There are dishes to do, the children's baths, and then their bedtime. The racket they make in protest to the day's end eases the awkward reticence between Kenny and Joy.

He lies down on the children's beds in turn, helping them to stave off the night with stories and songs and snuggling maneuvers. Their earnest nonsense soothes and reassures him. Steven says, "My Tonka truck can kill people's heads, right, Daddy?" Molly holds Kenny's hair in a lover's clutch while he sings "Good Night, Ladies." As her grasp loosens, the song grows fainter and fainter, until he's only mouthing the words and is almost asleep himself.

Joy is in the living room, smoking a cigarette. She hasn't smoked at all, until now, since her first pregnancy. They quit together then, and considered it their first gift to their unborn child. Kenny notices that she's using her old king-sized, cork-tipped brand. He likes the gestures she makes, and realizes he'd forgotten them: her precarious grip on the cigarette as she brings it to her mouth, its burning end too close to her fingertips; the way she sighs audibly when she inhales, and how the smoke comes out through her nostrils in two narrow, haughty columns.

"How long have you been fucking around?" she asks.

His heart slams. He hadn't expected her to speak, and she has never used that language outside of bed. It's almost as if he's hallucinated her voice.

"That's not exactly—" he begins.

She doesn't let him finish the sentence. "Is the fucking wonderful?" she asks.

He knows better than to answer this time.

"I see," Joy says. "One doesn't talk about it, does one? One just fucks."

Without thinking, he reaches for the pack of cigarettes and shakes one into his hand. He trembles, lighting it.

"I wouldn't really know," Joy says. "I never went that far myself."

What is she talking about?

"Feeling up near the coats doesn't count, does it? Or a little tongue-kissing?"

The smoke makes him light-headed. It's not dissimilar to the first sensation he gets from grass.

"A little cocksucking?"

Jesus.

"Gene practiced a lot at parties, you know, before he went pro."

It's a sad, vicious, childish lie. He finds it difficult to look at her face.

Joy stands and lays her cigarette, still burning, in an empty candy dish. "The children are the real business between us," she says. And then leaves the room.

Immediately, Kenny goes to the candy dish and extinguishes her cigarette, and his.

30

There is almost nothing besides work and school during these new days and nights. Neither totally engages Daphne, and she looks around for other ways to occupy herself. Anything not to simply wait in her room for Kenny's occasional, hasty, and surreptitious phone calls. She knows that he's suffering; he tells her so each time they speak. She knows that his absence now is necessary, and will finally lead to his constant presence. But in some hard internal place she's resentful and unreasonably impatient. In the past week, she's gone to the movies with Feliciana, and to a bridal shower for one of the nurses. The movie theater was crowded and they had to sit too close to the screen. At the shower, the bride received eight cheese boards, including the one Daphne had brought. She has turned down offers to go out with Marshall Haber, and with the instructor of her World Lit class. When Kenny calls from a gas station, with the highway roaring like the ocean behind him, she resists a strong urge to inform him of these spurned invitations. She does so by summoning up her better, bighearted self. He has enough troubles.

One evening, Mkabi tells Daphne that she's graduated from the bartending school and has her first job. It's at a private catered party in Santa Barbara the following night, a Saturday, when both women are off-duty. Mkabi says that the caterer mentioned needing another person for serving and cleaning up, and she wonders if Daphne might be interested. She says yes immediately.

They drive there together in Daphne's car. Later, after Darryl finishes work, too, he'll pick Mkabi up and take her home. The party is in a beautiful old mission-style house owned by a couple who run an art gallery. Almost a hundred guests are expected. The caterer's refrigerated panel truck arrives soon after Daphne and Mkabi. The two women are wearing their regular uniforms, without name tags, naturally, or cap or hairnet. Daphne has tamed and pinned her hair into a braided bun.

Everything in the house looks radically expensive and hardly used. In the kitchen, counters and appliances gleam like floor samples, and when Daphne peeks into the darker area of the living room and den, she can see the plush white of pillowed couches, and bold modern paintings hovering on the walls above them. An hysterical soprano dog is whining and yipping somewhere.

The hostess comes in with her husband right behind her, still buttoning the back of her long red dress. She looks at Daphne and Mkabi. "Are you serving?" she asks. "God, they look like nurses." She supplies them with tiny black organdy aprons to wear over their uniforms. They smile at each other after tying them on. Mkabi whispers, "Ooh, la la! Now we look like the maids in a dirty movie."

The caterer, an Italian woman, specializes in Greek delicacies. Trays and trays of phyllo-wrapped hors d'oeuvres are brought in from the truck. Portable ovens are carried in, too. No wonder the kitchen looks so pristine; it's just a backdrop for the action. The bar is set up in a far corner of the den, and Mkabi is banished to it. "Well, break a leg," Daphne says before they separate. Soon, she's toting a tray of miniature spanakopites, wedging it between groups of men and women who all seem to have arrived at once, as if they've been brought in a chartered bus to populate the house, to form a small privileged nation. Of course, they haven't come in a bus. The driveway and the street beyond it are lined with sleek shiny cars, like the ones in the Saks parking lot the day Daphne took the sweater.

She passes the hors d'oeuvres among the guests. "Hot," she finds herself warning an instant too late, and "Napkin?" as spinach filling oozes onto a shirtfront. She should have returned that sweater by now. It's just been lying at the bottom of the bottom drawer of her dresser. She's been too preoccupied, has not really thought about it until she entered this room filled with handsome, well-dressed people. Well, the money she earns tonight can be her first payment on the sweater, in case she decides not to send it back.

As she works her way through the crowd, Daphne tries to listen to some of the conversation. She can only manage to hear disjointed words and phrases.

". . . purple and the palest mauve."

". . . word processor . . ."

". . . riddled, *riddled* with cancer."

". . . like a couple of bitches in heat."

". . . moral imperative . . ."

". . . about sixty, seventy thousand . . ."

"Phoenix? Oh, God, don't go to Phoenix."

". . . signed, limited . . ."

". . . orgasms?"

On her fifth or sixth trip from the kitchen, a man grips her arm, so that the tray almost tips over. "Sweetheart," he says, "can you get me a refill?" He puts his empty glass on her tray, in the center of the dolmades she is about to serve. "Martini, dry, on the rocks," he adds, and winks, as if they've just shared a private joke.

At least this errand brings her to Mkabi, who had vanished from sight as the party escalated. They quickly exchange complaints as Mkabi mixes the martini. "My feet are killing me," Daphne says. "I should have worn my Palomar shoes." She looks down at her high-heeled white sandals with regret.

"All those drinks I learned," Mkabi says. "I'm thrilled to make this martini. Everybody's drinking white wine, or *Perrier* with a *twist*. Not one Rob Roy or White Russian; not even a Manhattan. Bobby could've worked this job. Okay, here you go." She puts the glass on Daphne's tray.

When she turns back into the crowd, Daphne realizes she can't remember which of the men asked for the martini. She wanders around, holding the tray aloft, hoping he'll notice her first and make some signal. It's so noisy and smoky. Everyone looks alike. There is too much laughter, in bursts like gunfire. Nobody is paying attention to a man in a tuxedo playing rippling cocktail music on a grand piano. Daphne feels odd, as if her metabolism has suddenly altered.

People put empty glasses on her lifted tray, and then

toothpicks, and then half-eaten hors d'oeuvres. Someone dumps an ashtray. The fresh dolmades she has not had a chance to serve are buried under the debris. If the caterer sees this, she'll be murdered. The hostess wings by in her red dress, and Daphne holds the tray even higher, her arms aching. She goes back to the kitchen and empties the mess while the other workers are busy. Looking into the depths of the black plastic garbage bag gives her vertigo. It is like peering into a lake at night. She takes the untouched martini and slips into a small bathroom near the pantry. A little white poodle, wearing a jeweled collar, escapes between her feet and joins the party. Leaning against the locked door, Daphne downs the drink. She chews the olive and drops the ice cubes into the toilet. With one hand to her breast, she wonders if she's about to die.

There's a telephone mounted on the wall. Although she has never called Kenny's number, it comes instantly into her head. I've always meant to do this, she thinks as she picks up the phone and pushes the buttons. A woman (Joy!) answers. She says, "Hello. Hello? Hello!" with increasing volume and annoyance. As Daphne hangs up, someone knocks on the bathroom door. She takes several deep, even breaths, and then looks around for a place to hide the glass. When she can't find one, she lifts the top of the toilet tank and sets the glass afloat.

After the work of cleaning up is finished, and almost everyone has gone home, the host beckons to Daphne, and she follows him into what turns out to be a study. He shuts the door behind them. Now what?

She's so tired. She longs to undo her hair and lie across

the paisley-covered daybed, among its inviting cushions. But she's not even going to sit down.

He's had too much to drink. She can tell by his dull, languid eyes. How did those thick fingers ever do up the tiny covered buttons on his wife's dress? "What's your name?" he asks.

"Daphne. Daphne Moss."

"You a college student?"

"Yes."

Slowly, his hand extends toward her. Lust crosses his face like a summer storm. "Good," he says. His hand lowers. After a few moments he says "Good" again, and reaches into his pocket to take out a money clip. "Tip," he says. "Nice job."

She takes the folded bills warily, without looking at them. They both watch his uncertain, empty hand as it retreats to his side.

In the driveway, Daphne splits the money with Mkabi. It's a stunning night. Masses of stars have congregated for their viewing. Darryl is waiting at the curb, leaning against his car. He and Mkabi kiss each other with leisurely pleasure. Watching them is like sitting too close to the screen at the movies.

Darryl has a surprise for Mkabi in the backseat of the car. Their son Bobby is sleeping there in his pajamas. She laughs out loud when she sees him.

31

The magician is a local dentist who does his legerde-main on the side, billing himself as Dr. Magic. He brings his act, without charge, to prisons, nursing homes, and schools for handicapped children. When he comes to the Palomar Arms, Joe is reluctant to attend the performance, but Brady advises him to go. "It breaks it up, kid," he says.

Brady goes to everything that's offered: juggling acts, lectures on Eskimo life and shell collecting, demonstrations of driftwood sculpture and macrame, prayer meetings of any denomination, art slides, poetry readings, palm readings, sing-alongs. He even accompanied Joe the previous week when four young musicians from a university came to give a concert of chamber music. Brady confessed that classical music always puts him to sleep, but it's still nice to do something different for a change. "It breaks it up," he said.

Live music! The pianist twirled the piano stool. The other musicians settled themselves on squeaky folding chairs. They raised and lowered their music stands. The two women arranged the drapery of their skirts with a kind of sensual modesty. They wore the colors of summer, rather than the somber black of concert halls. Even their tuning up, with the disadvantage of the tinny old upright, was lovely. Joe has always liked that joyful racket of preparation. The cellist's bare slender elbows sawed like a cricket's wings.

The room was too small, of course. Sound would bounce off the walls and be distorted. Sustained notes couldn't float slowly away as they should. But still, what a treat. The mountain coming to Mohammed. Joe sat in a trance of expectation.

Brady suggests they get into the front row for the magic show, so they can see what the guy is doing.

The magician takes out his baton and waves it with commanding majesty. It immediately droops in a rubbery dangle from his hand. He looks down at it, simulating bewilderment. Loss of power! Impotence! It's a universal symbol, and the audience laughs and applauds.

He brightens; the baton straightens up, too, and he asks for a volunteer to assist him.

Brady makes a megaphone of his hands. "Hey, Doc, you want to saw me in half?"

Dr. Magic stares at Brady, dismayed. But when the audience laughs again, he regains his composure. He points to Joe. "How about this gentleman?" he asks. "Would you care to assist me, sir?"

Brady guffaws. "That's no gentleman!" he shouts. "That's my roomie!"

Joe makes all sorts of protests, but they blend with the involuntary movements of his body. Soon the magician is pulling a vivid chain of scarves from Joe's bathrobe sleeves, coins from his ears, a skinny white rabbit from nowhere.

"Oh, God, oh, God," comes from the side of the room,

and Dr. Magic bows in the direction of such acclaim. He does card tricks and rope tricks, keeping up a light stream of humorous patter: "Please notice, folks, that my fingers never leave my hands! Are you wondering how I do this trick? Extremely well, I'd say."

Every once in a while, Brady calls out, asking for a little levitation. He's like the drunken heckler in a night-club who repeatedly requests "Melancholy Baby."

The magician ignores him, or puts him down with snappy, good-natured retorts, and no real break in his repertoire.

Brady whispers to Joe, "I seen all of this a hundred times," but he seems enraptured, eager to be fooled yet one more time. "Wait and see," he says. "He'll end with the birds. They always end with the birds."

Even sitting this close to the performance, Joe can't detect the mechanics, the trickery of the tricks. The man is an excellent amateur. He's probably a good dentist, too, with so much dexterity, and that gentle humor to distract patients from pain. But Joe is not enchanted by all this talent and kindness. He, too, has seen everything before. And when the doves do fly up for the finale, fluttering white and beating the air with their wings, he feels only a feeble responsive beating in his breast, and none of the old willing suspension of disbelief.

That night, after lights out, Joe tells Brady that he'd once bought a magic set for his grandson Kevin, to help the boy become more confident, more popular with other children. It was a deluxe set that came with a top hat and a magic wand. But Kevin did the tricks wrong or clumsily, always giving himself away. He even had trouble opening the collapsible hat. His parents and brother were sympathetic, and pretended to be impressed and deluded. Deborah, however, was driven by a cold honesty. She said, "The dime was between your fingers. You held them stiff and funny." And, "I *saw* you put that card in your sleeve, Kevin. It was sticking out the whole time." After he failed and failed to deceive her, Kevin became so frustrated he ripped the cards up, snapped the plastic wand in two, and stomped on the top hat, collapsing it forever.

"Yeah," Brady says. "Women can do that."

"Well, she was only a child herself," Joe says. "Only a little girl."

"Yeah, they learn early," Brady says. In the half-dark, in a voice that's slightly deeper because he's lying down, he tells Joe that his ex-wife, Alice, the blonde who visited him that one time, made him crazy in the same way. "If you think she's good-looking now," Brady says, "you should've seen her in the old days."

Joe doesn't think she's good-looking at all. With that metallic hair and heavy makeup, and her tough, inflexible jaw, she reminds him of a female impersonator. But he doesn't comment.

"You know how nothing you can do is ever right?" Brady says. "Not enough money, the wrong kind of friends, the wrong neighborhood. She wanted me to drink with her, but not get drunk. She wanted me home on time and out of the house! I couldn't even piss straight. Who the hell knows what she wanted? She made me crazy."

"You can't live with 'em or without 'em," Joe says,

amazing himself with his flowing articulate sentence, and by the way he's picked up on Brady's vernacular. And it isn't true. He *did* live with a woman, and now he's living without her.

"Anyhoo," Brady continues. "One night we both had too much, and we got to yelling and screaming at each other. She told me to do her a big favor and drop dead; it would make her real happy. Why didn't I just go someplace and die? So I drove down to the tracks, where the freights were. I was so plastered, I don't even remember driving there. I could hardly open the car door to get out. But you do. And I lay down on the tracks."

"My God," Joe says.

"It was some night, like a painting of a night. I was going to make her happy, that's all. I lay there for a long time. I must of fell asleep. When I woke up, the sky was lighter, or it was the lights of the train. And the noise of it was inside the rails, inside my head. Shit, I was sober! I was going to die! So I tried to get up or roll away and it was too late. I got halfway across when it came and came. The motorman saw me, saw *something,* but he couldn't stop until he was all the way down the line."

Joe waits for the rest of the story, as one waits in a theater for the last scene of a play. It is the same kind of mesmerizing darkness. But soon he hears Brady snoring.

Last week, when the chamber-music concert began in that inadequate room, Joe was lifted from the smaller room of his own body, from all the limits and restraints of his life, into the possibility of beauty. The musicians played some Mozart, and the Brahms Piano Quartet in C minor. In the third movement of the Brahms, there was a very long melodic passage for the cello. Joe watched the escape of other spirits around the room— the loosening of locked limbs, the changes in women's faces as they found objects or people misplaced in memory. Two lines from a lost Roethke poem came into his head then: "An old man with his feet before the fire, / In robes of green, in garments of adieu."

Next to him, Brady slept, missing the act of levitation, but he didn't snore or cry out the way he usually did at night.

32

Bench asks if he's been seeing the other woman.

"You mean *Daphne*," Kenny says. It's his only possible defiance. Bench is so coldly professional and impersonal, and Kenny lives with daily apprehension about the rise and plunge of Joy's moods. There have been no outbursts for two days now, but he can't be sure what she might do or say next, and he dreads being with her. His major fear, though, is of the correlation between her behavior and her legal intentions.

He has asked Bench to contact Joy's lawyer and find out what plans she has for the children. Kenny is willing to be reasonable and sane. He doesn't want to take them away from Joy, except for short periods of custody—weekends and holidays—and he would like to have easy access to them while they're living with her. It's the children's emotional welfare that concerns him most, and maybe the two lawyers can convince her of that.

Bench keeps harping on Daphne, and Kenny explodes. No, he *hasn't* been seeing her. He's been staying home like a good little pussy-whipped boy. How the hell long is this going to go on?

Bench's nostrils dilate in distaste. Have there been telephone calls, he asks.

Kenny sinks into the leather hot seat. Yes. So what?

He's been discreet, anyway. He uses pay phones, like a bookie. He talks so quickly he's reduced to phrases instead of whole sentences.

"You're jeopardizing your whole case," Bench warns, and when Kenny only sulks, Bench asks, "Letters?"

Kenny walks out, slamming the door behind him. Maybe he should have stuck with Larkin, who was simple enough to believe that goodbye is a lot like hello.

Joy continues to prepare meals. The dayworker still comes twice a week to clean the house. On the days she's not there, Kenny notices that Joy has stopped making their bed in the morning. He went to the room once to look for a jacket he had not yet moved to the guest-room closet, and found the bed a mad tangle of pillows, sheets, and blankets, as if olympic lovemaking had taken place there. Since then he checks it furtively every day, and it is always the same scene of disarray. His own chaste bed, now that he's learned to escape quickly into sleep, is as tidy and as spare as a monk's.

He looks for other clues to what she may be thinking or feeling, by stirring through the contents of the wastebaskets, the laundry hamper, and the refrigerator. He has become the house detective, an inspector of the heart. Aside from the disheveled bed, he doesn't find anything of significance.

In the middle of the day at the office, he has a sudden intuition that she's turning the children against him in some subtle and cunning way. His own mother had done that. Long ago, she started referring to Kenny's father as "he" or "him" with disparaging emphasis. She took away his name and title, and he became a dishonored general to his own men. When she bathed and fed Kenny and Robert, she told them what was going on, talking to herself mostly, scrubbing their arms and legs too roughly while she did so, or scraping the supper plates with teeth-shocking screeches. Although both boys were too young to comprehend much of what she said, they'd felt the chill of her contempt, and learned to share it. Later, when she'd say, "That bastard," they would know instantly who she meant.

Although he speaks to his mother on the telephone about once a month, Kenny has not heard from or called his father in a long while. Six months, or more. Was he really such a cowardly bully, or was he bullied and cowed into being one? Is he lonely now, heartsick with regret? Kenny is sure he's projecting his self-pity onto his father, who's married to another disagreeable woman and is as uncommunicative as ever.

Robert isn't married, and in his rare meetings with Kenny, he refers to their parents collectively as "them." Whenever that happens, Kenny feels the abrasive swipe of the washrag again.

He envisions a grown Molly and Steven, drinking cocktails in an airport bar, sharing distorted memories of their childhood, and he rises from his desk chair to pace. He tries to dredge up positive memories of his own. His mother whistled off-key sometimes, while she did house-work. And his father showed up once, in a daytime audience of women, to watch Kenny, as Columbus, discover America in a school play.

He sits down again, swiveling back and forth, holding on to the desk ledge the way Steven does when he comes to the office and plays at being Daddy. Kenny picks up the telephone, and wonders who he will call. His father, to offer false, long-distance absolution? His mother, to ask her to whistle a few bars for him? Joy, to say: What's going on there, stop immediately, I know what you're up to? Robert, to say: Guess what, I've become "him"? The children, to warn them against dangerous lies and subterfuge? Daphne, to squander his lust in short, staccato bursts? Instead, he dials Bench's number and apologizes for being obstinate and rude. He intends to be more cooperative from now on. He knows it's for his own good. Even the phone calls will stop.

33

So be it. Daphne is mature enough to accept a further delay of gratification. The phone calls didn't amount to very much anyway. She's had far less hurried ones from obscene strangers. And Kenny is such a wreck about it. If it weren't for the children, he'd be here right now, opening the bed, turning on the fireplace fan, unbuttoning his shirt.

In the meantime, he's going to send telepathic messages. There isn't any law against that, is there? All they have to do is think about one another with savage concentration at various times of the day. On the hour? They agree, murmur, send kisses crawling through the telephone wires, and hang up.

It's Daphne's day off again, and she doesn't have any classes. She intends to plan every minute of this unwelcome freedom. The people in the apartment above hers have started the day too early, by moving furniture and waking her. She lies there for as long as she can, willing sleep, feigning sleep, and then she gives in and gets up. It's only ten of nine. Daphne likes to sleep late, especially on mornings following work, and most especially today. She decides to wash her hair, to squeeze fresh orange juice (for a change), and to do some calisthenics. The body, love's main vehicle, can be terribly neglected during the frenzy of love. She'll use this respite to restore herself, and the restoration will help kill time. Just shampooing her hair, because of its length, can absorb the better part of an hour. On other days, Kenny had combed out the wet tangles for her, a sensation almost as lovely as flesh against flesh. While she's in the shower, her eyes shut against the streaming suds, she realizes that it must be nine o'clock by now, or even a little past that. She concentrates on Kenny's face, on his body, imagines him next to her, deflecting the water into a fine spray against her belly and breasts. He is thinking of her, too; she's sure of it. Daphne feels the electricity of his sexual gaze, and shivers under it, as she does in bed, saying his name.

She forgets to strain the orange juice, and swallows a few small seeds and lots of pulp, but it's delicious anyway. And it tastes healthful—a golden elixir, like a love potion. She makes a resolution to squeeze fresh juice every day from now on, and to take vitamins as well.

After closing the bed, Daphne has just enough room for the calisthenics. She puts some music on the stereo—Leon Russell's "Tight Rope," which she and Kenny had danced to in dreamy half-time once, just before he left the apartment. At ten o'clock she pauses during a series of sit-ups and gets to her feet. This time she conjures him clothed from the waist down, and barefoot, as they both were the day they danced. She holds her arms out to enclose a man-sized portion of air. It's easy to pretend, and sort of fun. Beyond Russell's aching, throbbing words, she's positive she can hear her own name said again and again.

Daphne calls Feliciana, who has a date, and Louise Weber, who's working. She dials two other friends in Los Angeles. The first phone rings and rings without an answer. A man picks up the second one and says that Jeanine is indisposed at the moment; can he take a message? Well, there's no law against being alone for a single day, either.

Daphne does some work on her Tolstoy paper, referring frequently to the marked-up text of *Anna Karenina*. She used to deplore the fact that other students wrote in books; it seemed like a sacrilege. But now, when she reads in the margins *Yes, yes!* and *This is absolutely true!* next to the passage about the birth of Kitty and Levin's baby, she is very moved. She turns the pages and writes similar comments about Anna's passion for Vronsky, even though she knows how it all ends.

Daphne puts the paper aside and gets dressed. Maybe she'll take a drive, head for the beach. She packs a picnic lunch and throws her bathing suit and a towel into the car, too.

There's a call-in talk show on the radio as she starts out, heading south on the freeway. The subject is euthanasia, and the show is titled *Pulling the Plug*. Her hand reaches for the dial, and then goes back to the wheel. Euthanasia is something she and the others have discussed in the lounge. Mkabi suggested that all healthy adults sign papers saying whether or not extreme life-saving methods should be used on them, and whether they want to donate their hearts, kidneys, and corneas for transplant. Jerry said that he can't see the point of living if you don't know up from down anymore. Monica asked what *his* point was, then, and he laughed, goosing her. Daphne began to be short of breath and had to leave the room. If something like that happens now, she'll simply turn to a music station, or shut the radio off. It wouldn't be the first time she was stricken by anxiety in an inconvenient place. At that party she and Mkabi had worked. And in class, when they analyzed the scene in *Madame Bovary* where Emma and Rodolphe go into the woods on horseback. God! Sex and death, sex and death, that's all she ever thinks about. Maybe she's seen too many Woody Allen movies.

The talk-show panel is composed of the host, a former d.j. who likes to play devil's advocate; a psychiatrist, who is also the founder of a hospice; and a fundamentalist minister. "Tell me, Dr. Carroll," the host begins, "do you think the taking of a human life can ever be justified?"

The psychiatrist relates in detail requests from dying patients that break his heart because he feels morally obligated to grant them and is legally unable to do so. The minister speaks of God's will, and the supreme plan that must not be interfered with. "Our time on earth is preordained," he says. "Read your Bible."

"And what about suffering?" the host asks. Does Reverend Fuller think a benevolent God wouldn't condone an end to human suffering?

Reverend Fuller says that God doesn't do talk shows, and we shouldn't try to run His business, either. And if there's an unnatural end to the mortal body, then the spirit assumes the pain, and assumes it for eternity.

They throw names at one another: Karen Ann

Quinlan, Freud, Christ, Lazarus, Elisabeth Kubler-Ross. People call in on the hot line. A woman with throat cancer whispers hoarsely of her consuming desire to die. A man calls and matter-of-factly offers to help her. He's helped many people. The host quickly takes another call. The question of abortion is raised, and that leads to a discussion of the general devaluation of life. Pollution. War. Assassination. The death penalty. Suicide. Genocide.

Daphne drives and drives. She thinks of the fever of maternalism that overtook her that night at the Palomar Arms—how she tucked Miss Nettleson in like an infant, how she tried to force-feed Mr. Axel. The nurses, those angels of mercy, could sprout awesome wings and become angels of death instead. Could she ever help some one die? The voices on the radio are interrupting one another, are growing louder with conviction and offense. But Daphne is calm. Now the whole issue seems intellectual rather than emotional to her. Lacing Mrs. Shumway's soup with real poison. Bringing it in a silver tureen instead of on a Styrofoam tray. Nursing them out as we nurse them in.

She has passed Oxnard and the show is over. The eleven o'clock news comes on. Time to make mental contact with Kenny. She realizes that she's driving in his direction, and if the physics of telepathy is like that of radio, their signals should be growing stronger. So she drives, thinking of him, and goes right by Malibu, where she had considered stopping.

After the news, there's music on the radio, and Daphne believes she's passed some critical test. She experienced no anxiety during *Pulling the Plug,* other than a brief flutter at the end when the show's title reminded her of that childhood fear of being sucked down the bathtub drain.

The beach is out for today, unless she decides to try Venice or someplace like that. It's clouding up, anyway, and she seems to be heading toward Los Angeles. Maybe she can drop in on Louise at work, or try calling one of her other friends again.

Less than a mile off the freeway, she pulls into a shopping center and eats her lunch in the car. How good everything tastes, just like the fresh orange juice that morning. It's as if her senses have been honed to a finer acuity.

After she's eaten, Daphne notices a health-food store and remembers her resolution to start taking vitamins.

Except for the clerk, a rabbinical-looking man in his thirties, the store is empty. Has everyone abandoned the American quest for perfect health? When Daphne hovers near the vitamin and mineral display, confounded by the abundance, the clerk comes up behind her and asks if he can be of assistance. Daphne tells him that she was hoping to just get a regular supplement, you know: A, B, C, D, and so on. She wasn't aware that the selection went all the way to Z, with zinc. Or that each letter offered so many choices. Why, under D alone, there's dolomite, dl-methionine, and desiccated liver. Maybe she'll settle for a standard one-a-day capsule. What would he suggest?

It's as if he's been waiting all his life for her arrival. He pulls two stools from behind the counter, and they sit facing one another. He tells her that his name is Carl, and asks what hers is. He tells her about lecithin and its dramatic effect on that killer, cholesterol; how L-tryptophan persuades you into healthful sleep; and that another amino acid, phenylalanine, controls the appetite and stimulates the memory at the same time. Even women her age, whose major need is iron because of monthly loss, should start thinking about the thinning of the bones that comes with menstrual cessation. Daphne's entire hormonal life whizzes by. Dolomite, yes, E, and a complex time-released composite of the various B's. C, of course, but how much, and what kind? Protein-coated? With bioflavonoids? With hesperidin?

He lifts a handful of her hair and remarks that it *looks* healthy. Daphne knows that her hair is always at its best after a vigorous shampoo. She glances down at the lustrous strand in his palm and would have to agree—it does look healthy. But he says that a proper chemical analysis would probably inform her otherwise. She could leave him a few hairs if she'd like, plus some nail clippings, and a urine sample. A friend of his, who works in a holistic lab, would give her a break on a complete survey, with Carl's intervention.

"I eat a pretty balanced diet," she says, remembering skipped meals, junk-food binges.

"Believe me, Daphne," he says. "Most commercially prepared food is designed to shorten your life. Read the labels," he advises, "for ingredients, for recommended daily allowances. And then remember that those are *government* standards, anyway. Think about the government a little, Daphne," he says with a grievous smile.

The hand he's holding, so that he can have a better view of her nails, is starting to get sweaty. She draws it away and puts it against her chest, where that awful pressure is beginning. "Thanks very much," she says. "But I'm actually only passing through."

"Where are you from, Daphne?" he asks.

"Indianapolis," she says, standing up, and Carl nods. "The accent gives you away. Pure Midwest. Well, I'll just have to guess your nutritional needs for now." He starts pulling various jars and bottles from the shelves.

She watches with growing alarm. "I'm a little short on cash," she murmurs.

"We take Master, Visa, American Express, and Diners Club," he says. "Even a personal check from you, Daphne."

She needs to get out of here, to get some air, so she gives him her Visa card without further argument, and then thumps her fingers on the counter while he moves in slow motion to process her purchase.

Despite Carl's declaration of trust, he still calls in for confirmation of her credit status. After he makes her promise to leave those organic samples the next time she's passing through, he lets her go, fifty-six dollars poorer, and with the weight of good health in her arms.

Back in the car, she realizes that twelve o'clock has come and gone without a thought of Kenny. She imagines his mental waves moving restlessly overhead, longing for their connection, like a spirit searching for its lost body. If Kenny had been thinking of her strongly enough, wouldn't she have been stirred into sensing it? She knows it's only a playful exercise in distraction, but she's disappointed anyway.

Daphne makes her phone calls from a supermarket, and discovers that neither of her friends is at home. She drives to the bookstore in Beverly Hills that Louise manages, and is told that Louise has just left for lunch with a salesman. For a while, Daphne wanders the aisles of the store, opening books at random and reading first lines: "The summer my father died, I plucked out all my eyelashes." "So you want to lose twenty pounds by Christmas!" "There were three bullet holes: a small one in the neck; a larger, gaping wound in the abdomen; and a space he could see right through, where her eye, probably a perfect match to the staring blue one, used to be."

There are other browsers turning pages, picking books up and putting them down again. Daphne wonders if either of the two attractive women in her aisle could be Joy, if she's ever passed her unknowingly on the street, or if they ever waited side by side in their cars at the same traffic light. Will they meet someday, inadvertently, when Daphne and Kenny are a public couple, and Joy the outsider? The woman she's looking at looks back, and smiles. Daphne flees the store.

Sherman Oaks isn't very far away. Kenny should be at work, marking the passing hours with their telepathic communion. Even if Joy wasn't in the bookstore, she's probably somewhere in Beverly Hills seeking her own kind of solace. Daphne just wants to see the house, and then go right by it.

She gets directions to their street from the gas-station attendant who fills her tank. When she enters the neighborhood, it's as if she's crossed the border, illegally, into a foreign country. It seems peaceful here; the landscaping is orderly; the houses handsome and well kept. There are signs establishing residency: *The Kaplans, Minetti, The Petersons.* Abandoned tricycles and toys in drive-ways indicate life going on behind the curtained windows. Children have been called home to lunch, for naps. Letters and newspapers poke out of the mailboxes.

There are no such clues at Kenny's house—just the large numeral 9 on the front door. She parks diagonally opposite. There could be a car inside the garage. Molly and Steven might be eating or sleeping only yards away. And Joy? Daphne could knock on the door and ask directions to another street, or say she's selling something: cosmetics, Bibles, vacuum cleaners. Vitamins. Money might pass between them. Their hands could accidentally touch. She won't do it, certainly, and hardly understands the impetus for her fantasy. She has let one o'clock go by, too, she sees, without attempting communication with Kenny. Perhaps because she is so dangerously close to his family.

Daphne sits in her car and stares at the house. The longer she looks, the less it seems like a real structure. It has started to flatten, to lose dimension. There are no people inside, or furniture, and she feels that there never have been. If she were to drive around the corner now, she would discover that 9 Shasta Drive is only a thin façade propped up on metal supports, like a movie set—a clever construction to fool the eye and the imagination.

That's why she has no immediate visceral reaction when Kenny's Toyota speeds around the corner and comes to a skidding stop in front of his house. It must be another illusion, this one embodied by desire. Only when he opens the car door and gets out, leaving it swinging, does she start to open hers, ready to call to him.

But he's running away from her, as if she's invisible, or the helpless figure in her own dream. He's at the entrance to his house, alternately fumbling wildly in his pockets and pounding on the door.

34

It's past noon, and it occurs to Kenny that he's hardly thought about Daphne today. The game of telepathy he'd suggested was only a silly scheme, something to say to her, something to keep a fragile thread of connection between them. He hadn't ever meant to play. But now, when he does think of her, it's with so much ardor that he's shaken. He sees the sweet slope of her ass when she turns away to sleep, only making him want her again; the way her breasts eye him from the disorder of the foldout bed as he's getting dressed. It would be so nice to call her and talk about that. *Christ, if my love were in my arms . . .*

He rings Miss Oberon and asks her to try his house once more. It's the fifth time since ten o'clock, and so far there's been no answer. Steven has an earache and was up most of the night, whimpering with pain. Kenny heard Joy go into him several times, and he went to the door of the boy's room himself at 3 a.m., offering to take over. But she'd said, "No, thank you," with revulsion, as if he were a street creep trying to press a porno circular on her. When she left the room to get something, she made a great show of avoiding contact with him in the doorway.

This morning, Steven was still cranky, and still running a low-grade fever, when Kenny was ready to leave for work. He couldn't help himself—habit dies hard; he said, "Are you going to take him to Evans? I could stay home for a while if you need me."

She smiled at him, a curiously vacant smile, and she staggered a little, probably from fatigue. "I don't need you," she said with exaggerated evenness. "Steven doesn't need you. Molly doesn't need you. *Get it?*"

Kenny might have been deaf, and expected to read her lips. He felt chilled, and when he tried to speak again, she went into the bathroom, slamming the door behind her.

As he'd attempted to tell Bench, Joy is an excellent mother. Alternately antic with the children and earnestly loving. Although she's a vain woman, and her apple breasts have always been an important matter of pride, she had nursed both infants, without hesitation. She'd been a wonderful geyser of milk.

Her current, bizarre behavior is only a way of avenging herself, of getting back at him. She's probably at the pediatrician's office right now with Steven and Molly. You could wait hours in that bedlam of screaming kids. If worse comes to worst, he'll get in touch with her there.

Miss Oberon comes in to say there's still no answer at his house. Should she try again later?

He tells her to go to lunch; he'll take care of it himself. She reviews his schedule of afternoon appointments, and lays a few letters on his desk to be signed. He remembers that he never retyped the one he'd made into a paper airplane, and wonders what it said.

"I'll be back in an hour," Miss Oberon says, and she leaves.

He hardly knows anything about her, except for her

extraordinary secretarial skills, her tortuous sobriety. He idly suspects that she's a virgin; even her glance appears closed, cautiously protected. She's Daphne's age, and has a decent enough figure, but in all the months she's worked here he's never really speculated on it, on what she might look like without the longish skirts she wears, that are usually the color of graphite, and the functional white blouses. At the bottom of all the letters she types, her initials, in lowercase, stand dutifully next to his bolder ones. Her note pad, though, is filled with the unbreakable code symbols of shorthand. She could be writing anything.

His thoughts are being diverted, and becoming more scattered. Where was he? Joy and the children. But he wants to go back even further, to settle into a pleasurable daydream. It was Daphne he was thinking about before, when he decided to try calling Joy again, a naked and sprawling Daphne, open everywhere to him. His groin begins to drum with need. He goes into the small bathroom right off his office and unzips. Oh, Jesus, he thinks, as he takes himself in hand. How pathetic. What lunacy. I have a beautiful, beautiful lover, and a beautiful wife.

He can't summon up either of them now. He's in his own frantic grip and Daphne's disappeared, and Joy won't materialize—a freaky punishment for the crime of duplicity, for hurting his family. Where the hell are they? A child doesn't die from a lousy earache because his father's fucking around, because his father's fallen in love. Cars don't crash. Come on. Come on. *Somebody.* It has to be Miss Oberon, then, the last real image on his retina, slipping out of her leaden skirt. Oh, come on, the blouse, the tits. What's her first name again? On her back, on her knees. Oh, take it, hurry up, oh, please, oh, please, oh, please.

Dr. Evans's nurse tells Kenny that Mrs. Bannister had brought Steven in first thing that morning. The boy's ear was inflamed, and Doctor had prescribed an antibiotic and bed rest. Over a chorus of wailing babies, she informs him that his wife left the office before nine.

Kenny dials his number again, and this time he lets the phone ring for a very long time. When he's about to hang up, someone picks up the receiver but doesn't say anything. Kenny says, "Hello. Hello! Joy? Steven?" He can hear breathing, followed by the bang-bang of the receiver knocking against a hard surface. "Hello!" he shouts. "Who is that?"

Then Molly says, from a distance, probably talking into the earpiece, "Okay, goodbye." A myna bird imitating bits of overheard human speech. And she hangs up.

His relief is enormous. They're home again; he's willed them safely back into the shelter of the house, out of traffic accidents, hospitals, morgues. "Ha!" he says aloud.

But why didn't Joy answer the phone? She doesn't encourage Molly to do that. So he dials again, and this time Steven answers—a coherent, reliable four-year-old, full of important news. His ear hurts. He has yellow medicine. Dr. Evans gave him a jelly monster for being good, and Molly got a ring. She's not allowed to put it in her mouth. Mommy is sleeping upstairs in the big bed.

"Tell her Daddy wants to speak to her," Kenny says.

He starts to walk around his desk, with the phone pressed to his ear. The cord keeps reeling him back in. Nothing but silence; no footsteps, voices, not even the television. It's taking too long. Could Steven have started to play, forgetting his errand as he climbed the stairs? Reliable, maybe, but still only four.

Kenny keeps calling the boy's name, and then Molly's, just in case. He whistles into the receiver, a long, piercing shriek. His office door opens and Miss Oberon, just back from lunch, with her purse and a package in her arms, looks in. "Did you want me, Mr. Bannister?" she inquires, and he shakes his head, waving her away.

Steven is on the phone again. Mommy is fast asleep.

"*Wake* her," Kenny commands, too severely, and Steven starts to cry. He bawls right into the phone, while Kenny tries to soothe and shush him. "I didn't mean to yell, honey," he says. "Steven? Come on, be a big boy."

"My ear hurts," Steven sobs.

"I know," Kenny says. "I know. That's why I want to talk to Mommy. I want to tell her to give you the medicine to make it better .Will you wake her up now?"

"She *won't!*" Steven says, and Kenny is like a mad dog on a short leash. "I'm coming home," he says. "Don't cry."

He runs past Miss Oberon, who calls something after him. "No, no!" he yells, and keeps going. He takes the emergency stairs, two, three, four at a time, his shoes bonging on the metal steps. There are fourteen flights and his breath is so harsh and quick that he's gagging before he gets to the final landing, and dying to be out of the dark, echoing stairwell. He lunges against the steel door that releases him into the glaring light of the parking lot.

All the way home he thinks that he should have called the police first, or a neighbor, yet he doesn't stop to do either now. A stubborn inner force insists that it isn't just help that's needed, but *his* help. Family business, private business. He changes lanes without caution, in and out, and the bleating horns of other, angry drivers disappear behind him in long, tapering streamers of sound.

Kenny is talking to himself, saying Joy's name and the children's again and again, a wishful abracadabra of names. And once he says, "Oh, *please*," and is horrified to remember his earlier, irreverent incantation of those words.

He's coming to his own street, careening like a Keystone Kop, amazed, in this bad dream, that he has found the way, that his hands move on the wheel, that his legs obey him and run, supporting his weight, which is as heavy as granite with terror.

The door is bolted shut. All those locks meant to keep intruders out won't let Kenny in either. His keys are lost, are in the car, or the street. He shouts instructions to Steven: "Push the button, damn it, turn the key, turn the knob! Open up! Open up!"

And then he's inside, at the top of the stairs in a few springy, carpeted leaps.

She's lying in the middle of the bed with her arms out. There would be no place for him if he had to lie down beside her. Her skin is like egg white, like ectoplasm. How can he tell if she's breathing when the room is rocking like this? How can he hear her heart against the commotion of his own? He scrounges in his head for the proper bargain, and when he finds it, he falls on her, swearing his part.

35

Nora McBride has pulled through, with the help of medicine, devoted attention, and her own passionate will. But when Daphne returns to work after her day off, she learns that Mrs. Bernstein is dead, having suffered a second stroke. It happened suddenly, while she and her sister were eating lunch and watching *Days of Our Lives.*

Mrs. Feldman, who has always been such a generous and reasonable woman, thinks an unfair exchange has been made. Pearl for Mrs. McBride. The next day, after the funeral, she pleads her case to anyone who will listen. "That one is much older," she says. "Does she have a friend in the world, or a kind word for anybody? My sister had years left. Nobody can tell me she didn't have years left. Do you know what she said just the other day? 'This year I hope Betty takes us for the holidays.' She was looking forward. She wasn't planning on dying. She wasn't even sick."

Daphne, moving in her own fog of confusion and grief, murmurs words of condolence and urges Mrs. Feldman to eat something from the wretched supper tray. Mrs. Feldman is inconsolable. And she's frightened that her sister will be replaced by someone she won't be able to live with. What if they like different shows? What if she won't talk, or talks too much?

"I don't know," Daphne says. "I don't know. Maybe it will all work out." As she speaks, she's thinking of herself and Kenny. How can that ever work out?

Joy is in a hospital, and she will either live or die. Daphne was still sitting in her car on Shasta Drive when the police cars arrived, and the ambulance. She watched Kenny running alongside the stretcher, one child in his arms, the other circling his feet like a dog. She watched as if she were looking through a one-way mirror, observer without being observed. A woman rushed up and took the children from him, and he climbed into the ambulance with Joy and it drove away. Daphne sat there for several minutes afterward. She saw the excited cluster of neighbors who gathered near the scene of the crime. No one noticed her, or her conspicuous alien car. When she finally pulled away, it was like leaving a drive-in before the end of the show. Neither of the police cars chased her; none of the chattering women ran after her car, pointing an accusing finger.

She went home and waited there in a rigid misery of exile and suspense. There was a thick letter from her mother that she opened after an hour or so. Both of Daphne's parents have been worried about her since her visit. She didn't look quite right to them. Is it an affair of the heart, her mother discreetly asks. Margaret wants to come down and stay with Daphne for a while, for a little change of scenery. She is such a pretty and popular girl. There is always a new boy on the doorstep! Yet something—maybe the pressures of her upcoming senior year—is making her nervous and unhappy. What's happening to everybody? Youth used to be such a gay and carefree time. Is it being wasted on the young (ha-ha)? Old Mrs. Jaffee says that Mount St. Helens is still taking its toll, that toxic particles are still in the atmosphere. She says the government should do something. If President Reagan had taken her advice, he would have bombed it right away and ended the whole thing.

Daphne laughs, and that releases the tension, permitting her to collapse and moan. Oh, what have I done? What have I done? Even children must know that you can't wish for disaster and make it happen. But she had gone far beyond the harmless game of wishing. She had become as willful and dangerous as a volcano.

Kenny didn't call her. She didn't expect him to, yet she sat close to the telephone, jumpy with anticipation. Sometime in the early evening, she called a few hospitals, until she found the right one. "Are you a relative?" the clerk asked, and Daphne knew she wouldn't be told anything unless she said she was. "I'm her sister," she said. "I live out of town." That entitled her to hear that Joy's condition was critical. After she replaced the receiver, Daphne wished she had asked for specific details. She wanted some of Kenny's precious numbers: a fifty-fifty chance? sixty-forty? She wondered what critical meant *exactly*, whether it was more hopeful than not. Her grandfather's condition, right before he died, had been listed as poor. The poverty of dying, of relinquishing the world. What would become of all Joy's things if she died? Blouses with price tags still hidden in their sleeves. Her Cuisinart, squat and silent on the kitchen counter. Kenny and his children standing among the valuable ruins.

She called several times that night, and Joy's condition was unchanged. Unchanged and critical. Daphne couldn't get a fix on the meaning of those words. She pictured Kenny at his bedside vigil, and remembered the way he'd sworn to leave his family and how, when he buckled his belt, she'd imagined a holster there.

She sat, holding herself, making an afghan of her hair, rocking back and forth on a rockerless chair. If only she *were* Joy's sister, and was privileged to be there beside him in innocent, loving commiseration. And then, astounded, if only she were *Joy*.

Unchanged. She sat there such a long time. When she stood up at last, her bones creaked and her legs were stiff and bloodless. She didn't even have the strength to open the foldout bed, but lay on its scratchy cover, under the blue sky of the starlit ceiling, trying to sleep. It was very difficult. She began thinking how older people say they don't envy the young their sexual freedom, that they wouldn't be young these days for anything. Daphne admitted that VD was scary; genital herpes was almost becoming a rite of passage, like acne. And no matter how careful you were, there was still a small risk of pregnancy. But what was that compared to the body's tremendous capacity for delight? Those middle-aged protests were only sour grapes, she decided. Because their own golden youth had been sacrificed to morals and custom, they just couldn't stand for anyone else to have fun. Then she remembered the dumb thing Jerry had said a few days ago, that the only difference between herpes and love is that herpes lasts. She'd laughed as much as everyone else.

Suddenly, in her awful wakefulness, Daphne knew

what the older people meant. It was that the old-fashioned idea of abiding love—what her generation called commitment—was endangered by the ease of casual sex. The faithful mind and the wanton body were only mortal enemies confined to the same prison. Did one always have to perish for the other to survive?

The next morning, Daphne could not recall dreaming, but she must have slept. There was a blessed moment of blankness before the reality of what had happened the day before crept into her consciousness, like fresh bad news. She wasn't able to go to school. Instead, she went back to sleep, still on the unopened bed, and dreamt a series of troubling episodes that had to do with school— the old examination dream in which she's unprepared, and her pencil breaks, or she can't find the right room until it's too late. On waking, she rushed to the telephone and called the hospital. Critical, unchanged.

When it was time to go to work, she put on her uniform, moving around the room like an automaton, and went out.

Poor Mrs. Feldman. The separation from her sister is almost surgical. Her great wound cannot be treated. "Pearl liked you. You were one of her favorites," she tells Daphne, although Mrs. Bernstein often didn't recognize her when she brought the trays in. "I want you to take something to remember her by. Go ahead, take anything you want."

Daphne's glance skims the room, which looks like one of those overstocked gift shops at the side of a country road. There isn't anything here she wants, and her own anguish makes it difficult for her to concentrate. "Thank you," she says, backing out. "There's really nothing. And you should keep—"

"No, no!" Mrs. Feldman cries. "A souvenir! You were kind. You asked her how she was feeling. Do you want one of her needlepoint pillows? Or a plant?"

"A plant," Daphne says, grateful for the option of a living thing. "A plant would be lovely."

Mrs. Feldman selects an overgrown philodendron in a clay pot disguised by a ruffled crocheted cover. The leafy stems twist themselves around Daphne's arm when she lifts the plant from the windowsill, and creep in trailing vines down her legs to the floor. She has an insane flash: Mrs. Bernstein, not in exchange for Mrs. McBride, but for Joy!

"Plenty of water," Mrs. Feldman instructs her. "Give it plant food. And see that it gets enough light." Then her face caves in.

Encumbered by the unwieldy plant, Daphne stoops to put one arm around the quaking shoulders, spilling some loose earth into Mrs. Feldman's lap.

She delivers the other trays with more than her usual speed, and a false cheeriness that takes all her energy to fabricate. Rushing the cart down the corridor and dashing in and out of the rooms is a little like driving too fast. The slow reflexes of most of the patients save her from the agony of small talk. She is there and gone before they can gather their words.

"Lovers' quarrel?" Monica inquires when Daphne appears in the doorway of the lounge. Everyone, it seems, turns to look at her as she enters.

"Why don't you ever mind your own beeswax,

Monica?" Evita asks, while Daphne attempts to rearrange her giveaway face. She goes to the refrigerator and takes her container of yogurt. "Illness," she mumbles, still staring into the open refrigerator.

"What?" Mkabi asks.

"Illness in the family," Daphne says with more clarity, turning to them. And when their complete attention remains on her, she adds, "Let's talk about something else, okay?"

When she goes to collect the trays in 219, Mr. Brady is asleep, and Mr. Axel is sitting in his chair, only a few inches from the windowless wall he faces. As soon as he sees Daphne, his eyes resume life. "Ah!" he says, like a birdwatcher rewarded at last by the sight of a rare specimen.

She takes his tray, reserving comment on how little he's eaten. Just minutes ago, her own yogurt could hardly be swallowed past the thicket of sorrow in her throat.

His scrutiny slows her movements, doesn't allow her to go. So she attempts normal conversation. "Too bad about poor Mrs. Bernstein," she says.

"Quickly," he answers. "No pain."

"Still, it's sad," Daphne says.

"*You*," he says, eyeing her sharply.

"Fine," she answers. Lately, when she speaks to him, she sometimes loses parts of sentences, too—articles, pronouns, adjectives—as if he's taught her a new, economical language.

"Oh, no," he says.

"Family illness," Daphne begins, and then can't continue the lie. His sympathy penetrates her very being. She puts his tray back on the table and sinks to her knees at the side of the wheelchair.

"Oh, Mr. Axel," she cries. "I wish I could die!"

36

Her head in his lap gives Joe the strangest sensation. Although he has been bathed by nursing aides, and embraced and patted during visits from his family, this feels like the first time in an eternity that he's been touched. How lovely it is to be touched! He guides his undisciplined hand, with a major effort at control, and brings it to her head. His fingers catch on the hairnet and pull it off of their own free will. Her hair tumbles across his thighs and over his knees. It is silken and aromatic, like Deborah's, like Sandra's when she was a girl, like Adele's in some remote planet of memory. He strokes Daphne's head and croons a wordless, tuneless song of solace.

There's no hurry for her to speak; he isn't going anywhere. It is the one advantage of his circumstance. Although he thinks: "The thousand natural shocks that flesh is heir to," he knows already that her despair is related in some way to love. What else? "Tell me," he says, only when he's certain that she's ready to do so.

Her voice comes up in a holy whisper of confession. "I'm a murderer," she says.

"Not." She can only have broken some man's heart, he's sure. They'll both survive.

"A married man," she says. "And his wife tried to kill herself. Maybe she'll die. I *wanted* her to."

Her head is still in his lap; his hand still on its burning crown. "No," he says, but it's not a denial, only some avuncular soothing.

She knows that, too, somehow, and continues, her voice so low he must strain to hear her. "And even now I'm jealous of her. I'm the worst person I know. Evil."

"Not evil."

"There are *children*," she says, as if that's an unassailable argument.

"Everyone," he says. ". . . some bad thing."

"Not everyone. Not you." Her tone is faintly colored by hopefulness.

"Oh, yes." In a rapid scan of his own history, he searches for evidence against himself to offer her. Two women, during his long marriage: one, a friend's widow with whom he'd lain for the sake of comforting her, and he had; the other, a hot, deliberate girl so long ago he might be mistaken. He'd never intended anything more than the act, though. And he was careful that Adele never knew. It's not the kind of thing to help Daphne with now. He can't save her with false assurances, either: the wife will live—she is more scheming than you; the wife will die, which is for the best, and you can atone by raising her children. The children are surely as unreal to Daphne as death. He needs a darker private secret than the few gray ones he unearths. Those selfish deeds of childhood, the grownup acts of vanity and pride. Not enough.

And then he remembers Tepper, whose pharmacy was close enough to Joe's for not-so-friendly rivalry. Also a married man, also a father, he'd fallen in love with a neighbor's daughter, a girl still in high school. It was a madness that terrified Tepper because he'd never felt so much in his life: a lust that raised the hair on his body when he thought of her; a galvanic urge for danger. The girl became pregnant, and she was too innocent and scared to tell anyone for a long time. When she finally did tell Tepper, he went a little insane at first. He wanted to beat her, and to enter her again and again in the dark, cushioned backseat of his Packard. The responsibility was clearly his. He was so much older, more experienced, a pharmacist.

If he let her tell her parents, they would kill him. The father was a butcher, and Tepper envisioned cleavers severing his head, his hands, his genitals. His own wife was a frail woman and he loved her. Even if he survived the butcher's wrath, he couldn't marry the girl. She was stupid, a bovine beauty.

Finally, he took her to the store late one night. The girl was weeping, clutching at him, as afraid as a child at the dentist's, but the slightest whiff of ether knocked her cold. She was too far gone, maybe five months, for what he attempted to do, and his fear made him inept. She bled like a slaughtered calf.

Daphne lifts her head from Joe's lap as he begins his halting narrative. Instead of referring to Tepper, he tells her that this is something he did himself many years ago. "See?" he says. "Love. Foolishness . . . nothing new."

She listens the way his grandchildren used to listen to the stories of the robberies. Wide-eyed, bloodthirsty, pure. But there's only one thing she really wants to know. "Did the girl die?"

Well, she didn't, as it happened. Tepper, released from his blinding panic by the spring of blood, did the right thing. He put an ice pack on her belly and drove her quickly to the hospital. It was a close call, and the consequences were brutal and scandalous, but the girl lived.

Joe looks at Daphne and decides to give her more than he'd intended, and by doing so turn her crime into a misdemeanor. Why not? "Yes," he tells her. "The girl died."

She draws a shocked breath. But then she makes a face. "Oh, come on," she says. "You're making it up, aren't you? You'd be in jail. *You* didn't go to jail."

There are bits and pieces of other stories he might use—newspaper items, rumors. Girls left to die elsewhere, far from the scene of amateur surgery. Parts of girls wrapped in rags and newspapers and not found for years. But does he want her to believe him capable of such horror? Besides, Joe is weary. He's been clubbed into weariness. The whole business, with all its complications, his exertions of recall and invention, has taxed him badly. His speech is stuck. He can't think so well anymore. And there go his hands in their harum-scarum flutter.

She takes his silence as an affirmation of her doubt. "I knew you didn't do it," she says, and she grabs his hands to still them. Her vitality sends a charge through him that is not exactly sexual.

He's failed her, but it isn't a fatal failure. There's a little more energy to her motions as she stands and takes his tray again from the bed table. And he's not done with what he can offer. Soon, he will let her start feeding him.

37

It's midmorning by the time they bring Joy upstairs from the intensive-care unit. There are no private rooms available, and she's put into a double already occupied by a woman who's had a hysterectomy. The room seems funereal with the scent of flowers when Kenny comes in. The other woman, whose bed is closer to the door, is talking on the telephone. Joy's bed is enclosed by a drawn curtain and he slips quickly into its tent-like privacy. She's deeply asleep, or unconscious, and is still that threatening color. They've hooked her up to an intravenous solution that's released slowly through the clear tubing, drop by trembling drop. He sits down in the chair next to the bed with excruciating care, as if the slightest sound might wake her. Shouldn't he try to wake her?

Kenny hadn't asked any of the right questions of the resident in the emergency room, who'd looked about fourteen and was in love with human emergency. He had a pack of Luckies in the breast pocket of his official white jacket. He'd said, with what seemed like pleasure, that Joy had actually *died* for a moment while they were pumping her out—a plunge in blood pressure, no breath, no heartbeat—and had then been revived. Everything fluctuated wildly on return, but now she appeared stable.

What they had to look out for was pneumonia—she might have aspirated some vomit—and for the less likely possibility of brain damage caused by that brief deprivation of oxygen. Her kidney function was being monitored, too, but his educated guess was that she had passed safely through it.

The man's casual, cheerful manner frightened and enraged Kenny. Who cared about his educated guesses. Wasn't this a fucking hospital? Why was it staffed by teenagers wearing name tags that proclaimed them doctors?

But he found himself muttering his humble gratitude. Joy's life had been saved, and no one harped on the fact that she had attempted suicide. The contents of her stomach were sent to the lab for analysis. The policemen asked a few questions and Kenny kept saying, "I don't know. I just came home. I just walked in on it." They filled out their forms and left. The real grilling would come later, he was sure, but at least he didn't have to deal with it now. In the five-minute visits to the intensive-care unit each hour, he could sit quietly next to Joy's bed and watch the understated miracle of her breathing.

Later, he was summoned by a resident in psychiatry. It was evening by then. The doctor asked about Joy's medical and emotional history, about the condition of their marriage. Everything was written down in a notebook, indelibly recorded. Kenny told the truth as best he could, looking into the other man's eyes for traces of judgment or empathy. Neither could be readily perceived. And Kenny's own mind wandered during the session. He thought: The children will have to be put to bed. Steven's earache. He'd never called and said about the medicine. The boy's sobbing on the telephone that afternoon. Molly in her underpants, screaming as he ran, hugging his neck too tightly. Daphne sitting in her car. Kenny blinked, jarred into attention. His exhaustion was making him superimpose images from other days, different places. He took the piece of paper the psychiatrist offered, with the names of three other psychiatrists on it, and put it in his pocket.

Afterward, Kenny slept for a while in a waiting room, with other clothed sleepers, the desperate stench of cigarettes and anxiety around them. Someone shook him awake to say that his wife had been taken upstairs.

The woman on the telephone says, "I have an ear-to-ear incision. They call it a bikini cut." Her voice lowers to a stage whisper. "I wanted them to take it out the other way, but it was too big. Letterman said *eleven hundred grams*. How much is a gram?"

Nurses come in and take Joy's blood pressure. She is so inert and hollowed out that it seems as if they're trying to inflate her with the pump and cuff. They take her temperature too, and check her pulse rate. She sleeps through everything, like a fairy-tale princess.

At eleven o'clock, visiting hours begin, and the husband of the woman in the next bed comes to see her. Kenny hears her say gaily, "Roses! Where will I put them?" Then there's a protracted silence, broken only by whispers and the rustling of fabric. He remembers parking somewhere dark in Brooklyn with a beautiful dark-haired girl. Another couple was in the backseat of Kenny's mother's car. They were all high-school seniors.

The girl he was with, whose name was Lorna, permitted him small, measured sexual favors. She was marked by boundaries he could approach but was not allowed to cross. Once, he glanced into the rearview mirror and the couple behind them had disappeared. But they were still there; they breathed like marathon runners, and there were other sounds. It's absurd to be reminded of that now, to experience the same kind of envious longing. His stomach makes a mewling complaint. He realizes that he's had nothing to eat for more than twenty-four hours, but he wants to be here when Joy opens her eyes.

Recently, he's been reading to Steven from a large, illustrated book of fairy tales, the same ones he knows from his own childhood. Younger sons sent on impossible errands that are accomplished with the help of benevolent witches. Sleeping beauties roused by a single princely kiss. Snow White in her glass coffin, no mist of breath to cloud it. Cinderella, suitably rewarded for goodness and poverty. For the first time, he thinks of the wicked stepsisters. Perhaps they were maligned. Perhaps they, too, could be loved in spite of their large feet and selfish ways. And elder greedy sons not made to come home in empty-handed defeat. Why was everyone always granted only three wishes? It's never enough.

Steven is too young to understand much of what he hears, but he loves the stories anyway, is also happily seduced by myth. Someday he will climb the ropes of a woman's unbound hair and enter a tower, her castle.

Kenny looks at Joy and remembers the terms of the fairy-tale bargain he'd made for her life. He whispers her name and she doesn't stir. He bends and places his lips on hers. Her breath has a rank, sweetish odor and taste—the morning kiss of marriage. She continues to sleep.

38

Daphne finishes her rounds and heads back to the kitchen. She helps the other women to put things away, to clear and sponge off surfaces. While she's doing these ordinary chores, extraordinary, irrevocable events are happening elsewhere. She hates this awareness. It's like thinking about breathing and losing its natural rhythm, or thinking about sleeping and then being unable to do so.

Right now, Kenny is probably planning how he will tell her one thing or another. It will be difficult, both the telling and the listening. She longs for protection from experience, from the necessity of ritual.

On the wall of her father's office at the insurance company, there's a sign: *When the going gets tough, the tough get going!* It's a senseless motto. When the going gets tough, Daphne no longer wants to be a vessel of feeling.

One of the women is singing in a clear sweet voice, made even clearer and sweeter by the tiled walls, as if she's singing in the shower. The song is sentimental and easy, yet it pierces the thin membrane of Daphne's resistance because it is, in the most elementary way, about love. Maybe *everything* is, and she'll be reminded forever by a relentless onslaught of innuendos. By books, movies, graffiti, the easy coupling of other people's hands. How will she prepare her defense? She considers making a vow of chastity. If she never wraps her arms and legs around anyone, she will never be made bereft by their emptiness.

When her work is finished and she takes off the hairnet, the weight of her released hair is startling. She thinks of Kenny winding its length around his hand, trapping her with the calculation of love. It's taken her ten years to grow this hair, and in an instant she decides to cut it. Not as a symbol of guilt or loss, but as a serious gesture of change. Short hair will modify her body's signals of need. The need itself might become diminished. There are a thousand ways she can alter her fate.

On the way home, Daphne is glad that she lives in California, where life never shuts down. Even past midnight, it's easy to find one of those large stores that carries everything, open and bustling with business. She needs a good pair of shears for the job, not the dull ones she has at the apartment. She doesn't want to just hack it all off and end up looking like those Frenchwomen who fraternized with Germans during World War II. Shoulder-length might be nice, and maybe an irregular fringe of bangs. When Kenny sees her, he'll be shocked by how different she looks. As if his pressing news is not essential to her existence. See, I'm already someone else. Why are you telling me this story?

The scissors are in aisle 16C, toward the back of the store, between hardware and beauty supplies. There's a dazzling selection, all of them blister-sealed and hanging on a cork display board. How will she decide among them? As she contemplates a choice, Daphne's fingers find a strand of hair and they slide down its slippery length to her waist. She remembers her head resting in Mr. Axel's lap and how his fumbling hand caught the hairnet and pulled it off. An accident of love. And she sees again, as in a revelation, the infinite varieties of attachment. In her outburst, she'd said that she wanted to die. Liar! But he'd believed her and called her back.

Once more, she touches her hair, slowly, turning an end of it into a loose curl. She picks the curl up and tickles herself with it just under the nose. Walking into the hardware section, she finds a saw blade in which she can see her reflection with its comical mustache—and around her head that nimbus of glory. To take scissors to it seems now like an act of self-destruction, not as terrible as Joy's, but with its own kind of violent intention.

Daphne continues down the hardware aisle until she comes to the subsection of Home Beautification. Again, there are myriad options, but she makes up her mind quickly. One gallon should do it, and she'll need a roller and a tray and a drop cloth.

In the apartment, she ties a kerchief around her head to protect her hair, and puts on best-loved jeans that have frayed past the salvation of mending. After the furniture is pushed against the walls, she moves her stepladder to the center of the room.

She scratches at the stars with her fingernails, and then with a razor blade. They're permanently adhered to the ceiling. There is nothing to do but paint over them. She pours the paint into the tray and lays the roller carefully into it. Not that she's happy, but she hums. At least two coats of this rosy-pink color will be necessary to cover the darkness. As she begins to apply the paint, the stars are obliterated, one by one, the way real ones are by the spreading dawn.

39

Kenny bathes his children before their nap, although they were bathed only that morning by the neighbor who cared for them in his absence. They're very playful in the tub, splashing and glancing at each other with sly interest. Steven no longer complains about his earache. Molly's perfect brow is smooth and untroubled. So far, neither of them has asked any questions about the past two days, or about their mother. How much is the protective forgetfulness of babyhood, and how much a shrewd evasion of what is impossibly scary?

When Kenny went next door to pick them up, his neighbor demanded her ransom of information. She pulled him into her kitchen, out of the children's earshot, and waited for her payoff.

"A mistake, Barbara," he said. "A lousy mess. I can't talk about it right now. I think everything will be all right."

Reluctantly, she moved aside and let him pass.

The children are wrinkling up, but he doesn't care. If not fish, they're at least amphibian. He caresses them with lather, and turns the faucet on from time to time to keep the water temperature constant. If there was enough room, he'd slip out of his smelly clothes and get in there with them. He feels as if he hasn't seen them for weeks.

Kenny had planned, on the way home from the hospital, what he would say to them. He'd had an impulse of honesty, tempered by caution. Joy had been the one who was always reading aloud to him about the grave responsibilities of parenting. For a long time after Steven was born, she'd drag out her dog-eared copies of Spock and Gesell, and look up *Teething, Night Terrors,* and *Strangers, Fear of.* Kenny has a bitterly ironic image of her thumbing another index, searching under S for *Suicide, Parent's Failed Attempt at.* He is newly astounded that she was willing to undo everything this way. It arouses his fury and his awe.

"Steven? Molly?" he says. "Do you remember yesterday when Mommy was sleeping?"

"Hey, look at me, Daddy," Steven says. "I'm swimming." He flails his arms, soaking the front of Kenny's shirt. "Uh-oh, I'm *drowning!*" And he plunges his head under the sudsy water.

"Drowning!" Molly echoes, shutting her star-tipped eyelids, submerging only her chin.

When he's toweling them dry, Kenny tries again. "Mommy will be coming home soon, you know," he says.

"I know that, dummy," Steven answers, closing the subject.

When they're bedded down, Kenny undresses and climbs into their tepid bathwater, with their rubber toys in a small flotilla around him. He sips from a can of beer, then balances it on the edge of the tub.

The baby-sitter from the agency arrives at two. She's a forbidding-looking giantess who can't seem to remember the children's names. More trauma. But he doesn't want the further intrusion of neighbors and friends, and he must see Daphne before she leaves for work.

Driving toward Ventura, he refuses recollections of previous trips in this direction. He's possessed by a fierce discipline, not too different from the one that used to help him dissolve thoughts of Daphne as he drove away from her.

The bath, a sandwich, and the time with his children have shored Kenny up. But he's considerably older than he was yesterday, and the manic energy he was once able to summon for his double life doesn't seem possible anymore. He wonders how he'll even tolerate the demands of an ordinary one once again.

When he'd planned on leaving Joy, all the qualities in her he'd loved at another time rushed back to admonish and seduce him: the serious intensity she brought to everything; that early sexual nerve; her courage in childbirth; her beauty. As he turned away from her, he found himself admiring, with a sense of loss, her quickness with numbers, the way she held a cigarette, and the sea color of her eyes.

Now he must do the opposite with Daphne. It's time to acknowledge her various failings, to help him turn away from her as if it's a reasonable thing to do. Sometimes she's childlike in ways that only lovesickness can make charming. Ingenuousness, he knows, would finally drive him nuts. As would the careless clutter of unwashed dishes, the spills of dusting powder, the spinebent books. That day in the parking lot at the college, she had hesitated too long before going away with Kenny. And she had referred to him as an "old friend." He remembers setting aside a freeze-frame of the moment, for different purposes. It will have to serve him now in breaking away. There is so much more to actively adore about her, to lust after, to mourn. But he'll do enough of that when he and Joy are lying next to each other again, and moving into the separateness of thought before sleep.

She had awakened today just as he was starting to doze in the bedside chair. She'd stared at him blankly for a moment, and he watched recognition and the gradual process of recall change the shape and expression of her eyes. "I'm here," he'd said, taking her hand, and she nodded and seemed to go back to sleep. But only minutes later she looked at him again, clearly focused this time. "Me, too," she said.

Their marriage will soon become a ménage à trois of man, woman, and therapist. As they were once joined by clergy and left to it, they will attempt to be rejoined by the trespass of a lingering third party. He supposes it's only another paradox of the new intimacy. And it will work out, or it won't.

But, oh, Daphne! Her insignificant failings fall away like the encumbrance of clothing. Dear love. Old friend. It pains him to think that she's unready for his news, that he's speeding toward her as a messenger of betrayal.

Under the picture of Kenny in his high-school year-book, someone had bestowed the title "Ladykiller." He seems to be working overtime at the fulfillment of adolescent prophecy.

Daphne doesn't even expect him, and he hasn't re-hearsed this scene because it has remained unimaginable. But when he knocks on her door, she is already opening it to let him in.

40

Mrs. Feldman's fears about a new roommate were not unjustified.

A week after her sister's death, a Miss Crane is brought into 225. She's senile, but in a different way than Mrs. Bernstein was. Often, Daphne is struck by the individual turns of senility. Something of the earlier personality must strongly inform the later one. Obsessions vary. A man who's always lived in California insists that the Mayor of Chicago has gotten him into this mess. He demands that telegrams of protest be sent, and letters to the newspaper. A few of the patients hide things against possible thievery: underwear, scraps of food, carefully folded brown paper bags. Others are haunted by their dead that refuse to go away; strangers assume lost faces and names. As she makes her rounds, Daphne is sometimes greeted as Gertrude, or Mother. She has fleeting considerations of reincarnation.

Miss Crane's crusade and cry are singular. She is simply intolerant of all activities that involve or affect her in any way. "I'm too old," she says. It is her constant refrain when they put the lights on in the morning and shut them off at night. When they wash or feed her. As soon as she's touched by anyone for any reason, she shrieks, "Stop that! I'm too old! I'm too old!"

Mrs. Feldman's resentment of Mrs. McBride is diverted to Miss Crane. She is truly the one who has usurped her sister's place. She's even sleeping in Pearl's bed! And she continually admits that she's outlived her functional self. "Shut up," Mrs. Feldman tells Miss Crane, giving her yet another provocation for her recital. She is also too old to be told to shut up.

Mrs. Feldman is changing. She's become less fastidious about herself, and has let some of the plants in her room languish for want of water. Once she confessed to Daphne that she was afraid she was losing her "flair." She no longer expresses curiosity about the outside world. And the soap operas and quiz shows that once gave her so much pleasure have become difficult to follow. But Mrs. Feldman turns the volume of her television set as high as she can, to drown the other woman out. "Lower that! I'm too old!" Miss Crane cries. A man in the neighboring room bangs on the wall with his cane.

Daphne considers this slow, merciless death of self even worse than the body's death. Yet it seems more within the realm of her control, and she is reassured by that. In the first lonely days after her breakup with Kenny, she found herself going frequently to the mirror, not out of sudden vanity, but to say, see, *I'm* still here. She contemplates the idea of loving without giving up the onliness of the person in the mirror.

And now she has company at her apartment. A few days ago Margaret came down from Seattle to visit. But she didn't come for the change of scenery their mother had indicated in her letter to Daphne. Yesterday, in the morning, Daphne accompanied Margaret to an abortion clinic, where a two-month pregnancy was terminated. Daphne stayed in a small waiting room, trying to read an article on trout fishing in *Sports Illustrated*. She exchanged awkward glances with the only other person there, a middle-aged man who looked at his watch every few minutes, as if his train were late. After rereading the same paragraph three times without making any sense of it, Daphne offered the magazine to the man.

She remembered taking Margaret to kindergarten for the first time and leaving her, tremulous, on a sunny threshold. Idiotically, she regretted being her little sister's first sexual informant, as if that made Daphne guilty of corruption or collusion.

When the operating-room door opened and Margaret came out, she seemed a little pale and shaky, but she was smiling.

"Are you okay?" Daphne asked, and Margaret said, "Sure." In the car she leaned back and said, "Get me to a nunnery."

The night before, they'd stayed up very late to talk. "Wouldn't the parents *die* if they knew about this?" Margaret said. "Daddy kept saying, 'Just don't drive over the limit in California, miss.' Mom made me pack an umbrella."

Daphne said, "I thought you told me you were being careful, Mags."

Margaret merely lifted her shoulders in a helpless shrug.

Daphne sighed, hearing a frightening echo of her mother in that sigh. "Doug or Randy?" she asked.

Margaret looked perplexed for an instant. And then she said, "Oh. It was Scott."

When they were undressing for bed, Margaret asked, "How about you? Are you still involved with Mr. Mystery?"

Daphne thought then that the word "involved" should be struck from the language. It was an evasive word that denied the memorable specifics of love. "No," she said. "That's all over." She waited, holding her nightgown against her breasts, for the inevitable wash of pain. It came on schedule, making her totter a little.

Margaret is at the apartment, resting, an alphabet of vitamins and minerals hastening her recovery.

Daphne is at work. Summer school is over, and she has given Mrs. Shumway notice. In two weeks, she'll be going to San Francisco to look for a new job, for a different kind of life. She's asked that her transcripts from U.C.L.A. and Ventura College be sent to San Francisco State. A high-school friend from Seattle lives near the bay, and has offered to let Daphne stay with her until she can find a place of her own.

She knows that she forms quick and lasting bonds with people and places, and that this makes separation very difficult. The Palomar Arms would seem to be an exception. Working here had only been an insane accommodation to her affair with Kenny. From the beginning, the place depressed her and made her uneasy. The underpaid labor of menial service, and the tragedies of aging and of ultimate desolation. No more microwaves to zap me, she tells herself. No more of Shumway's dirty looks, and Monica's cynicism, and Styrofoam, and that smell.

And yet there are friendships to be severed, and a further loss of what has simply become familiar. Mr.

Axel, who is starting to eat fairly well, with Daphne's assistance, may lapse into his old apathy, that slow suicide of starvation. She'll write to him, although he won't be able to write back. Daphne won't be here to witness Mrs. Feldman's continuing disintegration, but it will continue, anyway.

She knows that flashbacks of this place will occur in dreams and when she's awake, just like the ones she has of Kenny. These are usually from their early, best times together. She wonders if she must go through the whole chronology of their relationship until she comes to the moment of parting, and is done.

On her supper break, Daphne asks a question she's always meant to ask. "How did this place get its name?" she says. "I mean, it's pretty far from Mount Palomar."

Evita explains that "palomar" is Spanish for "bird shelter." "You know," she says, "for little doves—las palomas."

"And for pigeons," her sister adds.

Daphne thinks that it's sadly appropriate. Then she remembers that Kenny had once promised, while they lay entwined under her starry ceiling, that he would take her to Mount Palomar someday, where she could get a glimpse of the real heavens.

Miss Nettleson says, "I'm on the *Lady Godiva* set, but there are no cameras, no other actors. The scenery is very beautiful, but flat, because it's scenery. When I touch the trees, their green comes off on my hand."

Mr. Brady says, "After watching *Kung Fu*, I want to kick up my heels!"

Feliciana says, "Estás triste, querida?"

Mr. Axel says, "Tastes something . . . like food."

Kenny says, "You smell lovely everywhere. I'd like to keep your smell on me all day."

Miss Crane says, "Leave me alone, you! I'm too old!"

Margaret says, "This place is a fucking cage. That fireplace gives me the creeps. Do you want to go out for burgers and fries? As soon as I stop staining, I'm going to get a coil."

41

Nora is dressed with great ceremony. The women make a noisy fuss about it, shaking out the few dresses in her closet, exclaiming over them.

"Oh, not black! It's all shiny, anyhow. She'll look like an old black crow."

"Well, the moths got this one. It's air-conditioned."

"Should have called her family, asked for something new."

"Put polish on her nails."

"Lipstick."

"Hardly any *lips*."

They slide garments over her head, and with each one she's caught for an instant in the odor and texture of rayon or cotton, in the pebbled darkness of black crepe, or the miniature garden of a floral print. Long, cold stockings on her legs instead of the fuzzy ankle socks. But first they trim her toenails; the thick parings click into a basin like shelled peas.

"Jewelry!" someone cries.

Has she lost her wedding ring? She reaches for it and it's there, loose on her finger, and then caught on the swollen knucklebone.

Her hair is combed and crimped. They use an iron. She knows that scorch of curls, that fading heat against her forehead and cheeks.

She is being dressed like a bride. Something old—herself. Something new—the stockings. Everything else is borrowed: the strongly scented lipstick that makes her feel she's just kissed another woman on the mouth—"*Now* you're pretty, Mama!"; a heavy necklace of bright beads; a soft shawl that wafts across her shoulders. Something blue is the sky suspended over the lawn where the party will take place. There never was a bluer sky.

A corsage is delivered, and pinned in place, dragging down the rayon flowers of her dress.

Her wheelchair is festooned like the float for a princess in a parade. Crepe-paper streamers catch in the wheels. When she looks over the side, the spokes are too brilliant, reflecting light like a baton you can't really watch in its ascent toward the sun.

"Put her here."

"No, *here.*"

They settle on a shady spot, under a tree's leafy shelter, and then they leave her alone.

Daphne tries on several shirts before she remembers the sweater at the bottom of her bottom drawer. When she takes it out and puts it on, Margaret whistles. "Where did you get *that?*"

"I lifted it from a swanky boutique in Beverly Hills," Daphne says.

"Oh, *sure.*" Margaret touches the neckline of the sweater. "You look sort of naked in it," she says.

"Maybe I shouldn't wear it."

"If you don't, I will. Anybody under ninety going to be there?"

Brady is humming "The Darktown Strutters' Ball" as he shaves. Joe watches in wonder at his enthusiasm. "Like parties?" he asks.

"Breaks it up, kid," Brady says.

The band arrives as the sun starts to go down. Feliciana looks out of the lounge window and admits that her lifelong dream has been to sing with a group.

"Why don't you?" Daphne asks.

"Because she can't sing," Evita says. "She can't carry a tune in a suitcase."

Monica and Jerry and Lucille come in, all dressed up. Jerry looks uncomfortably formal in a jacket, shirt, and tie. When he comes closer, Daphne sees the pattern of high-kicking chorus girls on his tie. She introduces Margaret, and when she says, "My kid sister, visiting from Seattle," Margaret rolls her eyes and pretends to suck her thumb.

Lucille touches Daphne's sweater. "Where did you get this?" she asks.

"She ripped it off," Margaret says, and everyone laughs.

"Here's Mkabi," Jerry says. "We can start."

"Start what?" Daphne asks.

"Close your eyes, Daphne," Evita tells her.

"What for?"

"Just do it, okay?" She pushes Daphne into a chair. "Okay, now open them!"

There is an elaborately gift-wrapped package on the table in front of Daphne. "What's this?" she asks. "It's not *my* birthday."

"Going away," Feliciana tells her. "We figured, kill two birds with one stone."

"Don't kill this bird," Jerry warns them. "She looks good enough to—"

"Children present!" Monica says. "Watch your filthy mouth."

"I wasn't going to say anything. What was I going to say?"

"Open your present," Mkabi tells Daphne. "We have to get downstairs soon. They put Mrs. McBride outside already."

"I wish you hadn't done this," Daphne says, and means it. The greeting card she takes out of its envelope is thick, brown, and multifolded, and has an endless message in verse. Once she starts reading it aloud, she's committed to finishing it. The theme is Goldilocks and the Three Bears—how she tasted their porridge, and broke the baby's chair, and slept in his bed. When the whole thing is opened, it rattles and collapses back onto itself, and is too clumsy to handle. Evita helps Daphne straighten it out so she can read the last line: "But we can't BEAR to see you go!"

Everyone applauds, and Jerry stamps his feet and whistles with two fingers in his mouth. All their names are scrawled at the bottom of the card—this way and that. A few handwritten messages have been added. *Good luck. We're going to miss you. To a really nice person.*

Jerry takes a bottle of bourbon from a cabinet, and some of the little pleated paper cups used to give pills to the patients. He passes the cups around and fills them brimming. They toast Daphne's health, and Mrs. McBride's, and the Pope's, and the President's, and their own. Then they urge Daphne to open the gift, and her hands tremble as she pulls at ribbon and paper.

"Do you like it?" Evita asks, even before the layers of tissue have been lifted to reveal what's under them.

Maybe they bought this before she told them she wasn't getting married after all, and then they couldn't return it. Final sale or something. Because it seems like a trousseau gift, something purchased at a bridal shop. Daphne pulls out the lacy white confection, and there is a sigh of appreciation around the room.

"Put it on, put it on," they call, with the chanting insistence of a crowd urging a stripper to take it off. There is nothing to do but stand up and let them help her into it.

They lead her to the mirror near the coffee machine so she can admire herself. Perhaps she should have been wearing this peignoir when Kenny came to say goodbye, instead of that shapeless smock and those paint-stained jeans. The frilled cuffs, the cascade of white silky folds mock a glorified vision she once had of herself, like the cruelest parody. Daphne imagines that she looks exactly like her mother's dream of a virgin daughter, and she remembers a line of Keats from Allen Burdette's telephone courtship: "Thou still unravished bride of quietness."

They wheel her out from under the tree. "Say cheese, sweetheart. Smile! You're on *Candid Camera!*"

A woman shouts in her ear. "To what do you owe your longevity, Mrs. McBride?"

Nora thinks, and before she can answer, an interpreter says, "Why have you lived this long?" They are different questions and now she's confused.

Reenie brings a white satin Bible and a few of Nora's great-great-grandnieces, in patent-leather shoes and hair ribbons. The little girls are made to kiss her for the photographers. Another round of Catherines and Agneses. They spin out of her arms like dervishes.

The band isn't very good, but they're loud. Even the deafest patients will be able to pick up some strains of the old favorites. As people stream into view, Joe keeps looking for his own family. Sandra and Bud are still traveling on the other side of the world, but the grand-children said they'd try to be here. Invitations went out to all the relatives. Brady's ex-wife has shown up, which doesn't seem to surprise Brady. "She always liked a party, too," he says, before she wheels him away in the direc-tion of the music.

While Joe waits, there are plenty of children to please his eye. The paper lanterns are lit over their heads, and he remembers putting the big lights on at dusk in the store. Children used to come in when he still had the ice cream freezer up front. They'd slide the glass top open, letting vapor escape like genies, and take half the summer's night to choose a flavor.

In the elevator, Margaret says that you don't have to touch the buttons to make them light. Since they're acti-vated by heat, you only have to breathe on them. She demonstrates. With one quick hot breath she turns a dark plastic circle bright orange.

"Hey hey!" Jerry says, holding the doors open with both arms.

Evita giggles. "Maybe you can use your tongue, too," she says.

"Doesn't everybody?" Monica asks.

"Do it," Daphne tells Evita, and she obliges, lighting another circle.

They ride up and down a few times so that everyone can take a turn. They use their breath, tongues, elbows, knees, and chins. Feliciana says that men can do it one more way, and everyone is convulsed, except for Evita, who says now she has to wash out her mouth.

Above them, someone is banging for the elevator, so Margaret pushes a button the conventional way. They rise from the basement to the main floor, and wander out into the party.

Jerry asks Daphne to dance. He holds her very close, crushing the chorus girls between them. There's a wooden platform set up for dancing, and Daphne can see Mkabi and Darryl on the other side, with Bobby hanging on to their legs. Jerry is a good dancer, although he hums at the same time, like a mosquito circling her ear. Margaret is dancing, too, Daphne sees, with a sinister-looking older man in a dark suit. "Who's that?" she asks Jerry.

"That's Rauscher," he tells her. "You mean you never saw him?"

The song ends, and Daphne waits for release from Jerry's grasp. The band immediately swings into another tune, and she's off again across the boards in his embrace. After the third number in a row, she begs time out for some punch.

They pass Mrs. Shumway, who's standing with folded arms near the snack table, guarding the cardboard baskets of Cheezbits and pretzels. Her face is oven-red, and she looks like the chaperone at a church dance.

As Daphne and Jerry approach the punch table, she sees Mrs. Feldman sitting in a circle of visitors. "Excuse me," Daphne murmurs to Jerry, and walks away from him across the grass. "Hello, Mrs. Feldman," she says. "Are you having a nice time?"

"Very nice," she says. "But my heart isn't in it." She introduces Daphne to cousins and nephews. One of them, a tall man in a blue shirt, asks her to dance. "So *you're* the one," he says, when they're turning on the wooden floor.

In the midst of everything, she's dozed off, and even dreamed a little. The dream was of a white winter, so it's hard to come back again to the muggy summer air, to where this is. A voice is coming out of the heavens, booming and receding, calling her name. *"NORA Elizabeth McBRIDE!"*

"Jack?" she asks anxiously.

"CONGRATULATIONS on . . . HUNDREDTH! NANCY and I are . . . WARMEST wishes . . . HOPES FOR . . . and BLESSINGS . . . REAGAN."

Baseball fans are cheering, and then there's music putting out all the other sounds.

He hardly recognizes them until they're very close, and calling, "Poppy, we're here!" Deborah and her husband; Daniel and his oldest daughter. Daniel's wife had assured Joe after the girl's birth that she'd been named for Adele, but her name is Melissa Jane.

"Kiss Poppy," she's commanded, but she turns away, holding her nose and covering her eyes.

"Kevin?" Joe asks, and they hesitate, looking at one another, and then they tell him that the dumb kid's had himself transferred to Fort Bragg. He's decided to become a paratrooper.

Richard helps Daphne serve punch to the patients. When he tries to give a cup to Miss Crane, she says, "Go away, I'm too old." Daphne is ready to explain, but he seems to understand what Miss Crane means. "I'm very sorry," he tells her, and hands the cup to someone else.

Daphne and Richard start dancing again, and she thinks of Kenny. The chronology of their past is scrambled, because she's flung too far back, to the time they danced barefoot to Leon Russell in her room. And then ahead much too quickly to the last day. She shuts her eyes and can see herself opening the door and the way he came into her arms, weeping.

Her old roommate's daughter comes over to congratulate Nora. "All the best. You look simply lovely. My mother sends her regards."

There's a long lineup of well-wishers. They might use up the rest of her life. One of them throws an afghan across Nora's knees, and she's grateful. The air is turning cooler.

The band plays a fanfare, and a circle of fire comes toward her. "Make a wish, make a wish!" they all say.

"I'm only ninety-seven, you know," she whispers con-fidingly, but nobody hears. They're too busy singing. Well, let them think what they want. She can't blow out a single candle, anyway. Once, she was fourteen. Once, she could blow out the moon. She looks upward and can't see anything but the dark quilt of night. What if her brother Henry is hiding behind the moon now, waiting to jump out and yell "Boo!" at her? "I'm not ready," she says.

The first of the fireworks is sent up and bursts into golden rain.
"Ahhh!"

42

They go out to eat often, and they spend most of each day near the pool. Kenny has taken his vacation now, after hiring two recently graduated accountants to finish some overdue work. The ménage à trois he'd pictured has expanded into a quartet. He and Joy each visit a separate therapist, and the therapists consult one another on the telephone. His, Dr. Menkin, refuses to listen to Kenny's report of recent events. He wants him to delve directly into childhood, which makes Kenny impatient and fearful. When he merely thinks about that time, he uses the careful selection of memory, and still has a sense of control. But when he talks in the slanted light of that office, lying on the leather couch made soft by the bodies of other former children, he is much too vulnerable to hide anything; he becomes more and more the child whose experience he slowly reveals. Like Portnoy's analyst, Menkin wants Kenny to begin at the beginning. Eventually, he will be a grown man.

As if she knows that he's spinning backward in time, or because she's undergoing the same process with Dr. Blau, Joy won't let Kenny back into their bed yet. Her most intimate gesture, so far, has been to offer him bits of food from her plate in a restaurant.

They don't tell one another what happens in the

privacy of their respective sessions, although they make little comic asides. Joy sometimes refers to the two therapists as Cheng and Eng, Abbott and Costello, or the Captain and Tennille. Because of the phenomenal fees they charge, Kenny calls them Bonnie and Clyde.

The children are in the water, and Joy and Kenny are their lifeguards, the twin sentinels of safety. Their talk is lazy, intermittent, summery.

"Do you want some iced tea?"

"Let's put a jacaranda in behind the garage."

"Hmmm?"

Her hand is hanging limply in the green shadows at the side of her chaise, as if it were trailing from a canoe into a pond. He picks her hand up and holds it against his face.

She turns to look at him. "I'm an only child," she says. "It was always difficult for me to share."

It's dark inside after all that sunlight. Joy rests every afternoon at this hour, just like the children.

Kenny doesn't like going to his isolated bed during the day; it's more regression than he can tolerate. So, while everyone else sleeps, he roams the house like a caretaker, or a ghost. Sometimes he thinks about Daphne, but in a hazy, abstracted way. It could be his old defenses at work. Or maybe he just can't allow himself more than that. After all, they're turning him into a child, but one that isn't permitted to play. Only once he was caught without warning, and she spun across his mind's vision in a cartwheel, and was gone.

He looks at books, and is unable to read. Nothing in

the refrigerator tempts his appetite. Music, no matter how softly played, would be an intrusion on the quiet of the house.

Joy is taking an antidepressant that helps her to sleep, and to feel hopeful. On another day at this hour, Kenny went to the library to look up her medication in the *Physicians' Desk Reference.* Among the possible side effects, he discovered, is a lessening of the libido. His own is chastened, too, without the benefit of drugs. On the way home from the library, he stopped at a store and bought some magazines: *Playboy, Hustler,* and another one with an oiled woman on the cover, one knee tipped toward each border of the page. He looked at the pictures as he sat in his car, in the parking lot of a supermarket. His vagrant heart ached a little at the sight of all those slick, beckoning, impossibly beautiful bodies, but they didn't excite him. After a while he noticed the real women going by, pushing shopping carts, and felt a tremendous rush of recognition.

It is loneliness that makes him go to the door of the master bedroom and put his ear against it. Joy says, "What is it?" and he opens the door.

She's lying on her own side of the bed, a fact that gives him inordinate pleasure.

"May I come in?" he asks.

"Why?"

He considers the question, and knows that it's essential for him to be truthful. He's the youngest son, who has set out to seek his fortune, and now he's being tested by the most powerful witch in the kingdom. "I don't want to be by myself," he says.

It's the right answer, because she nods, bidding him to enter.

He steps out of his bathing suit and turns back the covers on his side of the bed. The pillow remembers his head. The sheets are delightfully cool and smooth, and he imagines his old dreams still trapped in them, waiting for his return. When he and Joy are able to make love again, will the sheets have to be brought to Menkin and Blau as proof of consummation? Kenny stifles a mad rising of laughter.

"Don't talk, all right?" Joy murmurs.

"All right," he agrees. He's happy to be relieved of the burden of conversation, although he knows there are things that must be said, sooner or later. Later. Not now.

She turns her back, but doesn't move completely away from him. He dares to come closer, finding an old, almost-forgotten position for sleep—arm flung over arm, leg over leg, as if they're running alongside one another and only giving the illusion of touching.